Tom Clancy's

OP-CENTER

CALL OF
DUTY

TOM CLANCY'S OP-CENTER NOVELS

ALSO BY JEFF ROVIN

Tom Clancy's

OP-CENTER

CALL OF
DUTY

CREATED BY

Tom Clancy and Steve Pieczenik

WRITTEN BY

Jeff Rovin

ST. MARTIN'S
GRIFFIN
NEW YORK

First published in the United States by St. Martin's Griffin, an imprint of St. Martin's Publishing Group

TOM CLANCY'S OP-CENTER: CALL OF DUTY. Copyright © 2022 by Jack Ryan Limited Partnership and S&R Literary, Inc. All rights reserved. Printed in the United States of America. For information, address St. Martin's Publishing Group, 120 Broadway, New York, NY 10271.

www.stmartins.com

Designed by Omar Chapa

Library of Congress Cataloging-in-Publication Data

Names: Rovin, Jeff, author. | Clancy, Tom, 1947-2013, creator. | Pieczenik, Steve R., creator.
Title: Call of duty / created by Tom Clancy and Steve Pieczenik ; written by Jeff Rovin.
Description: First edition. | New York : St. Martin's Griffin, 2022. | Series: Tom Clancy's op-center
Identifiers: LCCN 2022000935 | ISBN 9781250782861 (trade paperback) | ISBN 9781250861399 (hardcover) | ISBN 9781250782878 (ebook)
Subjects: LCGFT: Novels.
Classification: LCC PS3568.O8894 C35 2022 | DDC 813/.54—dc23/eng/20220114
LC record available at https://lccn.loc.gov/2022000935

Our books may be purchased in bulk for promotional, educational, or business use. Please contact your local bookseller or the Macmillan Corporate and Premium Sales Department at 1-800-221-7945, extension 5442, or by email at MacmillanSpecialMarkets@macmillan.com.

First Edition: 2022

10 9 8 7 6 5 4 3 2 1

CHAPTER ONE

Taiyuan Satellite Launch Center, Shanxi Province, China

February 12, 8:59 A.M., China Standard Time

Dr. Yang Dàyóu did not bother to follow the countdown clock. He stood at ease—more drained than relaxed—his pale hands poking from his creased white lab coat. His expression was neutral though his brown eyes were alert. His hair was prematurely white, reflecting a life fully lived over the course of sixty-three years.

The mood inside the steel-reinforced aboveground bunker was prickly with expectation. Unlike the cool, very dry air outside, the atmosphere inside was warm; part of that was the inadequate heating system at the over century-old facility, and part was the presence of seventeen humid, expectant bodies.

Most of the attention was on the two banks of console monitors. The narrow eyes of General Zhou Chang, military commander of the *Qi*-19 project, shifted impatiently between the countdown clock and the two-inch-thick window that looked out on the launch site. They moved in precise syncopation with each short breath, little machines set beneath the crisp military cap atop the general's six-foot-four frame. The official was very much like one of Yang's devices, an engine with just six cylinders. Chang was either watching or demanding; his language consisted of "yes" or "no"; and his associates and subordinates were either for him or against him. For better or worse, those qualities had brought the team to this point.

Standing close beside the general was his right-hand officer, Lieutenant Colonel Tang Kun. The short, bald stoic Kun ran security for the facility; ran it with a keen eye and steel will.

Yang did not need to see the clock. He knew where on the countdown they were by the actions of each man and woman in the room. Outwardly serene, the only visible sign of Yang's anticipation was an occasional smoothing of his gray mustache with an index finger. He was dressed in a crisp, white lab coat, starched so it would not wrinkle when he worked—a concession to orderliness which inspired confidence in others. There was a government-issued smartphone in his pocket; nothing went out without first passing before the eyes of Shen Laihang, the civilian chief of security at the center.

Dr. Dàyóu was chief engineer at the launch facility, also known as Base 25. The nation's leading aeronautical expert, the engineer had spent most of his career here, not only building missiles but helping to design every new building and every upgrade to the old structures. He spent more time here than he did at his home.

But it was not as a proud father that Yang gazed at the launch pad, a half mile away. It was as a cautious, watchful one. The morning sun shined bright on the result of two years of intensive labor, a brilliant and intricate device poised for launch.

A countdown is not just a ticking clock, Yang knew. It is potentially a ticking bomb, a series of coordinated, sequential events where countless mechanisms could fail. And in the case of the *Qi*-19, there were at least eleven points where that was dangerously true.

You did your best, he reminded himself as he ran through each of the countdown checkpoints in his head. Science was valid, but he had a staff of several hundred workers, and humans were faulty. *Not all of them scientists*, he thought without looking at General Chang.

"Mobile launcher lock—final check," said a voice.

The missile sat on Yang's adaptation of the Russian MA3-7917, a fourteen by twelve, twelve-wheel transporter-erector-launcher. The missile transport was both faster and more stable than the Chinese WS-51200 sixteen-wheel TEL, qualities this new missile would require. Because of the American Project Blackjack satellite spy network, all Chinese missiles had to have siloed as well as mobile variants. Counteroffensive algorithms were challenged when the launch profile was constantly changing.

Yang saw the countdown shift to the next-to-last technician in the front. Fifteen seconds from now he would learn whether that work would bear rich fruit or—

"Launch sequence commencing!" the technician's young voice broke the silent room. The man was not shouting but it seemed so. The process shifted to the last man, the ignition-checklist engineer, able to abort the countdown anytime in the next ten seconds. After that—

Yang Dàyóu had been through dozens of launches in his storied career, but none more important than this. Everything about the technology was new, his fingerprints proudly on every part of it. They were down to seven, six, five, four—

"Red light from the coaxial injector!" the checklist engineer announced.

General Chang shifted so he could see the man's panel.

"What is this?" he demanded.

Yang Dàyóu had already moved to where the young specialist was pointing rigidly, almost accusingly. Even without looking the engineer knew where they were, what had tripped things up: the last checkpoint in his mind, refurbish eleven. The red light was pulsing on an LED schematic of the sleek, silver-blue hypersonic missile. It was flashing between the hot gas intake and the sleeve.

"There appears to be a crack in the secondary plate," Yang said ominously as the count of two dissolved to one.

"Abort!" General Chang shouted.

But it was too late and Yang knew it. The rocket of the upright ballistic missile ignited, blasting fire at 1,000 degrees Celsius into the open silo beneath it.

The engineer's eyes pinched slightly as with fear rather than expectation he looked out at the *Qi*-19. His creation was a flattened cylinder, sixty feet long, topped by a twelve-foot-long glider. It was different from the 18, which had top speeds of five-times sound. His design would achieve up to six-point-three times the speed of sound, far outracing the latest antimissile defenses as it delivered its payload high in the stratosphere.

A moment after ignition, the bottom of the missile briefly inflated like a balloon and the two sleek tailfins of the *Qi*-19 blew outward. They tumbled away on clouds of heavy black smoke, which churned and grew and obscured the expanse of scrub-plains surrounding it. The underbelly of the dark clouds was a sea of fire that shaded from white to red as it stretched from the ruined blast walls of the silo.

Almost at once, the main body of the *Qi*-19 folded haphazardly toward earth, apparently buoyed by the rising fires. The skin of the missile turned its own shade of matte black in the inferno. The dark blue payload came loose next. It toppled from the ring at the top and fell over backwards, its delta wings sizzling and smoking and vanishing in a quick instant. There were small puffs of explosions from what was left of the glider as its own internal fuel system was ignited and quickly consumed. The sharp nose of the plane pointed earthward; it seemed to be directing, to their demise, the modular packets of electronics that slipped through large and growing holes in the aircraft's sides and belly.

The destruction was absolute and over in too few beats of the heart of the missile's creator. Everyone in the room, save General Chang, was held fast by the awful spectacle playing out before them, the low grasses between them and the launch site lost in the holocaust of burning fuel.

Then the shock wave hit the bunker with a rattling concussion. Most of the personnel were wearing headphones; those who were not, like Chang, like the guards at the door, covered their ears as the blast struck like a wrecking ball. The bunker stopped rumbling and shaking within moments and then the rolling heat splashed across the front, raising the temperature more than 20 degrees.

As though propelled by the impact, General Chang of the People's Liberation Army Air Force spun on the smaller scientist.

Lieutenant Colonel Kun stepped between them, more to moderate the general than to protect Yang. He unholstered his QSZ-92 semiautomatic. With his other hand the officer grabbed the engineer by the upper arm, squeezing hard.

While Chang's angry eyes pinned the man where he stood, the lieutenant colonel silently motioned for two guards to come forward. The pair was standing on either side of a bolted metal door. They wore open-necked jackets and Western-style trousers, all a deep sky blue. Sitting smartly on their heads were white peak caps with a blue brim. On their right shoulders was the red shield of the air force police. Armed with QBZ-95 assault rifles, the two men quickly made their way through the small concrete bunker.

"Remove Dr. Dàyóu to his quarters," Chang ordered thickly, all but spitting out the word "doctor."

"This is a mistake, General," the engineer said quietly. Though the man was visibly rattled, his mind was picking apart what he had just witnessed. "This was not a design flaw but a material—"

"No!" Chang shouted. His gaze burned deeper into the man, as if to remind him that this was not for the ears of those around them. "Take his telephone and remain inside with him. I will be there presently."

The military police moved to the left and right of the engineer and faced him. Their stern expressions were rich with condemnation: what the thirteen technicians and military personnel had just witnessed was Dàyóu's fault. The chief engineer had lost *his* face. The stain on the research unit, on the airborne branch of the military, on their nation itself, was all traceable to his failure.

Yang did not protest further as the men ushered him away, one guard in front and the other in back, Kun pulling him along with his punishing and demeaning grip. Yang Dàyóu was a patriot and, by word and deed, a loyal member of the Communist Party of China. But he had been working around the clock and did not have the energy to try to reason with the general. Besides, he knew that self-defense would be futile. He had cautioned Chang about reusing parts from the *Qi*-18 program, warned him many times. The specs for the shield that cracked and for other components were the same in the new design. But the conditions under which they had been stored could have compromised the chemistry of the alloys.

But the dual constraints of time and budget had propelled them along this course of action. And, ultimately, it was Dr. Dàyóu's signature on the top of every requisition form. Chang had merely countersigned. To the commission that would examine this debacle, it would be clear that the officer was granting to science what science had asked for.

Now Dr. Dàyóu would have to pay for that.

His only hope was that his family would be safe.

Especially his son, who would view this as a tragedy . . . and an opportunity.

CHAPTER TWO

Chase Williams did not know why he had been summoned to the Oval Office.

He had received a text from new chief of staff Angie Brunner while he was working out in the health club at the Watergate West apartment. Ten minutes later, showered and with his lean six-foot frame dressed casually—and having taken a few minutes to scan the morning update from Homeland Security—Williams had pulled from the parking garage and was merging with the traffic of Virginia Avenue NW. The sixty-one-year-old director of the National Crisis Management Center—informally known as Op-Center—was curious but not concerned.

She didn't call to fire me, Williams reflected as he donned sunglasses against the sharp wintry sunlight. Termination notices from the incoming administration had been hand-delivered by the White House Office of Mail and Messenger Operations. Williams' former Oval Office liaison, Deputy Chief of Staff Matt Berry, had his framed on his new office at a boutique conservative think tank. Williams wondered, a bit cynically, *Maybe Angie wants me to move to the West Wing with the rest of the worker bees.* As governor of Pennsylvania, now as president, John Wright was a champion of close interaction.

Whatever it was, Williams would listen and then adjust. That was what he had done his entire career. And a change of locale would not be a bad thing. For a man who loved the sea, he had spent an inordinate amount of time in rooms without windows. His present basement office in the sprawling but austere McNamara Headquarters Complex at the Defense Logistics Agency was not only steeped in recycled air but in the unnatural silence maintained by deep-state workers and black ops.

Williams knew the sentries at the West Wing parking area and at the security checkpoint. The latter two were former navy, and they threw him smiles and respectful salutes.

"Nice to see you again, Admiral Williams, sir," said one.

"You too, Kayser, Miller," he said to one and then the other.

It was a good way to start the business day.

Making his way through the West Wing, Williams passed the Cabinet Room which had clusters of people standing around the table drinking coffee. He recognized the mugs from the Navy Mess, which had been serving food at the White House for nearly a century and a half. He recognized the furnishings and carpet. He did not recognize any of the people, whose wide range of age, color, and dress reflected the obsessive priorities of the new administration. After two terms of the rigid meritocracy and occasional cronyism upheld in the previous administration, identity appointments would be an adjustment. The only identity that had ever mattered to Williams was "American."

Still, it had always been in Williams' nature to try to find common ground with everyone. One did not achieve lasting results by confrontation; all that achieved was fighting. As the former combatant commander for both Pacific Command and Central Command, Williams had witnessed too much of that. When he retired three years ago, his intention had been to lay down that lifetime of compromise and negotiation, buy a boat, and sail the East Coast fishing and clamming. Instead, he was asked to replace the ailing Paul Hood, founding director of Op-Center.

"Chase!"

Williams turned. Just behind him, emerging from her office, was January Dow. The new assistant to the president for National Security Affairs was formerly director of the State Department's Bureau of Intelligence and Research. Dow was a smart political creature who had always seen Op-Center as a threat to her fiefdom. She was dressed in wide-leg black pants and a large, white cowl-neck sweater. Her expression—at least when Williams was around—was a frowning and intense look that read "no trespassing." She had a short, peach-colored buzz cut.

"A familiar face!" she said.

"Good to see you, January," he replied diplomatically. Seeing her was the political equivalent of minefield training. "Congratulations on the new post."

"Thanks. I was pleased you made the cut as well."

"I'm low maintenance." He had continued to move away with small steps.

"What brings you here?" January asked.

He shrugged. "I was told to report, so I'm reporting."

The woman's eyes lingered. Williams could not tell if she knew something or was trying to learn something.

"Well, I've got a meeting to tee off," she said, crossing toward the conference room. "The VP is in the Middle East and needs scrimmage tools. Catch you later."

Williams smiled as he turned away. He did not even know what she meant by "scrimmage tools."

Perhaps on purpose.

January was very good at keeping secrets, especially when they directly involved the person she was talking to. Information about rivals was coin of the political realm, and sacks of coins were power.

But so was transparency and patriotism for its own sake. That was why, for two years, Williams had artfully deployed his diplomatic skills against career intelligence officials like January Dow, navigating shoals dominated by the CIA, the National Reconnaissance Office, the State Department, and the FBI, and relative newcomers like the Department of Homeland Security, U.S. Cyber Command, and the newly minted Space Force OGRE—Orbital Grid for Reconnaissance and Evaluation—among more than a dozen others. Williams already knew that arena well, having worked closely throughout his career with the Department of Naval Intelligence. He had enjoyed the work, and he respected many of the leaders along with their boots-on-the-ground personnel.

Until seven months before, when everything went to hell

and his career shifted once again. January Dow had had a firm hand in that.

Don't kick up an old stink, he chided himself. Williams reminded himself that the carpet he was walking on, the paintings he was passing, had witnessed more change than he could imagine. The republic had endured because people like him kept the center strong. With that thought firmly in mind, he presented himself to Thomas Deerfoot, the executive secretary to the president of the United States. He sat in a small office that had previously held just one staffer. Now there were desks the size of typing tables set in two rows; the others were occupied by the research secretary to the president, the social secretary to the president, and the scheduler to the president.

Not one of them looked to be over thirty, which was fine, Williams thought; the two striker-grade members of his own Black Wasp team were in their twenties.

Deerfoot glanced at his tablet, touched a button, a button was apparently pushed back, and Williams was directed to enter the adjoining Oval Office.

"Thank you," Williams said, smiling.

"You're welcome, sir," Deerfoot replied.

At least that level of protocol had not changed—though the doorknobs of the president's office had. Williams noticed that the white Victorian knobs of President Midkiff had been replaced with purely functional brass knobs.

A Secret Service officer materialized to open the door. Two agents sat in a small cubicle across from the executive secretary's office twenty-four/seven. They were part of the expanded West

Wing security mandated by the secretary of Homeland Security in 2021 to handle increased threats against the cabinet and staffers. Williams entered and the agent closed the door.

The decor of the Oval Office was the same as in the Midkiff administration, save for the beige paint on the wall and the color of the drapes. Midkiff's gold had been replaced by a more somber navy blue. The president was seated behind his desk, a laptop open before him. The desk was the same as President Midkiff had used—it had been used by JFK, among others—as was the large rectangular coffee table in front of it and the two sofas on either side. In the sofa immediately to the left sat Angie Brunner, Wright's chief of staff. An attorney and former Hollywood studio head, the fifty-two-year-old had been campaign director for the Pennsylvania governor. She was tall, with blue eyes and shoulder-length auburn hair worn in curtain bangs. She was dressed in a power-suit: black slacks with a matching notch collar jacket.

Angie rose, smiling, as Williams entered.

"Good morning, Admiral."

"Good day, Ms. Brunner." He smiled back.

"Admiral Williams," Wright said without glancing up, "I just need another moment."

"Of course, Mr. President."

Angie resumed her seat and indicated the other sofa. Williams walked over and pointed at a coffee carafe.

"Didn't have time for any." He smiled.

Angie nodded as she grabbed her own tablet from the sofa.

The how-do-you-dos apparently ended, Williams eased into the cushion. He did not believe he was summoned because of a major or looming crisis. No other intelligence officials were present, including January Dow, and these two did not display a sense of urgency. That suggested reconnaissance or a prophylactic, surgical strike.

The president remained engrossed in his laptop. Wright had longish, salt-and-pepper hair, restless brown eyes, and broad shoulders that had seen him through college football. Three seasons as a wide receiver had given him a broken nose with a distinctive ridge. The president was wearing a dark blue suit that matched the Oval Office drapes, his choice of colors emphatically signaling his politics. The president was a year younger than his chief of staff, though after twenty-six days on the job he looked several years older. He wore reading glasses, though he insisted on never being photographed with them.

Williams did not know much about the president, other than the accolades the press had heaped on the left-of-center superstar who was replacing a right-of-center warhorse. Of course, public policy told only part of any politician's story. Wright had been straight-to-the-point when they first met too. It had taken only five minutes for the president-elect to size Williams up and ask him to stay on the job. Williams had taken the measure of the other man as well. Wright had personally conducted interviews his staff might have handled and his questions were blunt and precise. A hands-on micromanager was Williams' assessment. That would account for the lean and hungry look so soon after taking office.

"Sorry to pull you from your workout," the president said, finally looking up.

Williams set the carafe down after pouring. "Not a problem, sir. The rowing machine knows how I feel about it."

"Probably the same way I feel about these," the president said. "Angie, is this correct? Homeland has it as the Wuzhai Missile and Space Test Center but DoD says it's Taiyuan . . . Shanxi Province . . . which is it?"

Angie sought the information on her tablet.

"If I may, Wuzhai was an early designation, sir," Williams offered in a way that did not seem to undermine the chief of staff. "The base lies just outside the county but that made its way into reports back in the 1960s, before we had the Chinese name."

"Thank you, Admiral," Angie said—in earnest, it seemed.

The confusion focused Williams on the only China-related matter contained in the HS report: the explosion of a hypersonic missile at Taiyuan during ignition. Surveillance from OGRE suggested that the payload was a dummy and the launch was the first test of missile avionics.

"Thank you, Admiral," Wright said. He removed his glasses and fixed his gray eyes on Williams. "You read about the explosion there, I trust?"

"I have, sir."

"I was just reading about your Black Wasp team member, Lieutenant Grace Lee. Impressive record. How would Lieutenant Lee handle a solo mission to China?"

Williams stifled his concern about sending any soldier on a solo mission to enemy territory. He also said nothing about her strict, objective moral code to wrongdoing. Corruption unbalanced the harmony of nature. Attacking it was quite literally a religion with her.

"She has demonstrated a flair for independent action," he answered.

Wright brought up a bookmarked section of text. "Your report on the pursuit of Captain Ahmed Salehi says, 'Parachuting alone onto the boat of the enemy, and armed only with a pair of knives, Lieutenant Lee neutralized the crew in the wheelhouse.'" The president sat back. "*Quite* a 'flair,' I would say."

"I won't deny it, sir."

"She was born here, her parents naturalized citizens," Angie said.

"That's right," Williams said.

He was going to make the chief of staff ask the question buried in the question. During the campaign, a plank of Wright's platform had been, *"Any human being born on these shores and dwelling here is an American. Period."*

"Is there a potential for NSI?" she asked.

"You mean Native Soil Impact," Williams clarified.

"That's right."

"Zero chance, Angie. None. If I had any doubt at all, I wouldn't send her."

That caught the president's attention. "*You* wouldn't, Admiral? You are a civilian and this is a military operation."

"I would not *recommend* sending her," Williams clarified.

"That kind of lax oversight may be how things worked under my predecessor, but that is not how they will function here."

"No, Mr. President."

The ensuing silence lasted just a moment but seemed much longer. It was deep enough to establish the chain of command as Wright saw it.

The president got back on-topic.

"Admiral, we want to know two things about that Shanxi test," Wright said. "First, what went wrong—technical malfunction or sabotage. Second, what was the payload? Satellite surveillance suggests an aircraft of some kind—but to do what? Finally, we need to find out what happened to the chief engineer, Dr. Yang Dàyóu."

"Obviously, getting close to Dr. Dàyóu would likely settle all those issues," Angie said.

"Would that include extracting Dr. Dàyóu to the United States if feasible?" Williams asked.

"We would not be averse to his defection, though we have no evidence that he would desire that outcome," the president said.

Williams did not say what was on his mind: that the request sounded like a form of Chinese-assisted suicide. Instead, he asked, "Where is Dr. Dàyóu?"

"We presume he is still at the Taiyuan Satellite Launch Center in Wuzhai County, but we don't know," the president answered. "Angie, you have the morning report from the embassy?"

She read from her tablet, "Ambassador Nell Simon in Tokyo says that at eleven fifty-five a.m. CST, on the twelfth, an agent of the Japanese Public Security Intelligence Agency witnessed Dr. Dàyóu's wife and adult daughter being put under house detention. That was less than three hours after the explosion. Dr. Yang Dàyóu has not been seen."

"I don't have to tell you that the Japanese are extremely concerned about this missile," the president said. "It can hit targets in the region quicker than we can scramble interceptors."

There was no question about that. Williams also knew from Department of Defense briefings that while the U.S. has its own hypersonic missiles, carried on the F-35, the load put the aircraft in "beast mode," a configuration that stripped the aircraft of stealth protection. The DoD's own surface-to-air variant would not be ready to test for another six months.

Williams took a swallow of coffee. "How long do I have to come up with a plan—or do you have something in mind, sir?"

Angie answered. "We want to put her on a plane to the embassy in Beijing as soon as possible. We've got the new ambassador's staff going over from Bolling AFB today at three p.m. on Janet Airlines. She will be credentialed as an army attaché for embassy security. That will give you and, we expect, Major Breen roughly twenty-one hours to work up mission parameters before Lieutenant Lee touches down. January Dow will furnish whatever documents and local intelligence you need."

Janet Airlines was an acronym for Joint Air Network for Employee Transportation. Operated by the air force, it consisted of a fleet of Boeing 737s and Airbus A321s that ferried government employees to domestic and, after COVID, international destinations.

"If that's the schedule, we'll work with it," the admiral replied. Trained in "can do," that was always Williams' answer.

"I'll have the ticket and documents sent to you for hand delivery," Angie said.

"Are there any other questions, Admiral?" the president asked.

"We get Class II gear from the general quartermaster when we need it—local clothing, perishables, smartphones—"

"She's with the embassy," Angie said.

"I'm not saying she needs local gear, but if she is questioned she should be carrying a phone with embassy contacts appropriate to her station and assignment."

"I see," Angie said, making notes. "We should be able to have that ready prior to departure. If not, then at Wheeler when they stop for refueling."

"Good job," Wright said to no one in particular. He seemed pleased that Williams had thought of that; no one in his immediate circle had. "Anything else, Admiral?"

"No, sir."

That was not true. But the president's slightly impatient tone had informed Williams that the audience was over and all that remained was to execute. There was no question about refusing the assignment. Both the intelligence function and Black Wasp capability of Op-Center were black ops. The four members of the team were an off-the-books entity that served the president exclusively and reported to him or his designated agents directly. The commander-in-chief could send them wherever he wanted on whatever mission he wished.

But a solo mission was new, and a cascade of logistical, tactical, and threat-assessment thoughts crowded their way through Williams' mind. First, the Black Wasp team had skills that were complementary and, together, formed a perfect whole. Grace

Lee, alone? That was an untested, undrilled proposition. Second, Williams had accepted this post in large part because it was not an armchair assignment. Their work in the field was neither routine nor constrained by normal rules of engagement. The admiral himself had performed an execution on their first mission, shattering every international law and one Commandment with his Sig Sauer 9 mm XM17. And third—

Third, Mr. President, you ignored one of the essential requirements of a good commander, Williams thought. *You didn't ask a single pertinent question.*

In fact, this would be Williams' briefest visit to the Oval Office since he came to Washington. Williams finished the coffee—he was going to do that much, dammit!—then rose and departed. Scrolling on their devices, the president and Angie had already moved on to the next order of business.

Five minutes later he was on the road, deeply and increasingly disappointed that Wright had not asked even the most obvious question, whether the rest of the Black Wasp team should be nearby in the event that Lieutenant Lee needed to be extracted. Handing an officer what was disparagingly called "a bare-naked order" was a sign of an inexperienced and possibly overconfident leader, dangerous to all concerned.

Williams would be sure to put that in his mission profile. He would *not* mention the largest concern he had, one that was as great threat to Grace as Chinese security.

Whether he could count on January Dow not to play politics with the lieutenant's life.

CHAPTER THREE

The Beijing Center, University of International Business and Economics

Beijing, China
February 15, 9:22 P.M., CST

During Wen's childhood, two things made an impression that had lasted twenty-one years.

The first was when he and his father, Yang Dàyóu, had gone to the sparsely populated village of Atulie'er where the engineer needed to test an ignition switch in the cooler air of the mountains. The boy remembered stepping from the train, a rickety pre-war transport with wicker seats and nearly impenetrable windows. His father allowed him a moment to watch a man check the big couplings, and he remembered saying proudly to the old gentleman, "My father is also an engineer." On the trek through the foothills, Wen saw a young man who was so hungry he killed and spit-roasted a rooster, cooking it without removing the feathers or entrails, and bit into the animal's seared flesh. Blood coated the youth's mouth but he did not seem to care. His father, who had grown up in nearby Zhaojue, said without emotion, "This is how we lived."

The second, greater event that shaped Wen's life was discovering numbers. Since his earliest days at Wuzhai Town Elementary School, Wen used them to expand his sense of wonder. In science class he learned that the sun was 93 million miles away and that the Earth was only 7,926 miles around at the equator but weighed four quadrillion tons. His favorite number was octillion, which sounded strong and had twenty-seven zeroes; it was his favorite until he learned about a googol, which was the number one followed by one hundred zeroes. And then he discovered a googolplex, which was one with a googol zeroes. And fractions.

The joys and challenges were boundless.

Wen was not interested in the numbers of his father Yang, which were used to build rockets and bombs—to destroy. As a teenager, Wen worked for a local grocer and became fascinated with using numbers to help people, to create businesses and build economies. When he entered Duìwài Jīngjì Màoyì Dàxué, the University of International Business and Economics, over a year before, his mission—and then, very quickly, his passion—was helping people to improve their incomes and thus their lives.

The community of students led Wen to a second obsession, one that found an ideal venue in Beijing.

Dissent. Masked in public, anonymous, online, but growing like the numbers he loved best: exponentially.

Only Wen's mother, Dongling, knew of his activities—though his father was not blind. As far back as high school, the young man had expressed concern about the suppression of speech and the arrest and execution of anyone who criticized the party. The elder Dàyóu sat with a disapproving expression that seemed hewn in granite. Only once had he spoken on the subject to Wen and his younger sister, Ushi, at dinner:

"You do not know how it was here or you would not be critical of what is."

Wen had never said anything of his activities to his father. The man would not have approved and, worse, might have forbidden his son to visit. Even though Wen did not visit the launch facility, it was nonetheless a high-security area in which social agitators would not have been welcome.

However, Wen revealed himself to his mother when they were together two months before. She was concerned, of course, but supportive. Her own family had been wealthy farmers displaced by Mao Zedong's Great Leap Forward in 1958. She confessed, in a whisper, that she had no use for Communists, save that they supported the work of her husband.

"Have you ever told Father how you feel?" the young man had asked.

The woman confirmed his suspicions about her husband's astute awareness when she replied, "Enthusiasm unexpressed is communication."

Housed in one of the Standard Housing units of the Huicai Apartments, Wen was fully dressed, his average frame lying in his purely functional bed, his textured black hair pointedly reflecting his natural but careless nature. His perpetual half smile suggested that while he took the world seriously, he took himself a little less so. His big eyes moved attentively as he turned the pages of *Thought Forest* magazine. He never missed an issue of the literary short story magazine, or *Youth Digest*, which were rich with thought and trends, respectively. He still read newspapers as well, so he could clip articles of interest. He wondered if he did it to be conscientious or because it was something he used to do with his mother, who saved recipes, weather forecasts, and news of giant pandas.

The phone lying beside him vibrated. Wen set aside the magazine and turned toward the wall to shield the screen from his roommate, Kong Yanyong, who was asleep just four feet away. Nothing woke the six-foot-three-inch bear of a man; not doors slamming, spring and summertime games in the park-like campus two floors below, or jets flying into Beijing Daxing International Airport. Kong *had* to sleep. The Beijing native joked that it exhausted him every time he had to tell people what his father did: the elder Yanyong was Director of the Office of the Committee for Comprehensively Governing the City by Law of Beijing Municipal Party Committee. Privately, Kong admitted that the title sounded more impressive than it was. Regardless, the young man was determined to prove that he could make it on his own, without a stipend. He not only studied hard, he worked long hours at a breakfast stand on the third ring road. He had to be there at 6:00 A.M. and always went to bed early.

Because of his outside activities, Wen had accepted an income from his father—tainted, though it was being put to good use.

Like fifteen percent of the population in China, Kong was

also a Buddhist. Short meditations sustained him, helped him compartmentalize his busy day. Wen, on the other hand, was an atheist like three-quarters of Chinese. He was driven by outrage against oppression.

Kong knew nothing of his roommate's active opposition to the regime and would be appalled by it. Kong was a patriot but not political. His goal was to support his homeland by securing an education in agriculture and helping to feed the impoverished provinces like Yunnan, Guizhou, and Qinghai. It was a good and noble ambition, Wen believed. When they spoke, it was not infrequently about Wen's experiences working for a grocer. At times, he envied that life of clear-eyed simplicity.

The young man turned down the brightness and looked at the screen. It was a text message from Dongling Dàyóu—his mother, in Wuzhai:

I am deeply sorry but we will not be able to visit you.

The message set Wen's belly on fire. The family was not scheduled to come to Beijing. He dared not dictate where his roommate could hear, but typed back at once:

Are you ill?

She replied:

I am not sure what is wrong.

His thumbs felt thick and clumsy as they banged out:

Shall I visit?

The stillness of the screen seemed to taunt him. His brown eyes stared at the unanswered text as though they could will a reply from it. He felt sick and then he felt guilty. Early in Wen's teenage years he had begun to discern the difference between an adult's introspective silence and strictly enforced silence. For those ten years he had become increasingly fearful that his father's work on secret government projects, projects that were too dangerous even to mention, would inevitably come to conflict. The Dàyóu family lived in the engineering block, and before leaving for university Wen had finally broached the subject with his father.

"*The fathers and mothers of my friends are silent and mysterious,*" Wen had said, "*but the officers are unfriendly and often hostile. Why do you continue to work with them?*"

The elder Dàyóu had answered, "*To make a great nation even greater.*"

Wen jumped as the phone vibrated. His mother finally answered:

We will make it another time. We love you.

Tears pressed behind Wen's eyes as he typed:

I love you all too.

The entire message was a code which mother and son had arranged when he visited between terms. That was when the young man had confided to her that he had grown up in a bubble. Seeing the real world, the hardship in Beijing, hearing the stories of other students, he had no choice but to oppose the restrictive social and financial policies of the Communist Party.

These texts had told the young man two things. Since his parents and younger sister had not been planning a trip to Beijing, the message told him that they were under house detention. It also told him that this was not a result of his own activism; otherwise she would have told him to postpone his visit.

This had to be about his father, who had never dissented a centimeter from party doctrine. If so, what could have happened? The man did everything as instructed. As quick as that text exchange, the young man's thoughts had turned from economics to fear—and hate. He felt as though he could breathe fire to release the fire inside, like one of the storybook dragons he had enjoyed as a child.

The short, lanky youth began erasing texts, then turned and grabbed a bottle of water from the floor, taking a long swallow. It did not ease the burning but it helped to keep it from spreading.

Calm down, he admonished himself. *Reason this out.*

He had not been to a gathering of the Counterrevolutionary Youth Organization in—he counted, on his fingers, like a boy—seven days. He had not posted a comment on the group's deep website Bagua for six days, a comment about illegal government debt-trap evictions costing people their home and lands.

He had not even looked at the site for two days. And he was not the most prominent figure there. The group was founded by the photographer Jiang Yiwu Dan and her husband, poet Chao Dan. They contributed every day. The authorities would surely go after them first, and they had not been arrested.

His heart was agitated now, thumping hard—even though nothing had happened. Nothing but *thinking*. The regime had successfully made *that* a crime.

Desperate for clues, for something he might have over-looked, he read the exchange once again before deleting the last one. Wen realized that he also had no idea *when* it happened. The event could be days old; this might have been the first opportunity his mother had to text. But the takeaway was clear. Members of the Dàyóu family were being held. At some point the authorities would likely come for him, even if it was not *about* him.

He started to text Anna, an artist and fellow dissident who lived in the Chaoyang District with her husband, Li. He taught Fundamentals of Statistics at UIBE; Anna had sponsored Wen's admission to CYO. He stopped typing when he realized that whatever had happened in Wuzhai, he might already be under direct surveillance. The government's Integrated Joint Opera-tions Platform might have been intercepting his communica-tions for hours . . . or even days.

He erased the new message and deleted the one from his mother after capturing the screen and saving it to photos. He might want to share it with Anna and Li. But Wen did not turn off the phone. That might seem suspicious to anyone watching and, besides, his mother might need to reach him again. Or one of the members of CYO. He used the phone to access Xinhua, the state-run media outlet. He did not search, but scrolled. There was no news about Wuzhai, nothing from the last few days anyway.

His options were narrow and limited to his next, immediate move. *Should I leave the room or stay?* he asked himself. *And if I go—go where?*

Wen was thinking that the best course—for tonight, at least—was to wait. In the morning, he would act as if everything were normal—

The decision was postponed by several quick raps on the door.

CHAPTER FOUR

Fort Belvoir North, Springfield, Virginia
February 15, 9:25 A.M.

Sharpshooter Jaz Rivette had never liked shooting ranges. Not the one run by the LAPD, not at Camp Pendleton . . . and not here.

Under most circumstances, the Marine Air-Ground Task Force lance corporal felt at home with the gunpowder-and-oil smell, the sharp report, the kick of any weapon in his hand.

Not just now. The twenty-three-year-old San Pedro, California, native liked freedom of movement and he thrived on risk, the kind he had enjoyed in Yemen, South Africa, and even in Pennsylvania. Standing here in his crisp duty uniform, spread-legged, with noise-canceling headphones, was the opposite of that. He was five foot nine, a slender man bordering on skinny. His movements had a restless, fluid quality down to his long fingers; the only time they stopped was when he aimed and fired. It was like a video had paused, suddenly and completely. His black hair was cut high and tight, giving greater prominence to his heavily lidded brown eyes.

As he emptied the Beretta M9A1, Rivette's annoyance was

even more pronounced because it was his birthday. He felt as though Major Hamilton Breen had brought him out here this morning just to spite him. It was true that Rivette needed to "re-certify" his sharpshooter status. That was one of the conditions under which he was seconded to Op-Center. But in the past seven months he had seen more action than many combatants saw in a two-year tour. All the major should have done was sign a paper and ship it back to Pendleton.

But no, Rivette thought as he finished a figure-eight pattern before drilling the bull's-eye. *Mr. JAG lawyer needs it to be official.*

He removed his headphones as he inserted the last clip. A red light came on over the target as the gunnery officer replaced the target. Major Breen was standing behind him, off to the left, entering check marks in a form on his tablet. Rivette used the break to glance back at the major.

"You know, it feels like playtime, all the drills we do in fake houses with cardboard cutouts, and assaulting cars with dummies inside. I used to do that stuff for real in the street damn near every day. But what we're doing here is unfair," said the young Black man. He added belatedly, "sir."

Though Admiral Williams was casual about rank—the years at Op-Center had tempered the man's formality—Breen appreciated the respect.

"How so, Lance Corporal?" Breen asked as he entered time and accuracy of the shots.

"Lieutenant Lee—she doesn't have to renew her black belts."

"Life is unjust," the officer agreed.

"*Or* her knife fighting. Way she uses them, they are lethal weapons."

Breen nodded ahead. The target was set.

Rivette turned toward it. "Hell, she can kill with anything she gets her hands on. Maybe there should be pencil or plastic fork certification."

The lance corporal hesitated before putting the headphones back on. He turned, his expression shifting from disapproval to concern.

"The admiral's text," the sharpshooter said. "Do you have any idea what their meeting is about?"

"I don't, Jaz."

"Dammit," the lance corporal said. "Military pays me to do what I love, but half the time I don't like what they do."

The thirty-eight-year-old major grinned as Rivette put three shots into the center of the target.

"We're done here," Breen said as he finished the form. "C'mon. I'll buy you breakfast at the commissary."

"Not the Officers' Club?" Rivette asked.

"Nice try," Breen said as they headed toward the gunnery office to return the weapon.

The Officers' Club was a three-story, antebellum-style structure located at 5500 Schulz Circle, Building 20. There was a self-serve breakfast bar, too small to be called a buffet, but there were coffee and pastries.

Lieutenant Grace Lee sat at a small, round table in the back of the room. The twenty-six-year-old wore her black hair in a short military style, tufted on top and buzzed on the sides; her eyes were dark brown but their intensity made them seem almost black.

This was not the usual table-for-four where Black Wasp usually convened. In his text to the team, Admiral Chase Williams had indicated that he wanted to see Grace alone. That was a first.

A concerning first.

The dining area was not crowded and no one here—no one on the base—knew the officer, other than to nod in recognition. Admiral Williams had told her that Op-Center had always been highly clandestine, known only to members of the intelligence community; its Joint Special Operations Command "Striker" rapid-deployment team had been even more secretive. When the entire organization was officially disbanded, a Memorandum of Understanding between the White House and the Department of Defense had created the new Op-Center: Admiral Williams plus three highly skilled members of the new Black Wasp unit.

Drinking black coffee, the woman did not bother thinking about the number of months she had been "on-loan," as Williams put it, from the U.S. Army Special Operations Command, Airborne. The military does not leave people in one unit permanently but rotates them every two to three years. It had only been seven months since she came to Fort Belvoir. That was not a factor.

Ordinarily, Lieutenant Lee did not contemplate events that were out of her control. Part of her Chan Daoist beliefs were that the past was a series of phenomena not guaranteed to repeat; the future was unknowable; and that by worrying about either, one loses today.

While the woman did not worry about it, she did think back over her actions on Black Wasp's three missions. She and Jaz Rivette had—what had he called it?

"Downscrolled," she remembered, smiling. That was it. He said it was a street term used when you put other gang members on the ground and rolled over them.

Grace's smile lingered. She had become very fond of Rivette and hoped that she had not been called here to be dismissed from Black Wasp.

She drank her coffee and watched the door, her dark eyes watchful.

Chase Williams arrived at ten o'clock exactly. Grace stood; the proud set of her shoulders made her seem taller than five foot two. She had grown to like—and, more importantly, to respect—the admiral and Major Breen as well. The man exchanged polite nods with others in the room. Even though he was not in uniform but in a quilted winter coat, slacks, and a brown sports jacket, Williams carried himself with authority. And it was in his eyes as well. Spotting her, he did not look around to avoid meeting her gaze. He expressed welcome with a little blink—it was his way—and came over. He moved easily but with the assured carriage of a commander. Williams was tall with a trim build. He had thinning, close-cropped gray hair and steady blue eyes.

Grace's lifelong training in martial arts had given her an uncanny sense to read people. The man's energy seemed good, positive. She relaxed. He was not the bearer of bad news.

He hung his coat on the freestanding rack, then sat and

adjusted the chair so that his back was to the room. Grace sat after he did.

"My *sifu* used to say that even among allies there are profiteers," she said.

"Keeping my face hidden?" he asked. He leaned in and said quietly, "I got burned a few times meeting people in public. Can't be too careful." Williams took a moment to collect his thoughts. Since leaving the Oval Office, they had been all over the geopolitical map. "Lieutenant, I'm going to get right to it since there isn't much time. The president wants you to go to Wuzhai County, China, to find out two things. First, a hypersonic missile blew up at the Taiyuan Satellite Launch Center. That was three days ago and the White House wants to know why. Second, they want to know what the payload was. The president believes—and I agree—that finding the chief engineer Dr. Yang Dàyóu is the best way to get that information. He may or may not still be at that location."

"Taiyuan is the jewel in the aerospace crown," Grace said.

"And protected accordingly," the admiral said. "Satellite photos suggest old-school fences and patrols."

"That makes sense. Low overhead and they don't have to answer for shooting someone who gets too close."

Williams waited for her to process that challenge before adding, "You're going over in the capacity of a security advisor to the new embassy staff. A civilian flight with embassy personnel leaves this afternoon at three. The president wants you on it."

The woman smiled faintly. Williams believed he knew why. He had felt the same rush of pride the first time a president had

asked for him by name. And he was twice the age of the lieutenant.

"Will the staff know who I am?" she asked.

"Only the job description I just outlined. The parameters
attached to the diplomatic notice from President Wright are 'to
conduct reconnaissance and gather intelligence without spying.'"

"An interesting distinction," Grace said.

"But a distinction nonetheless. You can approach but not
encroach. You can ask but not interrogate. You can observe but
not divert—"

"You mean do not touch?"

"Do not steal or relocate, so yes. Play safe."

The question had been slightly whimsical; the answer was
not.

"This grants you a measure of diplomatic immunity. In-
fringe upon that and you will be disavowed." He waited a moment for the gravity of that to sink in; he hoped it had. "Apart
from me, the president, his chief of staff, the ambassador, and
national security assistant January Dow are the only people in
the loop on your real mission."

"What about Black Wasp?"

"They don't know and I was not given a SAFE disposition
for them."

Support and Assist Function Endorsement was a command
order that allocated personnel, resources, and budget to assist
any military or intelligence operation. Absent such an authorization, help provided by any entity would be off the books and
legally illegitimate.

"What do we know about Dr. Dàyóu?" Grace asked.

"Nothing. I've asked Dow to send everything they have about him and also about the base."

"Shanxi isn't very far from Beijing," she said. "About two hundred and fifty miles by air."

"Have you ever been there?"

The lieutenant shook her head.

"Any family in the region?"

She grinned.

"Who?" Williams asked.

"An uncle—Sun Fenghe, my mother's older brother. A *crazy* uncle. He lives in Shanxi Province and works as a generator repairman in neighboring Wuzhai, at the coal power station. Both are near Taiyuan."

"Sounds promising. In what way is your uncle crazy?" Williams asked.

"The launch facility was originally situated in Taiyuan because of its power needs and the proximity of a rail line," Grace said. "I believe the proximity to the large lake there was also a factor."

"Like Cape Canaveral being on the Atlantic in case a rocket aborts."

"That is my guess. Uncle Sun's father was proud of the industrial nature of his home. It meant progress after centuries of stagnation. But lately, according to Sun, the region has begun to change. Jinzhou is the site of the new Greenbelt Development Zone Project, the planting and preservation of over ten miles of rustic beauty. It's similar to the Greenway in Nanxi, all of it to obscure the fact that China is still burning a great deal of coal. Uncle Sun wrote to my mother that he hates what is being done to his old, industrial home and has been disciplined several times for one-man protests against nature."

"He has a backbone, like his niece."

"Tempered, somewhat." Grace laughed. "He's a Confucian."

"Meaning?"

"His faith is in the social order, on Earth, not in spiritual matters."

This was the first time Williams had seen Grace show any levity about her family. The lieutenant grew up on Mott Street in New York's Chinatown where her parents ran the *Mulberry Community* newspaper, which advocated against the exploitation of undocumented Chinese and the institutions that supported them. Her father carried a handgun, but Grace had begun studying martial arts at age four to protect herself. On those rare occasions when she talked about her past it was with ever-present concern about her parents' safety.

"Are you on speaking terms with Uncle Sun?" Williams asked.

"I haven't communicated with him in over a year," Grace said. "But I will."

"Does he speak English—in case Breen or Rivette need to communicate."

"Unfortunately, no. Speaking of Black Wasp—"

"I'll meet with them when we're finished."

"Jaz won't like being left behind."

"None of us will, and we'll have to do some thinking about that."

Grace was about to say, *"Admiral, I can do this,"* but checked herself. After three difficult missions, Chase Williams obviously had confidence in her abilities. In each of those strikes absolutely nothing stayed within the POP, the Projected Operational Parameters, or went according to the MOM, the Mission Outline Manifest presented to the president.

"Assuming we go on a support footing," Williams continued, "there are cities that offer anonymity and are somewhat proximate to the target."

"Did President Wright give you that latitude, Admiral?"

"He didn't *not* grant it," Williams replied. "Back on Pennsylvania Avenue they call that 'plausible deniability.'"

Grace frowned. "Nothing has changed."

"How so?"

"For more than a century, gangs in Chinatown have protected their leaders the same way."

Williams sat back and took his cell phone from his jacket pocket. He did not want to think about that too deeply; he might not like the picture that emerged.

"I'm going to go see the others," he told her as he texted. "January will be sending me your personal documentation by messenger. We only chatted briefly—she had a meeting to get back to—but we agreed that you will use your real name and should stick as close to the truth as possible. You're going over to train the embassy guards in hand-to-hand combat."

"That makes things simpler. I can tell my parents, then. I'll also contact Uncle Sun."

Williams nodded. "I'll forward January's materials and her electronic files as soon as they arrive. Is there anything you want to discuss, any comments?"

"Just one comment," she replied. "Thank you for this opportunity."

"You're welcome. Now there's one more thing I want to say. I know you've had PUR training with Major Breen."

"Yes, and I've reviewed the outline he gave us."

"Good. I have some things I want to add."

PUR was the Department of Defense classification system for psychological disorders. One of them—and the most common—was Progressive Undercover Rapport, the idea that finding more and more to like in enemy territory weakened the resolve to act with hostile force. Breen said it was especially true when one is undercover—whether in a gang or a country—where there is a historic or ancestral connection.

"You're going to your homeland," Williams continued. "That's a compelling, I'll go so far as to say a seductive experience. While you're there you absolutely *should* take everything in. Let that comfort, that connection show in your expression, your walk. That will make you more credible as a local. Fighting it will only make you stand out. But do remember this. The leaders of China are not our friends. Even as the Midkiff administration cracked down, Beijing still planted thousands of nationals, with false visas, in key industries across the nation. Most had ties to the People's Liberation Army. These plants coordinate closely and regularly with diplomats in China's six American consulates to undermine our tech, financial, and energy businesses as well as the military. They do not just want to hurt us, Grace. They want to destroy us. And if this missile is ever perfected, that statement will give grave tactical meaning to that idea."

"What you're saying, sir, is school them."

Williams smiled. "Yeah. But don't overschool."

"Sir?"

"Germany, Italy, Japan, Korea—a lot of our soldiers who went over were embarrassed by what their ancestral homelands had done and went with a wipe-them-out attitude, like flagellants atoning for the sins of their brothers and sisters. Overkill is as dangerous as underperformance, especially in matters of espionage."

"Understood, sir. Balance. Yin-yang in equilibrium."

Williams got the general idea and nodded.

Grace rose and saluted, then excused herself as Williams lingered to text the others. Despite her intellectual grasp of the challenge, the admiral knew it would require constant vigilance on the lieutenant's part. She could play the native to near-perfection, but a single slip at the wrong time and the mission—and Grace Lee—were done.

The admiral told the other two team members to meet him at Soldier Statesman Park in ten minutes. It was cold but the park would be empty. Good for security and good for Rivette, who was going to need room to pace.

A great deal of it.

CHAPTER FIVE

The Beijing Center, University of International
Business and Economics

Beijing, China
February 15, 9:39 P.M., CST

The two insistent knocks were followed by a familiar voice,
raspy from cigarettes.

"Wen! Are you there?"

The young man's heart slowed like a fan suddenly unplugged.
It sounded like Chao Dan. Wen glanced over at Kong, who was
still asleep. Like a bear, when Kong slept he hibernated. The
young radical swung from the bed and hurried to the door, loudly
whispering, *Shh, shh, shh*.

During those few seconds the young man's mind shifted
from his own unresolved situation to the caller. Had something
happened to his wife? Was the poet here to seek asylum? Her
pictures were sometimes distributed globally on the internet,
unattributed—but someone in them may have been identified,
interrogated, pointed Wen out.

Even through the door, Wen recognized the clinging smell of the poet's Chunghwa cigarettes. Wen turned the lock above the knob and opened the door. Chao was wearing jeans and a heavy black-hooded sweatshirt. The front of the garment had the photo of a statue of Cáo Xuěqín, a great eighteenth-century writer. Wen looked past the visitor, did not see any students or police, then motioned him forward. The poet entered. Wen quietly shut the door and motioned the newcomer toward the small kitchen area. Chao was in his late thirties, tall, gaunt, and hollow-eyed, someone who had seen too much, too often. He did not seem agitated, though there was an urgency to his movements.

"What is it?" Wen asked in an urgent whisper.

"There was an explosion at the Taiyuan Satellite Launch Center two or three days ago. A satellite image was posted on Bagua."

"My father—?"

"Unhurt, we believe, but there is a report from someone that he was taken into custody."

"Someone who *saw* him?"

"Yes. A trainman on the Ningwu–Kelan railway saw him as they were helping to evacuate technical workers. This man saw someone under heavy guard placed in a staff car and driven somewhere inside the compound. He said it looked like your father."

That would explain, of course, his mother's text.

"They cannot believe he would sabotage his own project," Wen said. "Not Dr. Yang Dàyóu."

"Would you put any suspicion past the PLA or the Ministry of State Security? This is a very important defense project, friend."

"What about my family?"

"I was about to ask you," Chao said. "Have you had any indication of anything wrong?"

Wen shook his head. He was not going to explain how he and his mother communicated or give out any information that might be extracted from Chao Dan.

"Then maybe your family does not know," Chao said.

"They would have heard the explosion—"

"But they wouldn't know what caused it. The absence of the chief engineer after any mishap would be understandable. Perhaps you should contact them."

"For what purpose?"

"If they are all right, then you probably have nothing to fear. There is something else," he added. "Even if they are not involved, they might be held as leverage against your father. Talk to them. Find out."

Chao could not know that the family was already being detained. Hearing the dangers articulated, logically, was unnerving.

"I won't risk it, for their safety or mine," Wen said. "The MSS may be listening."

"Then they will hear nothing but innocent voices," Chao said.

"No. How would I explain my sudden concern?"

"You can say you were thinking of your mother and sister."

Chao was pushing and Wen suspected why: fodder for the website. He shook his head.

"Then at the very least you should consider leaving here, and quickly," Chao said. "If your family *has* been taken they will need someone on the outside to inform the public . . . the world."

"What do you suggest?"

"My wife thinks you should come to our place."

"That is kind of her," Wen replied.

"We can take the subway. We can lose ourselves."

Chao was right. At this hour students were returning from late shift jobs and night work. The young man looked down, took a moment to consider the offer. As he replayed the conversation in his mind, tried to reconcile what he knew to be true with his guest's concerns, a comment Chao had made jolted him. His eyes rose warily. "Tell me something."

"Yes?"

"How do you know I have a sister?"

Chao was guarded. "You must have told us."

"My father's work is classified. I make it a point never to discuss family."

Chao held up his hands as if in surrender. "All right, Wen. Jiang and I check up on every person we allow into the group. We have to."

"No, you didn't read about us online. My father's biography was scrubbed years ago. There isn't even a photo of him at one of his projects."

Chao's features became disapproving. "Wen, I come here

to help you and you accuse me of—what, collaborating with the authorities?"

"I'm merely asking a question, Chao, which you haven't answered."

"I risked my own safety to come here."

"Did you? My sister, Chao. How do you know?"

The poet hesitated and, standing frozen in the doorway, Wen grew anxious again.

"Let me ask *you* a question," Chao said, moving closer. "Do you have the courage to dissent?"

"What do you mean? Of course! I wouldn't have joined—"

"That isn't dissent. It's not sedition. It's provocation, earnest boys and girls throwing a little tantrum. It isn't bravery to wear a mask, stand in a group, thrust your fist in the air, then scatter. Crouching behind an online alias and 'bravely' quoting incarcerated activists is not courage. I'm asking if you would ever truly pit yourself against the authorities?"

It was another dodge, but that did not mean the question was illegitimate. Wen had often wondered that himself but had never been forced to decide. Chao was right. When the authorities brought in tanks or hoses, the Counterrevolutionaries usually dispersed.

"I don't know," Wen said. "But *you* wouldn't challenge the Communists. Does—does your *wife* know you're a collaborator?"

"Watch what you call me, Wen."

"Then you tell me what word to use. You *are* working with them, yes?"

The poet's unashamed expression was not just incriminating, it was sickening.

"How can you do this?" Wen asked.

"It was necessary," Chao said. He snickered. "Jiang thought she was being very clever."

"You're going to blame *her*?"

"Brother, stop talking and *listen*! The Counterrevolutionary Youth Organization was Jiang's idea. I believed in the mission and I supported it. She thought she was being very clever. She encrypted the data with military-grade software from a South Korean sympathizer, and we thought we were safe. We were not. I was approached at our apartment when she was out photographing a rally." He soured. "'Approached.' Three MSS men in plain clothes came and issued an ultimatum. Either I worked with them, furnished data on our members, or they would wait until my wife came home and arrest us both."

Wen was stunned. He shook his head. "I don't believe this. The protests—why haven't the authorities cracked down?"

"That's exactly my point! They stopped others, arrested people by the score. Why didn't they stop us? It's a tactic. They allow a little leeway, just enough so that troublemakers do not burrow back underground. Then they arrest the ones who start to become too well-known. You aren't nearly as strident as others, but your very membership may be one of the reasons they suspect your father of sabotage."

"He doesn't even know what I do!"

Chao brightened, and Wen instantly regretted having said

that. He seemed to fold into himself with the hopelessness of it all. Even though what he had said might help exonerate his father, Wen was disgusted by—what did Jiang once call it? The "soft confession," the truth collected by trust rather than through force.

Wen turned away. "I can't believe this. I can't believe what you've done."

"You know," Chao said, "it's one thing to put on a mask and stand in a crowd raising your fist, or to hide behind a foolish name online and quote some incarcerated revolutionary. It's quite another to truly challenge the authorities. I did not possess that kind of courage. Do you?"

"If the choice is to be a traitor to my family and friends, like you, I may have to find out."

"Don't," Chao cautioned sharply.

"Are they watching this building?" Wen asked, facing him. "Am I under surveillance?"

Chao nodded.

Wen leaned against the sink, filled a glass with water and drank it. He felt nauseated. His trust had been built on lies. The silence in the tiny kitchen was suddenly very heavy. He recalled ticking clocks in his childhood home. He wished he were there right now.

"This doesn't have to hurt," Chao said.

"Too late."

"The surprise and youthful disappointment will pass," Chao assured him. "Come back with me. You'll be safe and we can talk. You can *help* your father."

"How?"

"By clearing him. By talking about him, about his friends outside of the space center."

"By spying on my own father?"

"Don't be a ridiculous. It isn't spying to confirm a man's loyalty."

Wen felt cold, and it was not only because the heat from the sleeping area did not reach here. The chill was coming from deep inside. Chao was right about this much: whatever heroic lightning Wen felt marching with others or typing some post-worthy wisdom . . . all of that was ephemeral. Here and now, thunder did not rumble.

Chao laid a hand on the student's shoulder. "If you believe nothing else, believe that this is best for all."

The man's touch disgusted him. To have trusted him once was a reasonable risk. His poetry was passionate, with a sense of history and destiny.

But to trust him now? Wen thought. That was not possible.

And there was something else; two things, now that he thought about it. One was the awareness that for the rest of his tenure in school, and possibly beyond, he would be living in a glass cage, observed by the MSS. After the situation with his father had passed, as he was sure it would, his own activism would be remembered . . . and watched. The other issue was Wen's self-respect. It had evaporated under a stream of words from this fraud, this hypocrite. If he went now, he risked losing it forever.

But then there was this hard reality: *Not going with him is putting myself directly into the hands of the MSS.*

"All right," the young man said after consideration. "I'll go with you."

Chao smiled and squeezed Wen's shoulder. "It's the right choice. I promise, I will look out for you."

Wen returned to the sleeping area. He moved quietly, though Kong had not stirred. He recovered his phone, grabbed a knitted pullover from a peg on the wall, and slipped it on. He was still cold and trembling, gripped by fear and anxiety. He was not just alone but about to commit himself to the care of an admitted spy.

The young man turned back. Chao had moved to the door where he stood smiling benignly, like one of the *Sāncái*, the Three Augusts of Heaven.

"Let me ask you *a question,"* Chao's voice echoed in his brain. *"Do you have the courage to dissent?"*

Wen's legs moved mechanically for several steps. Then he ran forward. It was not courage but a sudden welling of rage and fear that caused Wen to lunge at the man, knocking him to the floor.

CHAPTER SIX

Soldier Statesman Park, Fort Belvoir North,
Springfield, Virginia
February 15, 9:54 A.M.

"We didn't have butt-freezing days like this in Southern California," said Jaz Rivette.

The lance corporal was sitting on a bench on the dry, yellowed grass; Major Hamilton Breen stood beside him with one foot on the iron armrest. He was leaning on his knee. Breen's head was bare, revealing black hair worn in a classic regulation cut. He was five foot eleven with gray eyes and a neutral expression developed over years spent in courtrooms. Around them were the skeletons of bare trees and empty trash cans. Both men were dressed in the sweat clothes they had been wearing at the shooting range, though each had slipped on a blue, Fort Belvoir Second Army windbreaker, a cherished relic of an inactivated unit.

Rivette was wearing his cold weather shooter gloves with synthetic leather palms and spandex backs and fingers. He was still cold and exhaled on his fingers.

"You were out here yesterday when it was below freezing," Breen pointed out.

"That was different. I was watching some guys playing tug-of-war and they went at it fierce. Big, beefy dudes. You could make toast off the heat they were putting out."

"They must have been getting ready for Able Forces Fitness Day," Breen told him. "I saw it on the calendar, a fundraiser for military families in financial distress."

"Nice. My Cajun grandma—she cooked stuff for needy folks in L.A. Most of it was too hot for them to eat, but she kept making that spicy jambalaya and those hot shrimp skewers."

"Stubbornness is a family trait, then?" Breen teased.

"The Rivettes and the Broussards—we got a backbone, yessir."

Breen called it obstinacy but Williams described it as youthful confidence. Regardless, neither man begrudged the re-markable young man his "backbone." Rivette had discovered his proficiency with handguns at age ten when he stopped a bodega robbery with the owner's .38. It was the first time he had handled a weapon, and the two assailants went down with matching wounds through the hip. The LAPD invited Jaz to take a gun safety program, where he excelled in the junior marksmanship class. Joining the marines at age twenty, Rivette had won a Distinguished Marksman Badge and a Distinguished Pistol Shot Badge, among other citations and medals. His goal, he had told his Black Wasp teammates, was to not just break but shatter the 2.2-mile pickoff record established by a sharpshooter of Canada's Joint Task Force 2 against an ISIS fighter in 2017.

The Black Wasp teammates had been there less than five minutes when Williams came striding across the park. Without stopping, he returned the salute of a captain who was walking his dog. The man must have known Williams, since the admiral wore no outward sign of his former rank.

Breen and Rivette were not surprised that Lieutenant Lee was not with them; it was the first time they had not met with the admiral as a group, and there was already a sense that this was a different kind of mission.

"Where do you think we're going?" Rivette asked as Williams approached.

"It's winter, so probably Siberia . . . maybe the North Pole."

Rivette chuckled. Breen was not a man inclined to levity. Even a hint of it was welcome.

For the major, his joke was a mild expression of the fact that the unpredictable ways of Black Wasp did not fit his nature. He was an attorney and a criminologist who thrived on order. As a respected member of the Judge Advocate General's Corps, he had done everything by the book and by the numbers. His unshakeable belief was that baked into the Constitution was the answer to every problem, every question, every fork in the road America might face.

Breen had been assigned to Black Wasp precisely because his mind worked with a proof-like progression from situation to resolution. He did not like not knowing what was coming, and having to prepare on the fly was a skill he was trying to master.

"Sorry to be late," Williams said. "I would have had you meet me in the chapel but they're renovating."

"Pray and fly, like they said at Pendleton," Rivette remarked. "Check in with the Lord before heading to the Middle East."

Williams remained standing. "*We're* not going anywhere. At least, not yet."

He had the sharp, sudden attention of both men.

The admiral explained the mission, which resulted in a rare moment of accord between the other two members: they did not like it.

"Lieutenant Lee has never gone undercover on her own," Rivette said, no longer cold.

"We haven't drilled for solo missions," Breen added pointedly. "Does the president understand that?"

"*I'm* aware of that," Williams said. "But I have no authority to refuse the president's order. Nor would I. You can't argue that there isn't a need for HUMINT on the *Qi*-19 project and that, like it or not, the lieutenant is the only one who speaks the language and wouldn't attract attention."

HUMINT stood for human intelligence, a resource that had been diminished by the proliferation of satellites, computer hacking, wireless interception, and other forms of ELINT— electronic intelligence. ELINT cast a wider net and tied up fewer resources. And it was certainly less risky in terms of human life.

"Are you saying, Admiral, that except for the essential task of finishing my recertification forms, we're supposed to do nothing while the lieutenant's in-country?" Rivette asked.

"Admiral Williams did not say that," Breen informed him. "Following protocol, he outlined the mission for us."

Williams and Breen exchanged knowing looks. From his years with JAG, Breen understood procedure—and commanders—in a way that Rivette did not. Even with allies, a commander said nothing about an off-the-books mission until he was certain everyone was on board. Breen knew that Rivette was not his concern: the JAG officer was. Williams was about to propose something highly illegal and, without the ET—Expressed or Tacit—approval of the president, that meant this was all on the admiral.

Williams sat beside Rivette, casually looking around to make sure no other dog walkers or runners were nearby.

"I'm thinking about a quick hat-up for 'field training,'" Williams said.

That fell within Williams' purview. Breen did not object.

"Major, you've run a great deal of tactical and weapons training here, and just recertified the lance corporal," Williams went on. "What we cannot do, except with cardboard cutouts and mannequins in a nondescript village mock-up, is infiltration."

"We did fine busting into Yemen, sir," Rivette pointed out, still harboring the notion that he was being benched.

"That was a hunt, Jaz. We had focus, and there were four of us covering north, south, east, west. I'd like us to drill in a foreign land, open-ended."

"What land?" Rivette asked.

"To be determined," Williams answered. "You on board, Major?"

"We'll be in the same global neighborhood as Lieutenant Lee?" Breen answered.

"That's right."

The major answered without hesitation, "Sounds good."

"Thank you," Williams said. "I'm going to get in touch with Matt Berry, see exactly where in that neighborhood he can put us."

Rivette smiled. "That's what I like to hear."

Matt Berry was the former deputy chief of staff and one of Williams' biggest boosters during the Midkiff administration. Berry had just accepted the position of managing director at the Trigram Institute, a Georgetown-based think tank—though Williams had described it as a "payday hustle." Berry and his associates bartered their access and intelligence for favors in areas where their reach was limited. These new contacts gave Trigram fresh insights that the firm then sold to interests ranging from the government to the military, from banks to energy and tech companies. Their only principle was to sell only to America and its historic allies.

"The administration will not know about an expanded Black Wasp involvement," Breen stated.

"They will not," Williams told him.

The counselor did not conceal his uneasiness. His next question did not surprise Williams. No one but Williams, Berry, and the president knew about the currency reserves in Op-Center's safe and bank accounts.

"Do you intend for Trigram to finance this trip?" Breen asked.

"I do not."

"Just so the lance corporal understands, if we were ever to accept outside funding it would violate at least a dozen federal statutes ranging from influence peddling to kickbacks. Even if Black Wasp never left Fort Belvoir, that shadow would fall over everyone."

"I broke a lot of Commandments growing up," Rivette said. "I like the part that sounds like we're not in danger of de-funding."

"We are not," Williams said. He regarded the major. "As for the rest, there is no potential criminality in Black Wasp following the direct order of the director of Op-Center. Execution is under your direction, Major, but the mission directive is governed by the JSOC MOU clause of the charter. You have a copy."

"I know the section," Breen said.

JSOC was the Joint Special Operations Command, the rapid-deployment, multi-service unit that was created in a secret Memorandum of Understanding between the White House, the Department of Defense, and Op-Center. It began with Striker under founding Op-Center director Paul Hood. It was relaunched as simply JSOC cell team under the reorganization overseen by Williams.

"Do I want to know more about our director's activities?" Breen asked.

Williams smiled thinly. "You do not."

Rivette said, "If this shadow talk that I still don't understand is done, sir, can we pick a spot we wouldn't mind living in for a while?"

"I'll do that," Williams said.

Rivette jumped to his feet, stamping out the chill in his legs. "Admiral, is Lieutenant Lee still here?"

"You've got a little time to see her," Williams assured him. "She's wheels up at three and she has preparations to make."

"Right."

Williams left and Rivette turned to Breen. "Can we finish my recertification? I feel like shooting something."

"Sure. I'll be along presently."

Breen lingered. The sharp sun and crisp air were an invigorating combination. The major was still unhappy. Breen's job was to advise the admiral on international law as well as to oversee investigations and forensics. What Williams implied was a violation of 31 USC, Section 1301, the Misappropriation Act, among numerous other federals laws. Slush funds for OCOs—Overseas Contingency Operations—were not specifically disallowed. So-called rainy day funds afforded the military as well as the State Department necessary flexibility above baseline budgets and the ever-present threat of sequestration—cuts mandated by Congress. But it was one thing to bank skimmed portions of an authorized budget. It was quite another to amass funds from outside sources, even if those sources were related government agencies.

Before joining Black Wasp, Breen had regularly conducted mock court-martials at the University of Virginia. He began each trial reminding participants of their heritage and duty by quoting lawyer-president John Adams:

"The fundamental law of the militia is, that it be created, directed and commanded by the laws, and ever for the support of the laws."

However many crises Black Wasp averted, regardless of the

bad actors they stopped or even terminated, a financial misstep like that would put Chase Williams in prison. For Breen, the challenge was at once simple and insurmountable:

Pointing out that risk would change nothing.

CHAPTER SEVEN

The Defense Logistics Agency, Fort Belvoir, Virginia
February 15, 10:29 A.M.

The Defense Logistics Agency was part of Fort Belvoir. Matt Berry and President Midkiff had made that arrangement for command and support so that as little electronic communication as possible passed between Williams and the rest of the team. Both men knew that the new Op-Center would not be playing by the rules. They did not want a digital trail that might lead to Black Wasp . . . or the Oval Office.

Williams drove the five minutes to his office. A division of the Department of Defense, the DLA was chartered solely to provide combat support. Because of its vast budget and secretive activities, the organization quickly became a repository of numerous unrelated black ops units tasked with secret military and technological operations.

These sanctioned and unsanctioned operations were housed in the McNamara Headquarters, nine connected five-story structures arranged in a semicircle. The complex was named for the first director of the DLA, Lieutenant General Andrew

T. McNamara, U.S. Army. The façade of the lower two floors was white, the upper floors were rust-colored, and they wrapped around a large reflecting pool, tennis courts, and basketball courts that created the feeling of a campus.

Williams had not availed himself of any of those since the day he arrived.

The admiral parked in the underground garage and took an elevator to a subbasement. His office was off a semicircular corridor that matched the curve of the building. None of the doors bore the names of agencies or personnel. Williams knew others down here by sight but not by name; there were sociable nods but nothing more. Though the admiral picked out erect, assured military bearing all around him, no one was in uniform. None of the faces had changed with the new administration. Williams wondered how many people in government even knew these people were down here. Even January Dow did not know where Chase Williams went every morning.

He closed the door, plugged his phone into the power cable, and set it aside. The office was spartan. He had hung no photographs, patches, or flags to indicate where he had served or who he was.

Williams unlocked his computer and accessed the WIPE program—Worldwide Intelligence Protective Encryption, an uplink to the Department of Defense orbiting X-40A. Launched six months ago, the automated spaceplane was twenty-two feet long with a twelve-foot wingspan. It protected communications by constantly shifting its orbit, incremental movements that baffled both the Earth- and space-based spy satellites of other nations.

Each office in the complex was soundproofed with electronic scramblers built into the walls and door. The technology was similar to that of the White House Situation Room
and the Tank, the conference room at the former Op-Center
facility. Even though he was in a nest of spies armed—he had
to assume—with bleeding-edge listening devices of their own,
Williams could not text fast enough to get done what needed to
be done. He put in a video call to Matt Berry. The familiar face
looked more relaxed than it had three months before.

"Chase! Haven't seen you since my open house here. I was
beginning to wonder if you were off on some mission. But you're
looking too rested."

"You too."

"Not rested . . . unstressed," Berry said.

"Then everything's good at the Trigram town house?"

"To paraphrase Neil Armstrong, it was a short trip from
Pennsylvania Avenue to Wisconsin Avenue but one giant leap,"
Berry said. "I love having conversations about ideas and policy
instead of dealing with politics and compromise."

"I envy that," Williams said, smiling.

"What's up, Admiral? Have you had a second meeting with
Wright?"

"Yes, and if I had time I would be talking to you over a
drink. All I can tell you is that I may need to get three of us plus
weapons airborne as soon as possible, likely destinations Beijing
or Taiwan."

"Unauthorized support for a solo mission," Berry said.
"That's an ideal way to start things off with Wright."

"I know the risks, Matt."

"I'd still think about them a little harder," Berry cautioned. "You're 'in' because of your accomplishments, not cronyism or deep-state connections. One screwup—"

"I know that too. Anyway, I can't use Janet Airlines if I want to go incognito."

"To put it mildly," Berry said. "Why not ask one of your old CENTCOM buddies? They go everywhere, a good fifteen percent of it unlogged."

"As far as anyone knows, I'm retired—"

"Right, right. There'll be questions. Look, I can probably arrange something—you know that or you wouldn't have called. But Chase—you *are* going to have to tell me where you're going."

"Yeah," Williams said.

The admiral knew it, too, and it would mean crossing a security line that could end in prison. A mission briefing by the president, with highly restricted access to said briefing, was automatically considered "secret." That was a step above "confidential" and below "top secret." The criteria were whether direct or indirect disclosure could damage foreign relations, national security, military plans, intelligence operations, and—most directly in this case—the study of significant scientific or technological developments relating to national security.

The failure of an understaffed mission could do all of that too, he told himself.

"Northwestern Shanxi province," Williams said.

If Berry suspected that the destination had anything to

do with the Taiyuan Satellite Launch Center, he said nothing. Williams could hear him typing.

"My initial thoughts were Beijing, Taipei, or Seoul," Williams went on. "We could lay low unless—"

"I wouldn't do any of those," Berry interrupted.

"Oh?"

"Beijing leaves you vulnerable to electronic surveillance, which just got an AI self-learning overhaul. They call it *Guǐ yǎn*, Ghost Eyes. It deputizes smartphone signals to spy on calls made within a quarter-mile radius. The program searches out languages and keywords in those languages. The user is never aware of having been piggybacked."

"I hadn't heard that," Williams admitted.

"You're a downsized operation, Chase. Ironically, Trigram got it from Matt Stoll."

"Paul Hood's IT guy?"

Berry nodded. "Class of Op-Center 1.0. Stoll went into business with Stephen Viens, formerly of the National Reconnaissance Office. They spot and identify dangerous new and emerging tech. We have them on retainer. Helps us formulate white papers."

"What's wrong with Taipei and Seoul?"

"They'd require an additional air or sea trip to China, with its own challenges."

"I remember using some off-the-grid ships and planes at Op-Center 2.0."

"That was then," Berry said. "A year ago, China's coastline was more porous than it is now. Patrols have trebled with satellites to back them up. Chase, you're a brilliant strike team now but without experts like Brian Dawson in Operations and Duncan Sutherland in Logistics. They were good."

"Top of the line."

"Right, and this is China we're talking about, not Yemen or South Africa."

Berry was not only right, Williams was annoyed that he had not thought to ask those questions.

"Got any suggestions?" Williams asked.

"If you're going for proximity and concealment, I'd suggest southern Mongolia."

Williams studied the familiar face in the monitor. That sounded like the kind of remark the frequently sarcastic Matt Berry might have jokingly suggested: a remote, unlikely destination where one *might* be able to get away from the ever-shifting, endless games and partisanship of the nation's capital. But Berry's expression said he was being serious.

"You won't be able to speak the language," Berry went on, "but that's a good thing. There are enough countries in the region with blended populations that the team could pass for anything."

"You're suggesting we go to—what, a village? A city? The desert?"

"You tell me and then I'll make some calls. And when you say 'we,' do you mean you as well?"

Williams had been wrestling with that. Not divulging it to Berry but deciding whether or not to go. Grace would need someone to report to if she found out anything, which meant him, here. But having an extra person in the field would help if she got into trouble.

"I'll get back to you on that," Williams said.

"Fine. Are you going in with papers?"

"No."

"Just wanted to know. I can work around that."

"How?"

"Putinomics."

"Sounds flip."

"Oh, it's real. Under Putin, Russia's black market has exploded to make up one quarter of the nation's GDP. Mongolia has a similar fat black market stratum even closer to the economic surface. Hell, it starts right there in the capital. The Khar Zakh in Ulaanbaatar is the go-to place for anything from guns to dinosaur fossils and stolen goods. A lot of it stolen right there, in fact, by pocket-slashers. You get to buy your own belongings back."

"You're saying we can buy anything we need right off the plane, including passage," Williams confirmed.

"Not just buy but shop and haggle, if you have the time. You can talk a man out of his only horse, if the price is right—though I think ATVs have become more common. The kind of things you'd need are in the open, within walking distance of the airport. I also have to know if you want your ride to wait on the ground. That will impact who I ask. The closer you are to China, the more it costs and the fewer the options. Not every pilot in a rabbit fur coat is anxious to drop wheels or anchor in that region."

"Give me an hour or so to figure all that out," Williams said.

"Take an hour and a half," Berry joked.

"Thanks."

The admiral ended the call and sat back. Berry was right, of course. Unless Williams divulged the nature of the mission, this was his decision. It was the first time in his career that Williams would have to make a decision without a staff or a team of outside advisors. Major Breen was the one Black Wasp whose counsel he sought—but only after a tactical determination had been made.

This was unfamiliar and it was lonely.

Like Mongolia, Williams thought.

The admiral opened the Op-Center files on the nation that was situated between and dependent upon Russia and China. The area Berry had proposed was largely unpopulated, and with good reason: it consisted largely of the massive Gobi Desert. But it was not the exotic wasteland of fiction and fable. At this time of year the region was dominated by air masses from Siberia, making the average temperature 15.7 degrees—some 20 degrees colder than it was at Fort Belvoir.

Before Black Wasp had assembled to track down the mastermind behind the attack on the *Intrepid* in New York, they had undergone specialized training that included weekends in Kodiak, Alaska. The individual members had already had survival training; this was, as Rivette joked, a "warm-up" course. They had worked in snow and ice and had trained in the newest Rewarming Drills—how to recover after being submerged for ten minutes, to the chin, in a below-freezing lake.

But those were forty-eight-hour ordeals, living in Arctic conditions, Williams thought. On American soil. With English-speaking support. *Wasps don't survive the winter.*

Horseback was apparently the preferred form of transportation in the region. Williams hoped that Berry came up with something better. Williams had ridden some but Breen was a motorcycle man and Rivette had dune buggies on his résumé.

Despite the challenges—and he would have to look a little harder at the other options—there was only one thing Williams feared more. And it was only a matter of time before friendly fire launched its first salvos.

CHAPTER EIGHT

The Beijing Center, University of International
Business and Economics

Beijing, China
February 15, 10:11 P.M., CST

Kong Yanyong woke to a racket that sounded like his food cart losing its brakes. The big man was in motion before he was fully awake, drawn to the light coming from the kitchen. As he hulked through the bedroom he could hear and then see two figures tangled fighting in the hallway.

Kong easily made out Wen in the spill of light. He was growling low in his throat, his lips pressed shut to lock the cry inside. He was lying on top of another man who was taller and flopping like a live carp on a griddle. Wen had his legs splayed; that, plus his weight, kept the other man pinned facedown on the gray carpet tiles. Wen's left hand was pushing the man's right temple down; his right hand was tight across the victim's mouth to mute his cries. If anyone had heard the commotion they would have remained very still and silent, listening and not interfering. For all they knew this was a police action.

Kong stood over the two. The eyes of the man on the bottom rolled toward him, imploring.

"What's happened?" Kong cried.

"This man is a betraying bastard!" Wen cried. With an angry grunt, the student pushed the man's head harder into the carpet. Chao's struggles left streaks of blood on the dark threads.

"Let him up," Kong said. "I'll handle this."

Wen eased aside and Kong forcefully grabbed the figure. The big man lifted the dazed fellow and, with one thick hand, held him upright by the lapel. The victim was wheezing and wobbly. Cigarettes from a torn pack in the pocket of his sweatshirt tumbled to the floor. Chao was also bleeding, his forehead and cheek rubbed raw on the industrial-grade carpet.

"Say, don't I know this man?" Kong asked. With the one fist he walked the poet into the kitchen, under the fluorescent light. "Buddy, it's your friend Chao!"

"No friend at all," Wen said.

"Why was he here at this hour?" Chao asked.

"Stinking business," said Wen. The student was unsteady and trembling from the violent struggle with Chao, his white shirt ripped and missing buttons. He ignored all that as he quickly considered what lie to tell Kong. "This traitor wanted me to join his revolutionary cult."

Kong was openly surprised. The big man was the maternal and fraternal grandson of men who had fought with Mao against the Kuomintang, the national party that was chased and contained on Taiwan. He was devoted to his heritage.

"No wonder he was skulking about in darkness," Kong said. "He's a poet, isn't he?"

"That's right."

"Ah. Mao said that there is no such thing as art that is detached from politics."

"Mao was right about so many things," Wen said.

"You . . . patronizing dog!" Chao spat.

"Shut up!" Wen said—though the man was right. It was lip service. He did not care for any Communists.

The student went back to his bed. Surprised by his sudden and unexpected conviction, he took a backpack from where it hung on the headboard and began gathering the things he would need—his laptop, phone, wallet, and identification papers. He turned off his phone so it could not be traced. Working with the Counterrevolutionaries had taught him that much. He went to the drawer and grabbed a change of socks and underwear, stuffed them into the backpack, then put it on the bed.

"Can you lean him against the wall?" Wen asked.

Kong pushed Chao against the wall beside the kitchen and pinned him there with a palm to his shoulder. Wen began to remove the man's sweatshirt.

"Hey!" Chao complained, coming around a bit and pushing back.

This time it was Wen who slammed him against the wall. A lot of disappointment went into that push. The poet exhaled loudly as the front of the jamb went into his spine. When the sweatshirt had been removed, Kong let the man slump to the floor.

"Stay there," Kong warned. Then he regarded Wen. "What are you going to do?"

Wen motioned his friend away from the kitchen, from Chao. He answered softly as he slipped into the sweatshirt.

"Chao has accomplices hiding outside. I want them to think I'm him."

"You better put the backpack under your shirt," Kong suggested. "And get rid of some things."

Dammit, Wen thought. He should have thought of that. He pulled out books, a water bottle—everything but his laptop.

"What are you going to do when you get outside?" Kong asked as he helped his roommate flatten the pack under the garment.

"That depends on what *they* do. This disguise will at least give me time to get away. By bicycle, I hope."

"Do you want me to come with you?" Kong asked.

"No!" Wen said. Realizing he had shouted, he lowered his voice. "No, stay here and keep him quiet. If I can get out of the basement, that should give me time to consider my next move."

Kong nodded, then asked, "Why do they want you?"

"Because of my father. He's an engineer, you know that— but he's chief engineer on an important project. Chao and his friends want to know all about him so they can use that information against the president and the republic."

Kong's expression turned disapproving. "He dishonors his nation and he dishonors family ties."

"That's why I have to get away."

"What do you want *me* to do?" Kong asked.

"If anyone shows up, just tell them you know nothing."

Kong shrugged his big shoulders. "It's the truth."

"Right." Wen grabbed his backpack and headed toward the door. "You're a good friend, Kong. Thank you."

"Loyalty," the big man said, clasping his roommate's hand.

It pained Wen to use his bighearted roommate, but he did not think any blame would attach to him. It also hurt to imagine what Kong would think when he learned the truth.

Chao rose a little from the floor. "Don't do this, Wen," he said and then his eyes sought Kong. "He's—he's lying."

"Traitor," Kong said.

"You're . . . wrong."

Chao was regaining his wits; it was time to get out. Wen patted his pants pocket to make sure he had cash in his wallet—a credit card was traceable—then looked around the room quickly to see if there was anything else he needed. He would not be coming back.

The young man opened the door halfway and checked the hallway. There were no curious students, no unfamiliar visitors. He pulled the hood up and exited.

"Good luck!" he heard Kong say behind him.

As he went down the staircase, Wen had two thoughts.

One was that he would miss his roommate. The other was that he hoped he got farther than the big door of the bicycle storage area.

"Dr. Dàyóu, tell us about your son's insurgent activities."

Looking weary but managing to stay alert, Dr. Yang Dàyóu sat in an armchair in an office of the Heavy Assembly Building at the Taiyuan Launch Control Command Center. That was where General Chang maintained his staff, among the ironworks and construction equipment.

With him were Chang, who was characteristically dour but uncommonly silent, and the official whose office this was, Chief of Security Captain Shen Laihang, a man in the olive-green uniform of the Chinese People's Armed Police Force. He had apple-red cheeks and narrow eyes that never seemed to blink. Chang stood to Yang's left and Laihang was seated across from him behind a gunmetal desk with a folder open beside him and a yellow pad in front of him. A pair of digital recorders on the desk preserved the interview.

The frayed-edge vinyl shades were drawn against the floodlights that lit the compound, and the steam heat hissed incessantly. Everything in this place, save for the rocket technology, was nearly seventy years old.

Many of the furnishings are older than I am, Yang had thought many times as he worked at the facility. *If they could speak, share what they had seen and heard, we would no doubt be wiser,* he thought now.

The chief engineer had already spent more than two days

in detention here, most of that in a windowless "bedroom" down the hall. He had been given nothing to read and nothing to write with. There was a lavatory, a desk, and an empty closet. He had seen no one other than these two men and the men who brought him his meals—his "keepers," he thought—just like the uniformed men in a zoo. There was an armed guard outside the door. Requests to talk to his family had been fruitless. He was told by Shen that they were at home and comfortable but that was all he was told.

There had been a half-dozen "interview" sessions during the extended "hearing," as Shen referred to them. The questions had all been about the engineer and his own activities, his friends, his foreign colleagues. He had answered everything truthfully. He had nothing to conceal and, in any case, he suspected that most of the information was already in his dossier. If the men hoped he would reveal something new under persistent questioning they were disappointed. There was nothing to reveal.

Until now.

"I do not know of any such 'insurgent activities,'" Yang replied. "I have not seen my son since he returned to school, and you monitor my communications. How *could* I know anything?"

"From your wife," Shen said. "From your daughter."

Yang shook his head. "If they knew of any such things they would not share them. They know my feelings about my homeland. They know better than to anger me."

"We know he is involved with a group called the Counterrevolutionary Youth Organization," Shen continued.

"I am sorry to hear that."

Shen perked. "Sorry to hear that he is involved or sorry that we know?"

Yang shook his head slowly. "Mr. Laihang, General Chang, I am sorry this interrogation is taking up my time and yours when we have a missile program to get back on its feet. I have told you what happened and why."

"A crack in the gas intake plate is not in dispute," Shen said. "We are trying to determine *why* you approved the use of a faulty part."

These conversations were like a Möbius strip, endlessly circling back on itself. Yang's eyes sought those of the general.

"Since the earliest days of the missile program—you remember, General, we were there together. Back then we improvised. I remember when we removed a pipe from a laboratory sink to replace a part on the first Dong-Feng missile. Do you recall that?"

Chang did not reply. His expression was unchanged.

"Beijing did not watch us as closely, then," Yang said, exhaustion finally creeping into his voice. "*We* told *them* when we were finished with development. We always met deadlines because pride drove us. I barely saw my family. That changed with the Yingi-18. Everything had to be done quickly. We both knew the risks of accelerated research and production but we made it work. And we were lucky. This time, we were not. General, my team was instructed repeatedly to do nothing that would delay the program. Ordering a new plate or a new valve when we had one on the shelf would have delayed the program. This interrogation is not about—"

"This 'hearing,'" Shen corrected him.

"This *inquisition,* sir—this is not about finding legitimate blame, it's about *who* will be blamed. It appears the result was predetermined."

Silence filled the room. Shen looked to Chang for the next move. The general came around so that he was looking down at the engineer. And Chang was looking down, in every sense of the phrase; Yang had seen it in his eyes back in the block-house. The past did not matter. Past service and sacrifice would receive no consideration. This was going to be Yang's fault, not Chang's. All the general had to do was build his case. Something in the man's eyes changed, one of those cylinders changing position from watchful to demanding.

"You are a Christian," the interrogator said.

"For three generations," Yang replied. "I don't know what you are implying, but my faith has served my patriot—"

"The state explores all the potential routes of treachery, and not just for you."

"What does *that* mean?" Yang demanded.

"Are you estranged from your son?" Chang asked.

The engineer seemed surprised by the question. "Absolutely not."

"Are you aware that he is active within a group of social revolutionaries?"

Again, Yang seemed surprised. "I don't believe it."

"Your son never discussed this?"

"No, and I question your information on the matter."

"It's sound, Dr. Dàyóu, which leads me to wonder if you approved this inferior part for use, hoping that the destruction of the missile would inspire and encourage your son and his allies—"

"A lie!"

"Individuals who seek to undermine the authority of the government of the People's Republic?"

"General, you know full well that I approved this part because you told me there was no time to order a new one from the factory in Shanghai."

"Is attacking General Chang part of the Dàyóu family's pattern of sabotage?" Shen asked.

If they had been hoping to bring Yang to some kind of breaking point, they had succeeded. He turned on the general and said, "If you are going to accuse me of treason, do so and end this perversion. Dr. Weiping was at my elbow through most of the design and construction and if he puts his ego aside and gathers the right team he will be capable of carrying on this project."

"Dr. Weiping is already carrying on this project," Chang informed him. "He will move the *Qi*-20 along until your replacement can be found."

"You weren't listening—again," Yang said. "Xue Weiping is brilliant but new, brash, and filled with hubris. He does not have a *sense* for things, only a mind."

"He will be monitored. He will come to me with concerns."

"*If* he recognizes them! General, I care about this project! I have given my life to this facility! And I tell you he will overlook many safety issues. Not intentionally—Weiping is a good man. It will happen because he has not lived with *Qi* engineering night and day."

"He knows enough to replace faulty parts. In fact, he has already confirmed my view about the *Qi*-19."

"And that view is?" Yang asked, though he was already certain of the answer.

"That we used the same shielding because we had surplus. It would have worked unless someone sabotaged us."

"We used eleven recycled parts from the *Qi*-18. If you want to know, it is miraculous only one of them failed. That speaks to the effectiveness of my team, not treason."

"Thank you for pointing this out," Chang said. "I will inform Weiping that all of the warehoused parts may have been tampered with. We will have to manufacture new ones."

"Of course," Yang replied, his voice tired. "Which is why we are here. I suggested that, you turned me down."

"There is no document to corroborate your desperate claim."

"No." Yang's eyes turned toward Chang. "I foolishly trusted the military overseer. You will use my reports on the reclamation of parts as evidence that I did not salvage them but weakened them."

"The valve failed. That is evidence enough. But yes, your reports will be entered as evidence. You see, Dr. Dàyóu, you are correct about one thing. This hearing *is* about fixing blame and it is your signature on all the relevant documents and files. The schematics and imaging of alterations in the proven design are on your computer—"

"Those were depictions of possible design flaws in the existing parts," Yang said. "You know that! Even if your monstrous notion were correct, would I leave corrupted designs where you could easily *find* them?"

"They are there. Several engineers on your staff have con-firmed them."

"Under penalty of being named as my accomplices."

"Then you admit guilt?" Chang snapped.

Yang did not reply. The question was insulting. Answering it served no purpose.

"Carelessness or treason, the record points in just one di-rection," Chang said. "I advise you to pick the former. It will go easier on you."

"Disgrace is not preferable to execution."

"Your family may feel differently about you."

Yang made no reply. This was madness and he was not mad enough to participate.

Chang's voice lost its urgency, settled into a recitation. "I am going to forward my findings to the political works com-mander of the People's Liberation Army Air Force. You will remain here until we have a disposition of this matter."

The words echoed in the ears of a man who was numb to his own fate. It was ordained the moment the missile exploded. Whether he ended up in prison or merely stripped of his security clearance and degrees—also predetermined—did not matter. He would be content to work in a grocery.

"One favor, perhaps in honor of the years of devoted ser-vice you know I have given," Yang said. "Leave my son and my family out of this." He looked up at Chang and added, "I implore you."

"Your family would have had no hand in your activities," Chang acknowledged. "If your wife and daughter have had no hand in your son's activities, then they will come to no harm, I promise."

Chang made it sound like that was a grand gesture on his part. Yang knew that his son had taken part in subversive activities. If a tribunal chose to be punitive, to make an object lesson of the once-celebrated name of Dàyóu, there was nothing that Chang or anyone else could do.

The impassive pair of keepers arrived to escort Yang back to his room. He knew what came next; he had heard it spoken of many times over the years, never expecting the fate to be his. The interrogators would write up their findings, it would be submitted to the political works commander, and he would render a decision or move it forward for adjudication by either the Military Court or the Courts of Special Jurisdiction.

Both roads led to the death penalty. Yang's choices were to accept a lesser charge than treason or hope that he could persuade the judges that he was innocent. That would mean proving that Chang was the guilty party, and that the general would never permit.

It all seemed as unreal as it was hopeless, and when he was locked in his room he stood in the center, raised both hands to his face, and wept.

CHAPTER NINE

Fort Belvoir North, Springfield, Virginia
February 15, 12:15 P.M.

All three active-military members of Black Wasp lived at the Army Family Housing residence on-post. Usually there was a waiting list for homes; President Midkiff had phoned the garrison commander and saw that they jumped to the front of it. Breen, Lee, and Rivette had no idea what neighbors made of the three of them living together. Rivette had jokingly dubbed it the Opium Den. Breen got the play on their name but did not approve; they simply referred to it as the Den.

Upon returning to the residence, the first thing Grace had done was call her uncle Sun. She had an email address for Sun Fenghe, but she did not know how often the fifty-two-year-old checked it. The only telephone number she had was a landline; she called that from her personal phone in the unlikely event that he had caller ID.

"Yes?" he answered, his voice raw from decades of coal dust, and tired, no doubt from a ten-hour day.

"Uncle Sun?" she said. "This is Grace Lee. Your niece."

"Grace?" his voice perked. "Is it really Grace?"

"It is, Uncle!"

She could practically hear him smiling.

"Precious diamond, how *are* you? *Where* are you?"

"I'm in America, but I wanted to let you know I am flying to Beijing tomorrow and want to come see you as soon as possible."

"Of course! I can't believe this! It's been, what, eleven or twelve years?"

"Something like that. Far too long!"

"Yes, yes! My dear! Will you have a car?"

"No, and I won't need one. I want to see you, maybe bike around a bit."

"You're serious?"

"Very. I have some personal days up front, so I thought I would fly down to Taiyuan Wusu International after landing."

"That would be wonderful! How long will you be here and why are you coming home?"

Though Grace had never lived in China, had never been there more than ten days at one time and less than thirty days in her entire life, Uncle Sun—like her parents—still considered it home.

She explained that she was coming to train the new embassy staff in kung fu, answering Uncle Sun as truthfully as possible. One of the first things Williams had told Black Wasp was that espionage was easier the less one had to remember. It was the same with martial arts. If a *sifu* had to overwrite a student's instinctive responses, rather than work with them, the result would be hesitation. Facing a gun with just your open hand, any delay could prove fatal.

Grace told her uncle she would email her flight information to Taiyuan. With a sparkle in his voice, he said he would be sure to check his messages. Uncle Sun did not see many family members, the clan having been thinned and disbursed by the same civil war that had sent her parents to America.

The plans generally made, Grace received a text that William was sending over both the physical and digital documents from January Dow. The latter had several high-definition photographs of the Taiyuan facility, including the likely location of any detention area. Grace was instructed to memorize those; the data had self-deleted at 1:30 P.M.

Rivette arrived at 2:00 P.M. with sandwiches and coffee. He went to Grace's room, told her he had them, then sat at the kitchen table. She came in a few minutes later and sat. He had gotten her a veggie special on sourdough.

"Figure it'll be a while before you have one of those," he said. "I know how you get when you get all wrapped up in something."

"Thank you. How did the recert go?"

Rivette ate his own fish filet sandwich. It was like Grace, too, not to forget what others were dealing with. "Passed. I mean, whoever fails a man holding a gun?"

"Good point."

He looked at her over a clutch of french fries. "You feel okay about this?"

"I feel great, actually. Danger in the home of my ancestors—what more could anyone want?"

"A Wasp watching your back?"

Grace smiled. "I'm going there to reconnoiter, pick up intel, nothing more."

"Major Breen says that being a member of the military, you won't have diplomatic immunity if you get caught."

"I'll be careful," she said. "The mission parameters are pretty narrow."

Rivette chuckled. "Can you tell me one mission parameter we have stuck to? Even a half of one?"

"I blame you for that."

"Yeah, like I'm the one who kicks open a door *and* a face in the same move?"

They both smiled and ate in silence for several minutes. Then Grace rose, coffee in hand. "I've got homework and packing to do."

"You need me to pick anything up from the exchange? Donuts for the trip? A puppy?"

She gave him a look.

"No, seriously. Back home, the gang used to jack cars while people were looking at me with a puppy. When the thing got too big we just snagged another one."

"You robbed litters?"

Rivette shrugged. "Gave 'em a home—briefly, right? At least I didn't eat them."

Her look became stern. "That's a sensationalized stereotype, Lance Corporal. Very, very few Chinese eat dog."

"Not judging," he said. "Just defending myself. Speaking of defending, I left the major in the park. Looked like he was in one of his thinking moods, for a change."

Grace smiled. "It's a dirty job but someone has to do it."

"Yeah . . . waste of time. Nothing ever goes the way anyone plans."

That, at least, was true enough.

Grace stood. "Thanks again for the food. I really appreciate it."

The lance corporal gave her a thumbs-up and Grace returned to her room. She shut the door, looked at her laptop and the open suitcase, and decided there was something else she had to do first, something she did without fail every week. It was not quite time for it, and they would know something was different, but they would not mention that.

She had to call her parents.

The call came while Williams was getting coffee from the single-cup communal brewer down the hall from his office at the Defense Logistics Agency. He checked the caller ID. Before answering, Williams got a power bar from an adjoining vending machine. Then he thumbed the ACCEPT button on the phone and said "Hold, please," as he made his way back to his office. He shut the door and sat before continuing.

"Sorry, January. I was not in my office. I got your materials and forwarded them to Lieutenant Lee. I'll bring the physical documents to her myself. What about the preloaded smartphone?"

"Deployment Operations is handling that at Wheeler," she said. "What does the lieutenant's flowchart look like?"

Williams' first thought was, *God save me from business terminology applied to military enterprises. Troops become numbers and death is just red ink.*

It was the first time the director of Op-Center had been asked that question outside the Oval Office—not by the president but by a subordinate. Intelligence had always been the highest coin of government; January Dow protected herself from oversight and political ambush by husbanding her wealth. That protected institutions, not Americans.

Williams told her the plan without mentioning Uncle Sun, only "some family" in the region. He knew that January would ask for names and he did not want her moving through a vetting process that the Chinese might well be watching. She knew that was a possibility; she might not care. He told her he would have to get back to her on that.

January did not press the matter. She pressed another.

"Now I have a question," January said. "Did you also talk to your friend Matt Berry this morning?"

There was a disease in Washington, D.C., which Williams called *Player Paranoia*. Every career bureaucrat in the nation's capital had it, a wide-ranging subconscious sonar that had no off switch. It constantly swept the landscape for human land mines, incessantly set off alarms. January would of course remember Williams' shoulder-to-shoulder work with Berry in the past; and like any longtime Washingtonian, she would feel threatened by it. Given the limited support Grace was getting, January had correctly concluded that Williams would turn to an ally for help.

"How do my calls fall under the jurisdiction of the national security advisor?"

"A question instead of an answer," she said critically. "A deflection."

"No, January. A question. Whether I talked to a colleague or not, I don't answer to you."

"I can have that changed, Admiral."

"Actually, January, you can't."

"Within the hour," she said threateningly. "Op-Center is not your personal fiefdom. Not any longer."

"January, I'm not questioning your ability to alter the command structure. I'm not even questioning the wisdom of civilian oversight, which is a separate issue. What I'm saying is that no one, not even the president, can prevent me from resigning. And I don't think anyone wants that on the eve of an important mission."

The woman was silent for a moment. When she continued, her tone was less strident.

"Admiral, you know—you *should* know as well as anyone— we have complex, fragile relationships in the region. We can't have the bravura of Black Wasp or its commander destabilizing that balance."

"When have we done that, January?"

"Consider it a localized policy injunction, not a service review."

"I don't even understand that."

"I'll make it simpler," January said. Her tone was patronizing, her patience feigned. "The People's Republic of China is not South Africa, Yemen, or Pennsylvania. The president and I are both concerned about the inability of Black Wasp to walk the tightrope between détente and intelligence needs. That is why he is sending Lieutenant Lee and just Lieutenant Lee. To reconnoiter."

"The punishment for espionage is to kneel on dirt and get a bullet in the back of the head," Williams said. "If the Central Military Commission decides to be lenient, a convicted spy might get a firing squad."

"I don't want to sound callous, Admiral, but that risk comes with the job."

Williams bit his back teeth together, hard. Yes, innumerable dangers came with the job. Any moment in the field could result in the loss of life, a limb, freedom. And that was just the physical. Williams did not know a single combatant who had returned from enemy territory or the field of battle without psychological challenges. And the scarring came young, when that hero, that idealist, that patriot was lopsided: physical resilience was deep but wisdom did not yet have the shoulders to support a new reality.

And then there were the January Dows. These smug, "big picture" bureaucrats dispatched warriors around the globe with lip service paid to "risks" and papier-mâché masks of concern. They were worse than the armchair generals—or admirals—who had at least come up through the ranks and knew viscerally what they were asking.

"Thank you for sharing your insights," Williams said, muting the anger with sarcasm. "I will do nothing that upsets American foreign policy."

"Make sure of that," she said and hung up.

Williams sat very still. Only now was he aware of having squeezed his power bar and that his hand was trembling. He eased back in the swivel chair, exhaled, and set the snack on his desk. He picked up his coffee.

"She will be checking to make sure I'm around," Williams thought aloud.

But that was irrelevant. As with President Midkiff and every superior officer he had served, as with every decision he had made since he had earned the authority to make them, all that mattered was the success or failure of the assignment. Success insulated him from Dow; she would want a part of that glory, not seek to bury him.

"Yeah, she'll be like a cat at a fishbowl." But that was nothing new.

If Op-Center failed, as it did when Captain Salehi entered the country and organized a terror attack, it was all on him anyway.

Williams drank some coffee and set his cup on the desk. He opened the power bar at the top and dumped the crumbs into his mouth. He wished he had been able to hire Captain Ann Ellen Mann, the officer who had been so helpful when Black Wasp tracked the Black Order terrorists in Philadelphia. He had put in the request for her to be seconded to Op-Center while Midkiff was still in office. But the outgoing president punted, Wright did nothing, and Mann was still busy getting the hard-hit Naval Support Activity facility in Philadelphia back on its feet. Williams was hopeful that Wright would eventually approve the hire.

He'll wait for the quota system to demand more women, Williams thought cynically.

January Dow was not part of his equation as he sat in his quiet, solitary surroundings to consider what was best for the nation and the mission.

CHAPTER TEN

*The Beijing Center, University of International
Business and Economics*

*Beijing, China
February 16, 12:16 A.M., CST*

Kong half walked, half pushed Chao Dan toward Wen's bed.

"I feel like I should call the police," the big man said. "They
will know what to do with you."

"You won't need a phone," Chao said. "Agents of State Security are right outside."

Kong pushed him down and crossed his arms. "Do you
want a washcloth for your face?"

"No, I want to go after your roommate!"

"I'll bet you do." Kong cocked his head toward the window.
"Tell me where these 'agents' are hiding. I want to see them."

"I told you, they're MSS. You can't see them. That's the point."

"Convenient," Kong said.

"Go to the window and wait. If Wen tries to leave the
building by the front, I promise, you'll see them."

Kong's expression registered concern.

"Believe it or not, I was trying to help him," Chao went on.

"From what? How?"

"What do you know about his family?"

"Not much, and I wouldn't tell you if I did."

"Fine. All I can say is that Wen will be safer with me than by going out alone. We may still be able to stop him."

"You lie."

Chao took stock of his head and back. They were injured when Wen charged him, but he could not stay here any longer. He rose unsteadily. "I'm telling the truth, and I'm also leaving. Which way would he go, out the front door or—"

"I'm not telling you anything, dirt."

"Fine. Then you're going to have to explain this—"

The poet's words were cut off when Kong punched him in the face, sending Chao back against the pillow, barely conscious.

During summer, one could find a large portion of the more than sixteen thousand students of the UIBE scattered about the campus in Northern Beijing. The grounds were nicknamed Hui Garden. For three seasons a year, students would have been out enjoying the lighted ponds, gardens, or even attending a sporting event at the stadium. Summer would have provided Wen with ample cover to make his way from the sprawling campus with its seven, five-to-eight-story-tall structures dominated by the towering white Chengxin Building.

At night, in the winter, very few students were about. The thermometer on Wen's phone read 23 degrees and he was only wearing the sweatshirt over his street clothes. He hoped that he would warm up riding his bicycle. If he were forced to go on foot, he would make for the subway and try to put as much distance as possible between himself and the campus.

Wen ran down the stairs to the basement. There were hundreds of bicycles chained to bars, side-by-side. Many were foldable; his was not. He unlocked the blue Fuji-ta city bike—sturdy for quick getaways after marches—and began to walk it toward the garage door. There was a door beside it for students with Segways, electric scooters, and skateboards. Both were operated by swiping a student ID.

Wen bent as the metal panels lifted automatically. He was looking for feet outside, saw none, and walked the bike out under the automatic spotlight.

He noticed, too late, a pair of men standing about ten feet from the door to the left. Wen did not stop. Peripherally, he saw the men look over. One held a cell phone. The other had his hands in his blue greatcoat, shifting from foot to foot against the cold.

His heart hammering, Wen turned his face away and got on the bike. The garage door closed behind him.

"Chao?" one of the men asked.

Wen swore to himself. The sweatshirt had not given him cover; it had called attention to him. Feeling stupid, he put his feet on the pedals and started pushing.

The men came toward him. "Wait!" the same man shouted.

His breath coming in icy puffs, Wen churned onto a long, narrow street that had a slight upward incline. Students usually

walked their bicycle up this slope they called *Qiángdà de sīdài,*
The Mighty Ribbon.

"Wait!" the man cried out again as they ran after him.
When Wen failed to stop, the agent said, "Position two requests
backup, Sunflower exit!"

Wen heard the men behind him. Through bare trees he saw
headlights come on at the road perpendicular to his position.
They could not come down, the path was not wide enough; but
they could block it.

There was no other way out. To either side were side gardens
with wood chips that would prohibit bicycling. As the car pulled
across the path and two men emerged, Wen stopped. He got off
the bike and let it fall. He felt he had a better chance on foot in
the dark. The men did not know the campus the way he did.

Wen heard the car doors open and saw two shadowy figures emerge; at the same time, the men from the garage were
nearly upon him. He heard the same sharp voice call for him to
stop, and part of him wanted to—an insistent part that had no
desire to be a hero. Maybe Chao would speak up for him. The
poet had failed in his mission, might support a lie rather than
face disciplinary action of some kind. Wen could accuse him
of—something.

His mind a muddle, he ran toward one of the gardens when
he felt a tug in the middle of his back. One of the men had
managed to land a strong hand on his sweatshirt and on the
backpack. Wen was stopped short and went back on his heels,
nearly losing his balance. Scared and angry, he pinwheeled his
arms, wriggled his body, kicked behind him—

He heard a cry and felt the hands on his back pop off, like an old train coupling snapping loose. He turned and looked into the darkness beyond the floodlights as the man flew backwards, his phone glinting as it fell to the ground. The man's companion had turned, reached, and his body was drawn forward. He had not lunged but was pulled ahead by his extended arms. Both men ended up in a heap as a strong hand grabbed Wen and yanked him back toward the door.

"Kong!" Wen said, his eyes wide.

The big man swiped his card, pulled open the door and ran through with his roommate in tow. He kicked it shut before Wen's pursuers could arrive. He doubted they had IDs.

"Come on!" Kong said. He did not run toward the stairs but to a door in back. "You can get out through the refuse room."

Wen followed obediently, mutely—gratefully.

"What have you got yourself into?" Kong asked. "Was Chao telling the truth?"

"Yes and no. He's an anarchist but he's in league with the MSS."

"You're saying those men I hit were government agents?" Kong asked.

"They were."

Kong nodded decisively at a thought as he opened the big, steel-plated door to the trash center. "It shouldn't present a problem. I'll say I heard a commotion in the room and found my friend being attacked."

"Chao will tell a different story."

"Your friend up there stinks like old shrimp." Kong grinned.

"He will modify his story when I tell him that my father is the Honorable Lu Yanyong, Director of the Office of the Committee for Comprehensively Governing the City by Law of Beijing Municipal Party Committee. Even the MSS shies from lifelong politicians."

Wen was more grateful than he could say, though when they entered the trash room doorway he tried to find the words.

"I cannot thank you enough, and I am sorry this has involved you." Wen hugged his friend.

"Where will you go?"

"I don't know. I think the subway will be safest, just to get away from here."

"It's after midnight. You missed the last one, I think."

"I'll figure something out," Wen said. He released his roommate, regarded him intently. "Listen, Kong: whatever you hear, my family are patriots and something is terribly wrong. That's why I have to get to them, to help."

"If I didn't believe that, Brother Wen, I would have let Chao and those men take you."

The two parted. Kong hurried back to the stairs to settle things with Chao before the agents arrived. He did not think the poet was accustomed to being roughed up and would probably wait in the room until the officials arrived.

Wen turned and ran through the rows of dumpsters. Before he had reached the outer door, he had turned the building around in his mind so he would know where exactly the exit would place him. From there he would leave the campus by the treed area near the administration building. The 5, 10, and 13 subway lines all had stations near the campus; he would make for one of those. His initial thought was to make for the Dongcheng District and the Beijing Station. A train with many stops and trunk lines seemed the safest way to travel the 330 miles southwest.

Awash with emotions that ranged from fear to gratitude, the young man shivered his way through the cold midnight hour, his senses alert and his thoughts returning to the only thing that truly mattered: his family.

CHAPTER ELEVEN

Joint Base Anacostia–Bolling, Washington D.C.
February 15, 2:12 P.M.

Bolling Air Force Base was one half of the larger enterprise, the other being Naval Support Facility Anaconda. It was situated directly east of Ronald Reagan Washington International, across the Potomac River, just sixteen miles from Fort Belvoir.

The officers at Fort Belvoir had a pool of cars and drivers. Grace was assigned a car for the twenty-five-minute trip. Williams did not go with her. The joint base was operated by the navy and Chase Williams was supposed to be retired.

The goodbyes inside the house were salutes from the three men of Black Wasp.

"You good?" Rivette asked as he walked outside with Grace.

"Never better," Grace replied honestly.

The driver loaded her grip and small carry-on into the trunk and they were underway. She did not look back, only ahead. Fifteen minutes before wheels up she was presenting her credentials to the air crew on the tarmac. No one on board knew her real reason for being there; only the ambassador knew that she was on a special mission for the president. Though the former chairman of the board of Pennsylvania-Ohio Steel was not a veteran diplomat, he knew what that meant.

The plane boarded and Grace took her assigned seat. The solo mission was not the only change for her. It had been the better part of a year since she had worn anything other than fatigues and sweat clothes; and it had been even longer than that since she had been with civilians other than those she was hunting or pushing out of harm's way.

It was a chatty group that boarded. Many of the people seemed to know one another. Grace sat in a window seat in a row two seats across, toward the front. She did not like to feel bottled up anywhere; for more than fourteen hours, definitely not. However, there were sensitive documents on her tablet and she wanted to be able to turn from whoever sat beside her.

An officer, a captain wearing the uniform of the marines, came toward her and stopped. Grace began to rise and saluted; the man saluted and smiled.

"Welcome aboard, Lieutenant Lee," he said, reading her name tag. "Good to have you with us."

"Thank you, Captain Petrillo, sir."

"I haven't seen you at any of the security briefings."

"I was only assigned this morning, sir."

The line was piling up behind him. "We stretch our legs at the Honolulu refuel. We'll have a chance to talk then."

"Yes, sir."

He moved on and Grace was relieved. She would have

time to figure out how to answer that question or else to get to the ambassador and punt it to him. In any case, it would have made the long flight longer, not so much having to listen to war stories—she had learned from her kung fu studies that there was always something for a wise student to learn in any situation— but to avoid sharing hers.

A woman in a double-breasted blue blazer stopped and swung into the row. She was in her mid-thirties with blond hair falling past high cheekbones. Out of the way of the last of the people boarding, she was already deftly unshouldering a bulging Gucci shoulder bag without disturbing the Canada Goose expedition parka folded in her arms.

"I'll take care of these things later," she said more to herself than to Grace as she flopped into her seat. "I don't want to hold things up."

The woman pushed the bag up against the seat in front, kept the coat in her lap, exhaled with an outthrust lower lip, and deflated into the seat. She finally turned to her seatmate and smiled perfectly.

"I'm Elsie Smith, by the way—Lieutenant Lee."

"Hi."

"You must be part of the security detail. I'm the deputy cultural attaché. I used to work with the president's chief of staff, Angie Brunner. In Hollywood."

Grace felt the gravitas of the nation's administration crumbling. She nodded toward the woman's coat. "You're set for the Arctic."

"LOL," she spoke. "I was told it gets cold where we're going. With the two-bag limit, I figured I could buy what I need for the rest of the year. Or send for it."

The chief flight attendant came on with an announcement and Elsie settled back. She hugged the garment as though it were her only lifeline to the familiar. She exhaled again.

"This is exciting!" Elsie beamed as the door was pulled shut and everyone took their seats. "Like a premiere, only more important."

Grace smiled politely, already missing Rivette. Fortunately, she had work to do and turned to her tablet as soon as the plane was airborne. The only destination she had to memorize fully was the Taiyuan Satellite Launch Center. That would not be on the phone she was to pick up at Wheeler.

The lieutenant opened the file from the national security assistant containing the data and maps of the TSLC. It was as thin as she had expected:

OFFICE OF JANUARY DOW
ASSISTANT TO THE PRESIDENT FOR NATIONAL SECURITY AFFAIRS

Subject:

Taiyuan Satellite Launch Center

Last Updated:

January 24, 2022

ALTERNATE NAMES:

*Taiyuan Space Center

*General Armaments Department Base 25

*Wuzhai Space and Missile Test Center
*Wuzhai Range
*Wuzhai Missile Test Center
*Wuzhai IRBM Test Complex

LOCATION
Taiyuan, Shanxi Province
Though site is frequently designated the Wuzhai Missile and Space Centre, Wuzhai County is 284 kilometers away from Taiyuan.

COMMAND
People's Liberation Army General Armaments Department

FACILTIES
Two carrier rocket launch pads and related support facilities including ground control and guidance facilities, spacecraft and booster testing and construction facilities, and two residential structures housing military and technical staff, respectively.

STATUS
Active

MISSION
Facility tests and launches ballistic missiles, carrier boosters, satellites for reconnaissance and meteorology, and Small

Spacecraft Mission Service Containers (SSMSC) for the transport, support, and linkage of single-purpose microsatellites.

HISTORY

The TSLC became active in 1967 to accommodate rockets and missiles too large for the Jiuquan Space Launch Center. Within the last five years the facility has tested and fired medium-range ballistic missiles, intercontinental ballistic missiles, and supervised the Julang-1 sea-launched ballistic missile.

SPACE OPERATIONS

Satellites

The meteorological satellite Fengyun-1A was launched in September 1988.

The *Yaogan*-1, *Yaogan*-5, *Yaogan*-6, *Yaogan*-10 and *Yaogan*-13 synthetic-aperture radar reconnaissance satellites were orbited from 2018–2019

The *Naxing*-1 and *Xiwang*-1 research microsatellites were launched in 2020

The KT-1PS military microsatellites and the ZY-1 and ZY-3 utility satellites were launched in 2020

MISSILES

Current activity consists of the Long March-5 and -6 series for low and medium Earth orbit satellites, 2021–2022

Launch status unknown: the *Qi* series hypersonic missile and payload. Tests in 2023 on Green Run checklist include core stage avionics, load and drain cryogenic propellants, and countdown simulation to validate timeline (ELINT via clone phishing intrusion).

Grace was troubled by the fact that the file did not include recent events. The administration was aware of the explosion; it should have been in the file. She could imagine Major Breen analyzing the failure, as he had with other lapses and gaps in the past: *Either an intelligence organization is not sharing; the Homeland Security Office of Intelligence Coordination is not making sure information was shared "equally and immediately" as it said in their charter; or an agency is withholding intelligence for their advantage.*

To that, Grace added her own concern: that the new administration is sloppy from the get-go, in which case they would probably always be behind.

There was also, surprisingly, only one surveillance map, a satellite image bearing a reference number indicating Air Force Orbital. It showed an L-shaped series of structures, so labeled, along with a pair of launch pads roughly a mile apart. There was a perimeter fence, but no indication of security cameras or even height. The briefing dossier had suggested there was unlikely to be video surveillance; the Chinese had people and used their eyes to watch the compound. There was a helipad in the northwest corner with what looked like a Z-20 medium transport helicopter. Obviously, no one in Air Force Intelligence had anticipated anyone actually entering the facility for reconnaissance.

She was supposed to contact Williams from Hawaii, to

let him know that she had everything she needed. She would broach these topics then.

On the other hand, she thought, *this suits my martial arts training.*

Taiyuan was an unknown quantity. If the flowing, water-and-wind nature of kung fu had taught her anything, it was to be ready to find a way over or around any impediment.

Certain only that she was tired from the nonstop preparations, and had to be ready from wheels down, Grace waited until her neighbor had noisily stowed her coat and bag overhead. Then the lieutenant pulled her cap over her eyes, leaned against the humming window, and went to sleep.

Chase Williams was still sitting at his desk in his office at the Defense Logistics Agency, trying not to dwell on the call from January Dow.

The conversation was at present a distraction, a manageable sideshow. But it was also the leading edge of a shadow that would fall across future operations. He could not afford to think about that now. The MAD—mission asset distribution—had begun with Grace's departure. Maximizing the success of the action and her safety came first, and while he waited for Matt Berry's call, the admiral was alternately weighing his own active, standby, or stand-down status.

What's more important? he asked himself. *Being here to answer January's certain request for in-person updates, or being on the ground where you might be able to help Grace?*

His careful consideration was interrupted when Matt Berry's

number appeared on Williams' smartphone. The admiral felt sanity and stability return as he swiped on the video call. People in combat formed a unique bond, and he and Berry had been in and out of geopolitical trenches for the better part of a year.

"Your face lights up a room," Williams joked.

"You forget, I know that room," Berry replied. "Nothing can save it." He regarded his friend for a moment. "You ready for the good news, bad news?"

"Yeah."

"I know the order you want it, so here's the bad news: I can't get you where you'd like to go until tomorrow, wheels up at four a.m. That's two days actually, since there's a layover. And it's almost three days if you factor in the twelve-hour time differential."

"That's not bad news, Matt. That's under-the-radar travel. I appreciate it."

"You better—it isn't so easy these days," Berry teased. "It was a helluva lot easier to work these things when my caller ID showed up 'White House.' Anyway, I've got you three on a cargo flight direct to Ulaanbaatar. They leave on the seventeenth. Because it's an early morning flight, no one is likely to see you coming or going."

"Cargo?"

"No arms or trafficked girls," Berry said. "That's cooled because of scrutiny on this end. They're carrying parts for stoves. When you land you take a puddle jumper to Tavan Tolgoi Airport in Tsogttsetsii, Ömnögovi. That's the province you want."

"Where does Black Wasp pick up that ride, if they're not going through the terminal?"

"Let the captain of the cargo jet know where you want to go. He may or may not speak English—you'll have to work that out. For three hundred thousand tögrög, about a hundred bucks, he'll direct you to what I'm told is a small plane holding area for all kinds of cargo. Once you're down south, how you get around will be up to you, though the local nomads are happy to deal. You've got that much Mongolian scrip in the safe in 20,000 notes—or for a couple of warm coats from that Walmart off-base, you can also buy their silence. Give them both and they will be friends for life."

"Wouldn't hurt to have some of those," Williams said.

"Stop feeling sorry for yourself. You're the one who opted to stay in government."

That was not a tease. Berry was right to point it out.

"I made the arrangements through Miyeegombyn Narangerel," Berry went on. "I'll text you the name. He's a big wheel in the Ministry of Construction and Urban Development, plants bugs in foreign buildings for the CIA so don't embarrass me."

"I'll do my damnedest. I mean that. Thanks again."

Berry regarded his friend. "Chase—did you get the sense that the president has Op-Center's back on whatever it is you're doing?"

"I think he may think he does. But the reality is something else. He's made January Dow my handler."

"He may not know about your history with her," Berry suggested.

"Or, worse, he does."

"You sure this isn't some kind of setup or a diversion for something else?"

"Not a setup," Williams said. "If he had wanted Op-Center gone, he would have laid the axe to the root before now. No, I think the president really wants what we are uniquely positioned to give him. I have to proceed under that assumption, anyway."

"Of course. Well, I've got to go peddle secret information to PAC clients. Talk soon."

"Thanks again," Williams said and hung up.

He found himself wondering, suddenly, how Captain Mann of Naval Support Activity would handle January Dow. Again, he told himself, that was not a matter for now.

Which was precisely why he had thought of it. He had a choice to make. And like most of the life-and-death decisions in his life, he made this one the same way he had made the others—with his gut, not his brain.

CHAPTER TWELVE

Fangshan District, Beijing, China
February 16, 3:00 A.M., CST

Wen Dàyóu's immediate destination was the small community of Shidu, located in the southwest corner of Beijing, east of the Taihang Mountains. His plan was to get to the home shared by Jiang and Chao Dan. Wen did not think that either Chao or the authorities would expect him to come here. That was more a hope than a belief. His other hope was that Jiang was unaware of Chao's duplicity and might help him get home. If Jiang were in league with Chao, he would be no worse off than he was now—a fugitive.

There was no one else to turn to. For their mutual protection, the other Counterrevolutionaries were not known to him by name or by sight. Even if that were not the case, he wondered if any of them would believe him about Chao. His lines about liberty were on the signs they carried, were the slogans they shouted.

In order to reach Shidu, Wen had to travel east to the Fangshan subway line, which would take him west. The last train had departed just before midnight; the rails would not reopen until 5:00 A.M. It was the same with the bus lines. Tired, hungry, cold, and sore from his fight with Chao, Wen could not even sit at a bus stop. The authorities were sure to be looking for him and they knew what he was wearing.

His best option, he knew, was the homeless encampment on the Chaobai River. Officially, Beijing did not have a homeless problem. The few times Wen had bicycled along the river he had not seen the police rousting the thirty or so people who lived on its banks.

Guided by the light of small fires in metal pails, Wen saw beds beside cardboard boxes and laundry baskets loaded with clothes and food. He approached a woman sitting on a tattered rug, her arms around her legs, her forehead on her knees. He came as near as he could to her fire without disturbing her. The breeze from the river stirred the smell of burning wood and old cigarettes that hung over the little settlement.

The woman had black hair, shoulder length and parted in the middle. She was dressed in a linen trench coat stuffed with newspaper for warmth. Her boots were ankle-high and the soles were coming loose. She turned to Wen as he sat. Her face was clean—with water from the river, he guessed—and she looked to be in her mid-twenties.

"Forgive me," he said. "I did not mean to wake you."

"You didn't," she said. "The shivering did."

She turned her face back, making herself as small and compact as possible. Wen followed her example, his arms folded on top of his knees. He sat there with the chill wind of the river dispelled somewhat by the fire, and forced himself to become smaller still. The straps of his backpack pulled but he dared not take it off. Then, overcome by the events of the day—and by the proximity of such suffering, the kind of pain he had sought to eliminate—Wen wept into his sleeve.

Dawn both warmed and woke the young man. The fire had gone out and his neighbor was already gone. He saw the remains of newspapers in the bucket, most likely pages from the woman's "lining." Some of the homeless were crouching on a hard-mud outcrop covered with dead, yellow grasses. Some had fishing lines in the water, others were cleaning hands and faces. Two men were urinating.

Wen rose and left quickly, somewhat refreshed from the two or so hours of sleep he had gotten. He hurried back in the direction of the school, the location of the nearest subway station. People were already on their way to work, bicycles and cars playing a dangerous game as they darted, angled, and raced through the streets.

Wen stopped to remove his sweatshirt and backpack. He tucked the hood inside before putting the garment back on and clutching his backpack in front to hide the portrait of Cáo Xuěqín. He had selected a subway stop near the school, one that he knew would be full of students arriving from off campus for class. He felt there would be less chance of his being spotted among his peers. As Wen neared the subway, he saw a bundle of morning newspapers being opened by an elderly merchant and set up in his kiosk. This was where Wen purchased his own magazines, and he walked over, acknowledging the vendor with a smile.

"Are you trying to get sick?" the man asked, jabbing a thumb at the sweatshirt.

"I didn't think it was so cold," Wen replied, paying for a newspaper and turning away.

What he saw froze him with cold-water shock, a sidebar declaring: "'CYO' Leaders, Members Arrested."

Wen turned to the newspaper and read about the arrest of Jiang Yiwu Dan and Chao Dan, along with members who had been identified by the pair.

The wages of failure, Wen thought. But it was more than that, he realized. The matter of Dr. Yang Dàyóu was of far greater significance than a local group of anarchists. They wanted to find *him.*

Staring at the paper, the young man felt sick and helpless at the same time. He did not know what to do next, where to go, his mind paralyzed and blank.

And then the matter was decided for him. Approaching him were two stern-looking men whom Wen recognized from the night before. They were led by someone who knew Wen's habits: Kong Yanyong, his expression devoid of the fellowship he had shown just a few hours ago.

"I'm sorry, Wen," Kong announced as one of the men twisted Wen's arms behind his back and the other fixed handcuffs to his wrists. "This was more serious than I had thought."

Wen had no reply, simply watched as a black sedan pulled to the curb. Onlookers gave room to the police action—including a woman with a sad, sweet face whose homeless state now seemed like freedom itself to the young man.

Wen did not pay attention to where the car was headed. It did not seem to matter. He sat in the back with one of the men; the other sat in the front with the driver. There was a plastic partition between them. That barrier was just the beginning of Wen's incarceration.

He was taken to Qincheng Prison, a maximum-security prison erected in 1958 in Beijing's Changping District. Surrounded by steep and barren valleys, Qincheng is the only penitentiary operated by the Ministry of Public Security and not the Ministry of Justice. It is not charged with holding citizens for due process but to detain and interrogate political prisoners. After driving through the heavily guarded orange-and-white-striped fence, the car passed under a tiled, stone entryway with classic bilateral symmetry and made its way up to the first of the compound's two jails. This cinder-block edifice was for high-ranking prisoners. The designation was an indication of social status, not the nature of the crime. The son of Dr. Yang Dàyóu would have been taken there for something as minor as shoplifting.

The car stopped in an iron-gated courtyard outside the three-story structure. Wen felt nauseated as the two MSS men firmly escorted him from the back seat; one on the outside, the other from behind. Wen breathed deeply but the echoing clang of the gate caused him to heave on the cobbled ground. The men held him until he was finished, then walked him through the gate to the prisoner receiving area.

He was photographed, fingerprinted, and ordered to turn over his backpack, wallet, and other belongings. Then he was taken through a gated doorway to the ground-floor cellblock. The long, high corridor smelled like musk and bleach. The faded blue paint of the vaulted ceiling was peeling; to Wen's added horror, he saw that the cells did not have bars but heavy iron doors.

Once inside, the outer door closed tight, Wen's handcuffs were removed, and he was handed over to two men in gray uniforms with long, black billy clubs carried in loops on their leather belts. The MSS men left and Wen was walked to a cell.

"What—what's happening?" he asked.

The men did not answer. Wen had not expected them to. One man opened a door, which creaked loudly on its hinges; the second man had removed his club, placed the end in the center of Wen's back, and pushed him inside. There was a small bed, a blanket, a pillow, a badly chipped porcelain sink, and a toilet made of stainless steel that, nonetheless, was rusted and dented.

The door shut heavily; the air in the room seemed to leave with the men. The only window was narrow, high, and covered with bars and mesh. There was no glass on the outside and the cell was bitterly cold. A radiator was affixed to the back wall but it furnished no heat.

It had been an inhumane delivery to a dehumanizing environment. Even in his near-panicked state, Wen realized that was the point. Trembling from fear and the penetrating chill, Wen eased onto a bed with weak and unreliable springs. They were rusted, too, from the sound of them.

Everything in the prison was bad, and it would not be long before that rot settled in Wen's body and spirit. Decay and not knowing when it would end—the entire process was corrosive.

That, too, was the point.

CHAPTER THIRTEEN

Fort Belvoir North, Springfield, Virginia
February 15, 5:21 P.M.

"I've decided not to go on the support mission."

The three male members of Op-Center were sitting around the small wooden dining room table when Williams made the announcement without preamble. Rivette seemed to welcome the news. He did not like being crowded and, having been plucked from his unit before socialization had taken hold, he was inexpert at concealing his feelings. Breen was outwardly neutral but inwardly uncertain. The day had begun with one unexpected turn, and here was another. He and Chase Williams had spent a lot of time together during their trips to and from theaters of engagement. He knew that the man would not bench himself without cause. If that cause were political, and if "political" would undermine sound tactics, he needed to know.

It came out as a simple, direct question.

"Why, Admiral?"

"Calculus," Williams replied. "The president's national security affairs assistant was instrumental in shutting Op-Center down when she ran the State Department's Bureau of Intelligence and Research. She seems eager to do it again."

"What did you do to piss her off, sir?" Rivette asked.

"When two people are in the same business they can compete, merge, or try to shut the other guy down. January Dow was not the share-information or join-forces type."

"I knew pushers like that in L.A.," the lance corporal said.

"I assume she doesn't want us involved because the president only wanted Lieutenant Lee and she's going to by-God keep it that way," Breen said.

"That's right. She wouldn't expect me to stay behind if there were a support leg of the plan," Williams said.

"You want to be here in case she checks," Rivette said.

"Not 'in case' but *when* she contacts me."

"Okay, but we're still going, yes?" Rivette pressed. "Can't leave a teammate without backup."

"Your part of the equation is still operational," Williams said.

Breen had been studying the admiral. "If I may, you don't seem one hundred percent, Chase."

"I'm not. I don't mean about giving Lieutenant Lee support but the bigger picture. Matt got to the heart of things in his own tactful, oblique way. So did General Patton, for that matter, when he said that a calculated risk was not the same as rash action."

"I'm not following," Rivette said.

Williams exhaled, exhausted by his own back-and-forth. "I send you off, a man down. That puts you and the support mission at risk. Which is more critical, that or my staying here and preserving Black Wasp to fight another day? If I cross January Dow on this, we're dead."

"You know the answer," Breen said, "but it's a sorry, unnecessary accommodation to have to make."

"No argument," Williams replied. "Which is where calculus comes in. I stay here, you go over. Ideally, Grace gets what the president wants and scoots back to the embassy. You two will have stayed undercover and come home."

"Our training objective achieved," Breen said knowingly.

"That's right. Win-win-win," Williams replied.

"Nothing rude about winning." Rivette shrugged.

"The clarity of young eyes," Williams said.

"Damn right, sir. I got 20/15 in my aiming eye."

Breen did not bother to contextualize what Williams was saying, and the two older men shared a knowing look. Even in JAG, winning a judgment against a soldier or an officer was never really a win; morale and honor, the sacredness of duty versus humanity and compassion always took a hit. For a career warrior and proactive patriot like Williams to "stay" because a functionary said so took some of the polish off the entire system. Knowing how difficult this decision had been for Williams made Breen respect the admiral even more.

"So now that that's decided—where *are* we going?" Rivette asked.

"Mongolia," Williams said.

The lance corporal grinned. "Damn me. The birthplace of Genghis Khan Jones."

"Who?" Williams asked.

"That's what the guy called himself. 'Genghis Khan Jones, the Street Mongol.' Got to this country and put together a team of looters from his tent on Twenty-Fifth Street and Long Beach Avenue. He was smart enough not to step on anyone's gambling or drugs or trafficking gigs. In fact, those dudes came to him when they needed stuff. Most honest bad dude I ever met."

"How well did you know him?" Williams asked.

"Saw him a few times when I was sent to buy ammo or iPhones, which was pretty much all my guys needed."

"Did you pick up any of the language?" Williams asked.

"I learned 'hello' and 'thank you' in his lingo."

"That's more than I know," Breen said.

"We made it through Yemen not knowing Arabic," Williams said, "but we had a trail and a single purpose there. This is different. This would be more jury-rigged than anything we've done. We were also on the move when we were hunting Ahmed Salehi. This could be a sit-down of days, maybe a week or more. And there are a lot of moving parts—Grace, her target, elements of the target that will be looking back, and not even being in the same country. You'd have to move and adapt quickly."

Rivette was smiling.

Williams looked at Breen. "I know where the lance corporal falls on this. How about you, Major?"

"Not a secret that I like order and organization. But we'll do what's needed."

But his mind was elsewhere. "We have a lot to get done—by when?"

"Berry is working to get you over in two days or less."

The major rose. "Jaz, we better get going."

"Where?"

Breen replied, "To check some weather forecasts and then go shopping."

"I simply do not trust Chase Williams to stay within mission parameters," January Dow told the president.

The intelligence official had been summoned to the Oval Office to brief the president on the status of Lieutenant Lee. January had not been asked to sit and knew that the audience would be brief; General Eileen Petrillo, chair of the Joint Chiefs of Staff, was in the vestibule outside the Oval Office. She had arrived at the same time as January and was not a patient woman.

January told the president that Lieutenant Lee had been airborne for two and a half hours; that the White House Travel Office had rushed her paperwork through, and provided the parameters of the plan, as far as she knew them. The president seemed satisfied with that.

Then it was on to Op-Center and her concerns about Williams. The president listened and then was equally blunt.

"Your solution?" the president asked.

"Admiral Williams is subject to UCMJ Articles 77–134 governing the actions of retired officers," she said. "If necessary, I would like to remind him of that fact before the admiral goes off half-cocked, as he has in the past."

"That won't impact Lieutenant Lee or her assignment?"

There was impatience in the president's question; January knew it was time to button this up.

"To the contrary, sir. It is designed to protect the integrity of mission parameters."

"Fine," Wright told her.

"Thank you, Mr. President."

January turned smartly and left promptly. She smiled and thanked General Petrillo for her patience without delaying her further by slowing or waiting for a reply.

There were several articles among the Uniform Code of Military Justice that could be applied to Williams. As a civilian, the retired officer would not be subject to a court-martial but it would provide the framework for civilian charges. In any case, the prospect of prison time would put Williams on notice that renegade action would not be tolerated by this administration, and it would give his JAG officer Major Breen something to think about other than shadowing Lieutenant Lee through the plains of China.

This was not a move January wished to make, but it would protect her flank against blowback from rogue action . . . and it was the kind of preemptive strike at which she was expert.

This was the way Washington D.C. was run, from the West Wing down to the smallest office in the Farm Credit Administration.

CHAPTER FOURTEEN

Qincheng Prison, Changping District, Beijing, China
February 17, 4:00 A.M., CST

It had become swiftly and emphatically clear to Wen Dàyóu that in a year and a half of university he had amassed very little useful knowledge. He had learned numbers and their application, but that did not help him now.

What he had needed—what every Chinese citizen clearly needed—was a working knowledge of the world. Knowledge about how to secure and preserve freedom. Knowledge about people and the psychology of caring for them . . . of breaking them. He had not even learned self-preservation, a skill Kong Yanyong had evidently acquired.

Psychology. That word clung in his mind when every other thought fell away incomplete and helpless. Awakened before dawn and not permitted to urinate—the only question that Wen managed to articulate—the young man was escorted by two guards along a corridor that smelled of mildew. He was walked into a dark room, thrust into a wooden chair, and left there in complete darkness. The door closed hard and the only sounds were the hiss of a radiator somewhere in the room and the sound of his own rapid breathing.

He stayed where he was and said nothing. The room smelled musty; almost like a doghouse he once had in Shanxi. He thought back to the pranks of his childhood. His captors might have their own sinister versions of mousetraps or trip wire to help break him.

Or was just thinking about them more psychology? he wondered.

He was too confused now even to risk thinking.

After a time—it seemed like a half hour or so; enough time, anyway, to make him drowse in the chair—the door opened and an overhead row of fluorescent lights flicked on. Wen awoke with a gasp as a man in a dark green uniform walked in, quietly closing the door behind him.

In a wide-eyed moment, Wen took in the room. He was in a small, spartan office with old office furniture: a gunmetal desk, a swivel chair behind it, and a row of filing cabinets behind that. There were a black telephone and a lamp on the desk—nothing more.

Nothing modern . . . nothing hackable, it occurred to Wen. For some reason that was unnerving. From Counterrevolutionary posts he knew that this was where people disappeared. Now he knew how.

Wen had been slumping but now sat upright against the straight back of the chair. He made the effort with a half-cooked sense of dignity. He watched as the short man with red cheeks and unblinking eyes walked slowly to the desk. He was carrying a manila folder, thick but neat with papers, and set them on the desk. It remained closed long enough—intentionally?—for Wen to see his name on the tab. With precise movements the man opened it and began scanning the documents and photographs. The official had not yet acknowledged the prisoner. Wen knew it was pointless to say anything and sat with fear that, to his surprise, still had room to grow. Not only did his heart race, but his hungry stomach burbled and his bladder ached.

"May I use a restroom?" Wen asked.

The man did not acknowledge that Wen had spoken; he simply turned the papers over slowly, now and then lingering on a section. Now the young man realized why the room smelled like a doghouse. The odor came from the chair he was on. Wen grew resolute, at least about that: he would not give this man the satisfaction of wetting the chair. He would not cross that next line of dehumanization.

He also did not want to appear to be a coward.

"How are my mother and sister?" he asked in a stronger voice.

This question, too, went unanswered, but Wen felt better for having asked it.

After some fifteen or twenty minutes of no sound but the movement of paper and Wen's own breathing, the man closed the dossier and removed a pen and yellow pad from the desk. His looked at Wen.

"I am Taiyuan Chief of Security Shen Laihang," he said in a rigid manner designed to impress, not inform. "You are being held here as required under the Statutes of Criminal Detention for documented infractions of Articles 17, 123, and 154."

Wen had nothing to say, though his mouth was too dry to say anything.

"This investigation is being conducted under the direct supervision of General Zhou Chang of the Taiyuan Satellite Launch Center in Shanxi. You are familiar with that facility?"

He nodded.

"Speak!" the chief of security barked.

"I . . . I am."

"When was the last time you were in Shanxi?"

"November."

"The date?"

"I don't recall."

"Would it have been the fifth through the seventh?"

"It—it might have been."

"Are you familiar with General Chang?"

"By name. I may have seen him. I don't know."

"How do you know the insurrectionists Jiang Yiwu and her husband Chao Dan?"

Wen had not expected that sudden turn. He hesitated.

"Jiang Yiwu. Chao Dan," the official repeated.

"I—I know them from a page on social media."

"The name of this page?"

"Bagua."

"That is a site on the dark web. You know that the dark web is forbidden."

"I—I am a student, and other students were—"

"I am not interested in other students," the interrogator

said, raising his voice for the first time. "You have met Jiang Yiwu and Chao Dan?"

"Yes. Your men know that Chao came to see—"

"That was last night. Previously, you collaborated with them in activities related to the Counterrevolutionary Youth Organization."

"Not collaborated. I attended—activities, you might say. Peaceful."

"In the streets, marching and carrying banners. You are aware this kind of public display has been outlawed under Article 17."

"Not . . . not specifically." The steam heat had gotten louder and Wen began to perspire.

The interrogator sat stiffly, his eyes neutral as he thumped the file with an index finger. "Your presence at unlawful protests designed to agitate unrest has been photographically documented by Jiang Yiwu. This is an infraction of Article 123."

"I . . . I'm sorry. I was not . . . thinking."

"Last night you ran from members of the Ministry of State Security in their execution of official business. This is a criminal action punishable by five years in prison under Article 154."

Wen's composure unraveled and he began to sob. Sitting here, it all seemed so pointless. He did not understand what had compelled him to take those chances, stupid risks. Safety in numbers, a false feeling of anonymity, a sense of support from international posters on Bagua, the sense that Jiang and Chao knew what they were doing—all of it had given him misplaced confidence. He saw that now. He wanted to communicate to Shen Laihang that he was contrite, reformed . . . but he did not have the words.

"We want to know about the people your father associated with at Taiyuan," the interrogator moved on.

Wen felt the pressure lift.

"I don't know them," Wen replied.

"Are you aware that your father is under suspicion of sabotage?"

"I only know what Chao said, that there were suspicions of that. They cannot be true, of course."

"Why 'of course'?"

"My father is a patriot."

"Yet you were active on Bagua."

"We are patriots in our own way." Wen did not know where he found the courage to say that but he was glad he did.

Shen Laihang left the office and, when the door shut, Wen deflated. There was a guard outside and the young man considered asking him to go to the lavatory. But the interrogator returned promptly and this time the guard followed him inside. The official returned to the desk and began making notes on the pad. Wen could not see what he was writing. The young man looked away from the guard and the billy club he wore and dreaded what would happen when the writing was finished.

The telephone rang with a jangle that caused Wen to gasp.

"Answer it," the interrogator said when it rang a second time.

The young man had to get up to go to the desk. He did so

unsteadily, his head briefly throbbing, his knees like sand. He managed the three steps and raised the receiver to his ear.

"Hello?"

"Wen? Is that you?"

"Father?" Wen was forced to plant his left palm on the desk to keep himself upright.

"Are you all right?" the elder Dàyóu asked.

"Yes! Mother and sister—where are they?"

"At home, I'm told," the engineer answered. "I don't know."

Wen noticed that the chief of security had stopped making notes. The diminutive man sat back, watching his prisoner.

"Father, hold on please." His hands shaking, Wen covered the mouthpiece and glared down at Shen Laihang. His voice, when it came, was as close to a demand as he could make it. "What can I do to help him? What do you want?"

"Hang up."

"What?"

Wen heard the guard take a few steps forward.

"Put the receiver down now," the interrogator instructed.

Wen did as he was told. His empty palm joined the other on the desk. Shen Laihang's eyes shifted slightly to the guard, who grabbed the student by the upper arm.

"Return him to his cell," the chief of security ordered.

"Wait!" Wen said. "I want to help—"

"You have."

"I don't . . . please, my mother—?"

The billy club slashed across the small of Wen's back and he lost control of everything below his waist. He crumpled to the floor and lay there gasping, moaning, trying to feel something other than the electric pain that shot, then throbbed, up his backbone and into his shoulders and down his legs to his heels.

"Get him up and take him away," Shen Laihang ordered.

Wen was aware of being hoisted to his feet and having his own limp, right arm slung around the neck of the guard. Then he was half walked, half dragged from the interrogation room to his cell. The fire that raced from Wen's neck to feet had centralized in the backs of his legs, causing two burning welts to rise on the skin behind his knees. Just the pressure of his trousers caused intense pain; he would have screamed if he had the energy.

And yet, as he was returned to the cold cell and the iron door was locked, Wen's thoughts were not on his own plight. They were on his mother and sister and the horrors that might be inflicted on them; and on his father, who Wen hoped would stay true to his ideals in spite of whatever pain might be inflicted on himself or the women.

Right now, the greatest strength Wen possessed was not inside but in the solidarity that had always marked the Dàyóu family.

Dr. Yang Dàyóu returned the receiver to its cradle. A guard unplugged the phone from the wall and carried it away. The engineer placed a hand on the night table that had held the phone. He rose, his movements slow and contemplative. He could hear, in the distance, the shift change: guard dogs were barking at one another. They snapped and fought because they were animals.

What was Chang's excuse?

Drawing his shoulders erect, he regarded the man who stood before him. General Chang, who had not stopped scowling since the explosion of the *Qi*-19.

The two men were in a small room at the workers' quarters of the Taiyuan Satellite Launch Center. Yang had been kept locked in these quarters since his arrest. It was not an uncomfortable prison but it was a prison nonetheless. There was a window, but it was three floors up with bundles of barbed wire on the ground and a high electrified fence beyond. Workers at all levels, from welders to chief scientists, were relied upon; they were never trusted.

The general did not speak until the guard had closed the door.

"Well?" General Chang asked in a low, firm voice.

Yang looked at the taller man and waited a moment before answering. He wanted to make sure his own voice was as steadfast as his posture.

"Is saving your name worth losing your honor, General?"

The officer gazed dispassionately at the engineer. "That is not the relevant point, Doctor. Is saving your name worth losing your son?"

Yang did not doubt the earnestness of the general. In the decade since Zhou Chang had come to this facility as Captain Chang, Deputy Chief of Missile Operations, he had been single-minded about building the nation's missile offense system. He had viewed his own rise and China's security as a lockstep partnership. Over the past two years, the People's Republic had faced a severely shrunken economy and technological advances in the United States and Russia. Subjected to the dual challenges of reining in costs and accelerating schedules, Chang had made gambler's choices on the *Qi* project. Until the other day, he had been lucky.

But that was no longer Yang's problem. If the engineer did not exonerate Chang by accepting full blame, Wen would suffer. The young man would be punished not for his foolish but youthful counterrevolutionary activities, but for being Yang's son.

"Are my wife and daughter aware of Wen's status?" Yang asked.

"They have not been told."

"May I speak with them?"

"I will arrange it when you have acknowledged the haste and negligence that caused the *Qi*-19 disaster." He moved closer. "It is either that or treason, Dr. Dàyóu—and disaster for your son."

Yang knew what he must do but his heart refused to accept it. His profession was built on equations and ideas like work-energy integrals and coordinate acceleration—measurable, reducible, transferrable from machine to machine. The human mind was equipped to approach problems in the same way. But mechanisms did not have heart and that was Yang's struggle.

"I need time to think," the engineer said.

"How much time?"

Yang regarded the other man. "How much time does one require to quantify loss?"

Chang was not sure he understood but said, "You have until I return. After that, events will continue as I have outlined."

"I will make my case before the Court of the Political Works Commander," Yang said. "I may fail but—"

"You will fail," the general said. "You will be nowhere near the Most Honorable Pan Jinping. Because this pertains to national security I have requested that this be by command paper."

"Who is writing *my* defense?"

"The charges will be brought by the People's Republic of China, directed against the *Qi* project. As commander, it is my responsibility to defend this operation and its members."

Yang's mouth twisted as though he had stared into a face of cold evil. "Lies. That's what you will tell them."

The general went to the door. "That is for His Honor to decide based on documentary evidence."

"Then why did you need me to confess to anything?"

"It would be cleaner to have that in writing," Chang replied. "Not necessary, just thorough and complete." He rapped once and was let out by a guard.

Yang stood still, in a state of despair that did not show on his face but filled every paternal part of him.

He sat on the bed, exhaled a long and tremulous breath. He felt lost, empty, enervated. He had been trusting and had suffered for it. They held his family. For the sake of his wife and daughter there appeared to be no option but complete surrender.

That was not true. There was another choice.

His eyes went to the small table in the middle of the room. His lunch tray was on it, the food untouched. There were metal utensils.

They don't care if you take your own life, he thought. *They left a knife. They seem to desire that.*

The thought was heinous. It would confirm Chang's allegation and the fallout would likely stain his wife and daughter forever. It would not do Wen any good either.

Besides, that is not like you, he thought. *There is a problem. That is an end, not a solution.*

As Yang asked himself that question, something he had said to Shen and Chang came back to him. Something that might hold the seed of an answer. . . .

CHAPTER FIFTEEN

Xinzhou, Shanxi Province, China
February 17, 4:00 P.M. CST

Lieutenant Lee was able to sleep more than she had expected. Between rest and reviewing the files from January Dow, the flight to Beijing was not as onerous as she had anticipated. As soon as the seat belts came off, Elsie Smith unstowed her carry-on and was gone, introducing herself to anyone who looked her way as she aisle-grazed. Grace heard the phrase "in Hollywood" float back like the smell of C-4 at explosives demos. Each utterance caused the officer to mourn the continued erosion of gravitas in Washington.

The refueling layover on Oahu had been scheduled for a half hour. Deployment Operations in Washington had not been able to finish Grace's documentation before she left, and the job had been tasked to the Directorate of Plans, Training, Mobilization and Security at Schofield Barracks. The home of United States Army Garrison Hawaii was located at Wheeler Army Airfield where the passengers were allowed to deplane for fifteen minutes.

Williams had texted Grace that Captain Eric Moreau would meet her on the tarmac. Even as she was walking down the mobile stairway, an officer and an MP had identified her and walked over.

Grace saluted and the exchange was brief: the captain confirmed her identity with a security question provided by Williams—the hometown of her youngest roommate—then handed her a souvenir shoulder bag from Hawaii, the kind she might have purchased at the Schofield PX. Before the captain departed, Grace went to the freestanding eyewash station and examined the documents. Everything she had been expecting was there. Since the papers were unregistered forgeries, and the Janet Airlines flight was headed to China, Captain Moreau knew Lieutenant Lee was on a separate assignment.

"Good luck to you, Lieutenant," he had said after walking her back to the stairway.

The sentiment was in earnest and Grace was grateful for it.

The plane was soon airborne and touched down in Beijing at 1:00 P.M. local time. The flight to Shanxi was not for ninety minutes. Standing with a fat carry-on bag, Grace made sure to talk with the ambassador before the staff left the terminal for the embassy bus. The ambassador wished her well on her visit to unspecified family and double-checked the date she was expected at the embassy to begin her duties. The well-wishes were all theater. In addition to studying surveillance footage of the new arrivals—which the Ministry of State Security would compare with files of known American operatives using facial recognition programs—the MSS would subject the recordings to AALR analysis. The Advanced Automated Lip Reading technology used in China was not as sophisticated as the F.B.I. and C.I.A. versions, which circumvented privacy and profiling laws by limiting its search to words and word groups. The Chinese software provided full transcriptions and translations which were scrupulously read by intelligence technicians. As far as they knew, Grace was going to do exactly what she and Ambassador Simon had discussed.

Grace did not feel the looming pressure to act that she usually did on these missions. Previous Black Wasp operations were enveloped in urgency wrapped in the unwelcoming seats and sounds of military transports. By contrast, though the journey was long, it was organized.

She changed from her uniform into jeans and a heavy gray sweatshirt with a hood, then spent her time in the terminal browsing in small shops, looking at faces with a warm feeling of kinship, and listening to conversations. The last was something for which she had insisted on allowing time. There were hundreds of spoken languages in China, from Sino-Tibetan to Turkic to Indo-European. She wanted to separate these from the Mandarin-based "Standard Chinese" that she would be using. Even though she was not pretending to be a local, it had been years since Grace heard colloquial Chinese back home, and she knew that Chinatown slang and even profanity was different from what she heard here. She wanted to attune her ear since she expected to be eavesdropping more than talking.

The woman was grateful for the chance to settle into the pulse of her ancestral home, and also for the fact that there was no smoking in either the international or domestic terminal. In a nation where more than one in five people smoked, that was something Grace would have to acclimate herself to.

The three-and-one-half-hour flight from Beijing was to the airport roughly seventy-four miles northeast of the city. Grace had texted Uncle Sun before boarding and he replied, excitedly, that he would be there to meet her.

The Airbus A321 was new and uncrowded and made for a relaxing flight. Fully half the twenty-odd passengers were men, but there were a few women, all wearing sports jackets and serious looks. A few knew each other. She suspected they were technicians headed to Taiyuan; she would know when they deplaned.

Grace experienced alternately warm and melancholy thoughts as she flew over the countryside, which was mostly rivers and hills. She was drawn to it by an ancient or genetic or spiritual connection; she did not know which it was, most likely all of them. Because of that she was sorry that it was *enemy* territory.

Hostility toward people with the same blood as yours, she thought.

It was a conflict that bordered on lunacy, yet here she was. Grace wondered if anyone at the White House or in Op-Center had harbored any concerns about sending her here. And if they had, did her ability to move freely among the locals make it a calculated risk?

Don't get tangled in thoughts like those, she cautioned herself as the late afternoon winter sun painted shadows across the countryside below. *You have Black Wasp firmly on your side.* To them, there would be no doubts.

The wings of the Airbus dipped, the sound of the engines changed, and soon the aircraft was descending. The terminal was a single long structure, modern and white. From the air it looked like a bird of prey with sleek, straight wings resting on a body of skeletal girders. That impression was reinforced when they deplaned via another mobile stairway, with a curved, central beak angling down.

Grace's credentials moved her through customs and her documents were not closely examined. Smiling brightly, she addressed the agent in Cantonese, and the young man found her both an engaging and a welcome change from harried travelers. She moved through the room with its opaque glass walls to the arrival area where Uncle Sun was waiting. He stood with ten others who had come to meet passengers and there was no mistaking him.

Whatever sense of homecoming Grace had felt flying to Shanxi was amplified by the sight of her mother's brother. Sun Fenghe spotted her from the photo she had sent and she from his. He was fifty years old, five foot six, and powerfully built, with gray hair buzzed short. He wore a knee-length black parka and well-worn work boots. But Grace's strongest impression was seeing her mother's face in his, especially in the big, dark welcoming eyes and genuine smile.

That, plus his enthusiastic, nearly jumping crisscross wave of both arms from behind the aluminum gate.

A final presentation of her documents to a guard, and

Grace was permitted into Arrival Hall 1F and at liberty in the People's Republic of China.

Sun stopped waving so that he could embrace his niece—but briefly. After a tight hug he held her at arm's length.

"Let me look at you!" he said, still beaming. "These eyes saw you as a child and then just like magic, you're a woman! I see your father's determined mouth . . . your mother's beauty!"

"You are kind, Uncle Sun."

"Kind nothing! I am proud, *so* proud, and honored that you have come to see me!" He hugged her again then released her. "Do you have any luggage?"

"Just this bag. The rest went on to the embassy."

Sun scooped the suitcase in a strong hand and pointed ahead. "The car is right outside. Wait—do you want anything to eat or drink?"

"I'm fine," she assured him.

Still grinning, he hooked his free arm in hers and they walked together to the glass doors and the bright, chilly street. He slipped sunglasses from the top of his head and covered his eyes.

"The American Embassy in Beijing," he said as they exited the terminal. "Will that mean I will see more of you? You must tell me everything!"

That was all she said about her coming to China, that she was stationed to the mission on an open-ended project. She did not want him to know anything about her real reason for being here. In the event that her real reason for being here were discovered, Sun could plausibly tell everything he knew.

They waited for the WALK sign at Taohuayuan Road. A pair of vans was parked outside; several of the men and women she had observed were boarding.

"Is there a convention in town?" she asked Sun innocently.

"Those are the buses to Taiyuan," he replied. "Too many of them now, making ruts in the dirt roads."

The sign changed and they left behind arriving passengers and smokers who were on departing flights. As they entered the open parking lot, Grace spotted a bicycle rack and asked if her uncle had a two-wheeler.

"I have two," he said, "one for good days and one for snow and mud."

"I was thinking I'd like to take a ride in the morning. Maybe loosen up after being boxed in a plane for the better part of a day."

"It's a wonderful idea, but it will be cold," Sun cautioned.

"I know, I looked at the forecast. That means there will be fewer people for me to run over. It's been years since I've been on a bicycle."

Sun laughed. "A wonderful idea, then! I find the cold invigorating. I have to work or I would come with you. If you get lost, just tell anyone you meet that you are the beautiful niece of Sun Fenghe. They will give you help, a meal—anything you want."

They got into a battered red truck, a ten-year-old Chang'an-made Kuayue Kuayuewang pickup. When they set out on the refurbished suspension it reminded Grace of the five-ton 6x6 trucks that used to take troops into the wilderness for survival training.

The area around the airport was a ribbon of roads and service buildings. Sun drove onto the expressway as dusk was settling and Grace could see, in the distance, the lights on the buildings—mostly hotels—of the city itself.

"It's too cold for the parks or I would insist that we visit the city for an outside dinner," Sun said. "Good local produce."

The conversation shifted almost at once, and the ninety-minute drive to Uncle Sun's home was full of family updates and reminiscences. Grace told him about her parents and about her military career.

"So then we are rivals," he joked.

"No, Uncle. The governments are always rivals, not the people."

"That is true," Sun said. Then he sighed. "I miss having these talks with relatives. No one else cares about my ancestors. Why should they? They have their own long histories."

"What *do* people care about where you live?" Grace asked. It felt deceptive but not awkward or ungainly, sliding into intelligence-gathering that she would need.

"My concerns are different from those of most people," he said. "We old-timers, the few of us who treasure the character of our land, do not approve of the Greenbelt Project."

"You mentioned that in an email to Mother," Grace said.

"The authorities call it 'renewal' and 'beautification,' but it is like Disneyland. It's a place for young families to frolic. But it is destroying the character of the area."

"The young people are coming for—?" Grace asked because

she wanted to keep the conversation going; the intelligence January Dow had furnished already told her the answer.

"The Launch Center and the facilities that are rising around it," Sun said. "I am not telling secret tales, you will see it for yourself. As close as you can get, anyway." He snorted. "This is not America. Here, they shoot and then command you to withdraw."

"There are bases like that in the U.S.," Grace said.

"Not like here, I'm sure. Perimeter fence after perimeter fence with patrol dogs—it's like your great-grandfather Yan used to describe when he talked about Japanese prisoner-of-war camps. People cannot get in or out but they cannot hide what goes on there, though."

"What do you mean?"

Sun gestured upward with a hand. "The missiles. The sounds, the fire in the sky, the smoke when the wind blows our way, the smell of fuel that gets into everything. I actually like that. It's China at work—acrid, like the factories once were."

Grace decided not to ask her uncle if he had heard the explosion and what the local talk was. She knew it happened; any details she might pick up were not worth exposing her interest in the site.

She asked about her uncle's life, about the repair work he did at the local power station.

He told her, then asked, "Do you want to know a real secret?"

"Sure."

"I work all day with grease and coal. Do you want to know why I don't smell of it? Milk and a spoonful of vanilla. I grind the beans myself—or rather, I pound them to powder." He raised a hand. "See? No smell. And I'll tell you another secret. Dogs love me. I smell like a bovine, not a carnivore."

It was the kind of insight one did not find in a dossier, one that was worth remembering.

Despite the long sleep on the intercontinental flight, the darkness brought on a restful feeling and Grace found herself eager to get to her uncle's home, bathe, share a modest meal, and then sleep.

Tomorrow, her work would begin. That was when she not only undertook her mission but would try very hard to do so without losing the love and friendship of Uncle Sun. . . .

CHAPTER SIXTEEN

Dulles International Airport, Washington, D.C.
February 17, 4:19 A.M.

It was a busy and productive day and a half of preparation for Hamilton Breen and Jaz Rivette.

The first task the three members of Black Wasp undertook was to review meteorological data and study the terrain of the area the two men intended to visit. None of them knew how long Breen and Rivette would be there; it could be days or even weeks. That would depend on the ground reports Grace transmitted to Williams, but Breen and Rivette had to plan for all contingencies. Carrying anything but emergency rations—power bars, mostly—would be burdensome so the three men checked the names of Mongolian merchants in the target zones who were identified on travel websites.

They would still need to bring clothes and personal gear. Black Wasp had cold-weather attire, which they had not had the opportunity to use, but the sands and rugged stone required specific footwear, gloves, and facial coverings. There was also a question of whether or not to bring a tent or at least bedrolls.

Williams had left those decisions to the two men. Since they could not telegraph their actions by going to the base quartermaster, the major and the lance corporal took Williams' car and headed to the Outdoor Adventure located in a civilian shopping area three miles from Fort Belvoir. Breen discovered that shopping with Rivette was a mission unto itself.

From the first, for sleep, Rivette had favored a dome or cabin tent. The sharpshooter grasped the need to be compact and mobile but he also put forth the need to be warm.

"I read that Ulaanbaatar is tied with Ottawa and Moscow for the world's coldest capital city," Rivette said. "If I need to shoot, we both want to be sure my fingers are warm." He crouched beside a large plastic package and read from it. "Windproof, water-resistant. Look what else it says—'super easy to carry.'"

"Bright orange and green, designed to be visible from the air," Breen pointed out.

The Southern California native shook his head. "I did the sleeping bag thing when we were in Kodiak, and when I was in the mountains for Marine-training 101. Gloves caused my fingers to overheat and swell. Can't shoot like that. So both times I lay on my back with my hands in my armpits, and each of those was only for two nights."

"Fortunately, you'll have time to figure it out."

"What do you mean?"

"Except for the crew cabin, which we will *not* be in, these old, commercial cargo planes are poorly heated."

"Some kinda manhood thing to be freezing at 35,000 feet?"

"A cost thing," Breen explained. "No one is supposed to be back there, and crates don't care about heating. When it breaks, why fix it? You will be cold for about sixteen, seventeen hours total. Plenty of time to figure out how to keep your fingers warm."

Over Rivette's ongoing complaints, they went with a pair of charcoal-gray, waterproof canvas bedrolls. They also purchased oversized boots to accommodate two layers of socks, fleece-lined gloves with touchscreen fingers, and body warming pads that worked off AAA batteries. They each had a standard military-issue compass but purchased two more that strapped on the wrist. They also bought two dozen energy bars and stopped at the pharmacy for sodium chloride tablets to help stay hydrated.

When the men returned to Fort Belvoir, they made sure their to-go backpacks were not overstuffed or lumpy. If it became necessary to hide, they had to know their shapes without looking. It took some rearranging—soap and shaving materials were tucked into the bedrolls so guns and a knife could be concealed in the backpacks—but the men made it work. Rivette had selected a pair of Colts for the mission: an M4 assault carbine and an M1911 semiautomatic handgun. He had taken each one on the two cold-weather training trips; it was as important to know how they withstood the cold as how they functioned. Breen carried a 10.5-inch fixed blade knife. Lieutenant Lee had recommended it, calling it the "idiot proof" version of the butterfly knives she wore in ankle sheaths. He was not expert in the blade's use but would feel better having it if they encountered a snow leopard or some other predator.

Breen and Rivette divided the cash equally between them

and kept it in their pockets. If they had to separate—by intention or not—each would have one thousand dollars in Mongolian tögrög, American dollars, and Chinese yuan. Williams had rejected the idea of bringing warm clothes to swap; it was too much to carry and money was universal barter.

Breen had the only D-GLAS—Department of Defense geosynchronous low altitude satellite—device for communication. If Breen became disabled, the phone would respond to Rivette's facial scan as a default and allow him to talk to Williams. Because of the satellite's perigeal orbit over the region and its ability to piggyback signals off neighboring satellites in the event of interference from weather or geography, communications were clear and uninterrupted.

"Feels okay," Breen said when they had dressed and hefted everything on their backs for the first time.

Rivette agreed. "Seems kind of a waste not to climb Mount Everest while we're over there."

"Next certification," the major promised.

The packing done, it was time to study. Rivette learned key words in Mongolian while Breen spent a great deal of time going over maps of the region and intelligence about Mongolia. Geographically, there was good news and bad. The bad news was it is landlocked. The good news was it has the sparsest population density of any nation in the world. Though the country had a market economy, it also had close political ties to its neighbors Russia and China. He did not know the bounty on American spies but he speculated it was substantial. On the other hand, one-third of its population was nomadic and half of those were Buddhists. Breen made sure to download some overviews of the religion as well as key texts like the sutras. Glancing at the *Diamond Sutra,* he saw a quote from the Sixth Patriarch Hui Neng, one that gave him hope: "Where there is a sincere request a response will follow." He was greatly ashamed that he knew so little of a faith followed by 520 million people.

Preparations completed, it was time to eat and sleep. There usually was not time for Breen to contemplate missions ahead of time: there was a crisis and Black Wasp was on the move. Having the night to think elbowed the major's characteristic confidence to the side. His concerns about illegally entering a sovereign nation were one issue, especially in support of espionage against China. The fact that the incursion was not authorized by the White House meant that if Black Wasp were caught, Wright would likely spend zero political capital trying to get them back. Finally, there was the matter of Rivette's go-get-'em approach to problem-solving. Rivette's style was impulse, not reason, and he hoped he did not have to expend too much effort wrangling the lance corporal.

These and his fears for Grace's safety tag-teamed him for nearly two hours. Breen eventually fell asleep but 3:00 A.M. arrived quickly. That was when Williams showed up in his unarmored but heavy-duty SUV for the forty-minute drive to cargo services at Dulles International Airport. They started out in a light drizzle that threatened to turn to sleet. Rivette sat in the back and resumed his interrupted sleep.

"You good?" Williams asked Breen.

"Yeah," the major answered. "You?"

"Fair."

"Undecided, I'd say."

"How so?" Williams asked.

"You weren't wearing this parka when we were shivering in Soldier Statesman Park and your go-bag is on the back seat floor next to Rivette."

"You've always had a good eye, Counselor."

"Are you coming with us?"

Williams sighed. "I don't think so."

"But you wanted to get there, see how you felt, give yourself the option," Breen said.

"Something like that. I've been struggling with this, Major."

"It's not like you have anything to prove, Admiral."

"It isn't that. It's the bullying that I resent."

"The bullying, or who is issuing those commands?" Breen asked.

"Fair point," Williams agreed. "When I ran CENT-COMM, I had a senior enlisted leader, Fleet Master Chief Roger Murdoch, who would go around quoting Douglas MacArthur as if the general's words—because they were that general's words—inoculated him from any other viewpoint. But until now, until today, I never entirely bought into the one Murdoch said damn near every day: 'It is a dangerous concept that men of the armed forces must owe their primary allegiance to these temporary occupants of the White House, instead of to the country and the Constitution to which they have sworn to defend.'"

"It's a subjective truth, Admiral. By the Constitution, those 'temporary occupants of the White House' *are* the commanders-in-chief."

"I suspect General MacArthur was being oblique, not subjective," Williams said. "I see the subtext now. He was warning complicit officers that they could not put politics and ambition over good judgment and patriotism."

"A debatable point," Breen said. "John Milton applies, I think."

Williams snickered. "'They also serve who only stand and wait.' That's never been my way."

"I know," the major said. "And I was always a courtroom combatant. The world is upside-down."

Except for the wipers and the heater, the car was silent. Williams wondered how much the global axis had to tilt before everyone went spinning off. More immediate than that, he wondered how long it would be before he went spinning off.

The highway was deserted at this hour, and in this weather. They left 495 and Williams drove to the cargo area. Williams accessed the tarmac via a keypad-activated gate. Berry had given him the daily passcode and informed him that the aircraft was a decommissioned Russian military cargo aircraft, an Ilyushin Il-76, circa 1977.

"I'm told it's not pretty," Berry had warned. "But if it gets here, it'll get out again."

The men pulled up to the covered carport and stepped out. Williams saw that Breen was watching him expectantly. The admiral did a gut-check and, decided, left his go-bag in the vehicle.

The short, stocky, big-winged jet looked like Williams felt: dirty gray and world-weary in the frozen rain. Fueling was under way and one of the crew members came over to meet them.

"Pel Dogsom," said the new arrival, a scruffy, bony man who was probably fifty but looked seventy. "English—eh."

"Chase Williams," the admiral replied.

"From Berry."

"That's right."

The man's brown eyes turned to Breen and Rivette, who were carrying their gear.

"Come," the man said, and led the way toward the aircraft.

Rivette was impressed as they started after the man. "No-hassle security."

Williams pulled up the hood of his parka and followed the men to the stairway. Though he had done this before with Black Wasp, he could not at this moment imagine what it would feel like to be going. The problem, he knew then, was not with January Dow, Douglas MacArthur, or John Milton. It was with him.

Though Williams was retired, Major Breen and Lance Corporal Rivette saluted him at the foot of the stairway.

It was not a "Godspeed" or less solemn "Watch your ass" moment. The members of Black Wasp had become Williams' friends. It was a solemn expression under the salute and then the men were gone.

A disinterested, wet member of the Dulles ground crew wheeled the stairs away, the hatch was shut, and Williams backed away. The sleet sounded like nearby gunfire as it pit-pat against the polyurethane of his hood.

Williams turned sharply and left. The problem was him and he knew how to fix it. As he got into the SUV, he realized that he had not stayed behind to accommodate January Dow. He had stayed behind to teach her and the new administration a lesson in tactics and command.

CHAPTER SEVENTEEN

Jinzhou, Shanxi Province, China
February 18, 6:04 A.M., CST

Grace had not bothered to set her alarm. If her body needed sleep, she wanted to have it. Better to go out alert than early.

Sun had made her bed on a foldout cot in a small alcove that held a bookcase packed with books in tumbling stacks, record albums—bamboo flute music, mostly, with a separate pile of meditations—and boxes of maps, blueprints, and instruction manuals.

She did not wake with the sun but, rather, to the muddy, distinctive smell of Dong'e E'jiao coffee. Flavored with donkey hide, the brew had become popular in Chinatown before she began her enlistment. It was a bracing blend that was surprisingly smooth.

The lieutenant texted Williams to let him know her schedule. The two had agreed that unless he had something to report, the communication would be one-way. The less her phone was in her hand, the less anyone would be curious about what she was writing. When it was not in use she kept it in a customized "holster" that did not inhibit her movements. She wore a matching case on the opposite side for compact binoculars. Both were tucked in her armpit for concealment.

There were precious few ground-based images of the launch site, and none of a launch itself. Regardless, she would not bother taking any. Sunlight glinting off the phone could call attention to her. Being caught sending a photograph could be a death sentence. The Department of Defense had all the satellite imaging it needed in the event a missile strike was ever necessary.

Grace then dressed and went to the kitchen to greet Uncle Sun. Her room, Sun's bedroom, the living room, and the kitchen were the entirety of the place. The two had a breakfast of rice porridge and biscuits, along with their coffee. Sun had to work and Grace offered to buy food for dinner.

"That would be a treat!" he said gratefully. "If you'd like a scenic adventure, Ho's Market is the best for fish. Ho and I grew up together. His wife catches them fresh. He's ten miles to the north and the roads are flat and reliable. It's the only 'benefit' of the Greenbelt invasion."

"Then that's where I'll go," Grace said. "It's the same direction as Taiyuan, yes?"

"Yes, but the missile base is halfway between Ho's place and Taiyuan, and you want to avoid going anywhere near there," Sun warned.

"That's why I asked," Grace replied.

"I'm serious, Grace. *They* are serious. The military patrols stop at Ho's for coffee and snacks, and your papers identify you as a U.S. Marine. Being attached to the embassy will mean nothing down here."

"I understand."

"If you want to see a city, Jinzhou is quite nice, I assure you. You'll see that's true as you ride through. There are parks and new buildings with shopping, and cultural exhibitions—a lot to see and do."

"I think I'd rather go see some of the countryside," Grace said. "The ride to Ho's sounds like a perfect way to stay warm. And—I'm like Mama that way. We enjoy a challenge."

"I probably won't see you until eight or so," he said. "The round trip will take you at least that long."

Sun kissed his niece on the forehead and cautioned her again to be careful.

The thermometer hanging outside the kitchen window registered just below freezing and Grace asked if she could borrow her uncle's windbreaker to wear over her sweater. It was not just for warmth that she wanted it. The garment smelled like the power plant, a combination of grease and smoke; it smelled local.

Sun's house was little more than a cottage, set at the bottom of a hill in an overgrown field in the old section of Jinzhou. The sparsely populated area was dominated by a block of mid-twentieth-century brick apartment buildings. These were separated from Sun's home by an old stone wall in disrepair. The aboveground electrical wires hummed with life. Though Sun had a small vegetable garden growing in a mix of soil and compost, and several dutifully attended window boxes, he enjoyed the old wooden poles and cables more.

"The cables don't come down in wind. I never lose power," he said proudly. "Energy people, we know our trade."

There was a shed behind the house. It was just large enough for Sun's pickup, a pair of bicycles, and a shovel and pail for garden work. Stacked haphazardly beside and behind the shed were mechanical odds and ends he kept when he upgraded equipment at the power plant. He kept them, he said, in case he had to make emergency repairs; if he left the materials on-site his superiors would sell them to other countries for personal gain. Her uncle's life would be considered lower class by American standards but he seemed genuinely happy.

Simple does not mean impoverished, she realized.

Sun left for work and Grace got her bearings before setting out. There would be many people commuting on bicycles, but Sun said that would thin once she hit the outskirts of the city.

Grace rode into the bright sun that did not mitigate the cold. As Sun had said, the road was new and level. As he had not bothered to say, the air was surprisingly clean. That might be a virtue of winter winds or it might be the efficacy of Beijing's efforts to improve the quality of life with its Greenbelt and Greenway projects.

Careful, she thought. *PUR.*

Major Breen had taught that the way to prevent this was to stay in your head: think, don't feel. That was a challenge as she saw the faces of fellow humans with the same habits and smiles and concerns as people back home—in some cases, biking, walking, and driving under the same global brands on billboards.

Grace looked straight ahead as she pedaled and advised her brain to do the same. Except for the knowledge that she was not at home, Grace could have been riding through Chinatown.

It had the same narrow, crowded, elbow-bend streets with the same faces and signage she saw in New York.

But it isn't, she continually reminded herself.

Leaving the city proper, Grace rode along freshly paved two-lane roads that seemed to represent the world Uncle Sun was fighting to maintain: they were bordered by old stores, some of them no more than shacks, and quaint homes that increasingly looked more like shacks than houses the longer she rode. It did not seem like miles she was covering, but years . . . decades. The past was alive in the structures she passed, the faces she saw. She agreed with Uncle Sun. It was worth preserving.

It was nearly noon when Grace reached Ho's Market. It was a long, one-story shop with wooden shingles and a red tile roof that had seen better seasons. There were tables outdoors, empty of diners or tea- and coffee-drinkers because of the cold. The tables and chairs were rusted, often-repainted iron; she guessed there was nowhere to store them and they were too heavy to move, judging by the imprints they had made in the oak planks underneath. Then she noticed a smell like a fireplace, and saw small, newish metal fire pits in a woodshed. Coronavirus-inspired outdoor dining had obviously come full circle, from China back to China.

The market was crowded inside with both late-morning shoppers and vendors delivering vegetables, homemade honey, dried fruit, and other goods. The fish counter was marked not just by the display case but by a fossil that hung on the wall behind the clerk.

"You are visiting?" asked the white-smocked woman behind the counter. She was short and white haired with a welcoming face.

"Yes," Grace said. "I am visiting my uncle Sun."

"Sun Fenghe?" she asked.

"That's right."

"A lovely man, always cheerful," said the woman. "I am Chu Hua and this," she pointed up, without being solicited, "is *Lycoptera muroii*. He swam the seas during the Jurassic era and was found on this very spot."

Grace acted suitably impressed. "Since you know fish, and my uncle, what do you recommend I make him for dinner?"

The woman suggested two Pacific mackerel with side orders of sugar buns and vegetable spring rolls. Grace accepted the woman's judgment without question and asked if she could pick it up after her tour of the Greenbelt. Chu Hua told her they closed at six thirty unless they had customers—and Sun would not be happy if Grace was late and he had to eat vegetables from his garden. Grace thanked her and departed. Though the lieutenant could have made the purchase on the way home, she had wanted to be seen and known there before continuing north. She had not seen any military personnel, but they must come for morning coffee or lunch and the time was not right for either.

The Greenbelt Project began a half mile beyond the market, a work-in-progress of promenades and trees, an artificial lake, and memorials to figures and events that defined four thousand years of Chinese history. It was not an aesthetic match for the countryside, though young scientists and engineers accustomed to urban living and a university education would likely not care.

Though it was past lunchtime there were no other walkers or riders out in the cold.

The neat, new road and its pleasant surroundings suddenly ended—not because the Greenbelt was unfinished but because the grounds around the Taiyuan Satellite Launch Center had begun.

Dead grasses from the field blew around her as Grace stopped pedaling and drank from her water bottle. She knew she could not stay long—she had worked up a sweat and the wind from the north was cold. She also did not think it wise to approach in the daytime and took it all in as quickly as possible, as Major Breen had trained them to do with maps and other memory drills. She did not use her binoculars, lest they catch and reflect sunlight.

There was about a mile of heavily treed forest—planted, not natural she suspected, given the careful spacing of the trees. It terminated in a fence that was everything Sun had said it was: even from this distance it was a formidable construction, a corrupt version of the Great Wall. There appeared to be three layers of barbed wire strung between heavy wooden supports. Dogs and militia could be seen beyond, indistinct because of distance, sunlight, and dust stirred by the breeze.

Beyond the fence were cinder-block structures that were probably offices, residences, laboratories and—from the smoke churning beyond—manufacturing facilities. She saw three permanent gantries, though intelligence suggested that the missiles were launched from mobile units that could be raised to target specific areas. The only indication of where they were came from what looked like maybe launch-control blockhouses or bunkers. Or they might just be housings for underground facilities.

They could even be bogus targets, she thought. Those structures might be nothing more than dummy buildings or staircases to the real facilities underground.

Grace stowed the water bottle in its loop behind the seat. She took a last look toward the facility. She did not even see the entrance; satellite images suggested it might be underground, lending support to her feeling that the real research and construction was done underground.

She got back on the bicycle and turned it around, started back. There was no getting around the fact that the place was designed to prevent the kind of infiltration she needed to perform. That was Chase Williams' call, however, and she would do whatever he wanted.

However, she resisted sending him her assessment. If Uncle Sun was correct, there might be another way to find out what she needed.

CHAPTER EIGHTEEN

Qincheng Prison, Changping District, Beijing, China
February 18, 12:06 P.M., CST

Wen Dàyóu had spent the morning the same way he had spent most of the previous thirty-two hours since his interrogation. He was lying in his cot, staring at the ceiling, waiting for people he did not want to see or news he did not want to receive. He had not slept well since his interrogation, nor for more than an hour at a time; the echoing clang of a metal door, the cries of someone arriving or departing, or the sounds of banging pipes made it impossible to sleep. He missed the freedom he had taken for granted: to get a snack, to text a friend, to read or study.

There was too much time to think and it plagued him, worrying about his family. Though he often felt like crying he refused to do so. If the guards came for him, he did not want to face the interrogator again with red eyes. He was ashamed of his behavior during their last session. If he did not marshal some steel, at least, they would own him. That was the goal, after all.

Wen was thinking about Kong, hoping that his roommate was all right, when the cell door groaned open. The prisoner sat and swung his feet on the floor as a female guard appeared. Instead of his lunch being brought to him, as Wen expected, she brought an unexpected visitor. The figure was dressed in gray prison garb and, prodded by the billy club, stumbled toward him.

Wen rose, uncertain who it was at first. When the newcomer stopped under the single overhead bulb, the young man saw with horror that it was Jiang Yiwu.

The photographer was a head shorter than Wen but looked smaller still. She was bent slightly to one side and looked as though she might fall over. Wen walked to her side and as Jiang looked over at him she raised a hand to shield her eyes from the light. Her long hair was cut short and she wore a wan, uncomprehending expression.

"Jiang . . ." was all he could say.

The guard shut the door but he did not hear her leave. Wen put his hands on Jiang's upper arms and she winced; he loosened his grip but, still holding her, he eased her toward the bed.

"Sit," he said.

She did not resist. She *could* not resist. When he had lowered her to the thin mattress he went over and filled his dirty glass with water from the dirty sink. She sipped some through dry lips and then Wen sat beside her. His companion was staring at her feet. They were clad in black slippers, the tops of which were stamped with the number 102720. Wen wondered how long it had taken the jailors to reach that number and how many of those prisoners, over one hundred thousand, were innocent of any crime.

"They tied me," Jiang said.

"To what?"

"Heavy rope . . . around . . . under . . ."

Wen did not understand at first but then he realized what she was describing, why she was bent. Their captors had bound her and left her. He lightly drew down a corner of her blouse and saw raw, red marks where a thick rope had passed over her shoulder. He replaced the garment with care.

"*Why* did they do this?"

"I did not . . . answer questions."

"About me?"

"About . . . anyone . . . to start. They wanted names. Counterrevolutionary names." She raised and lowered her shoulders weakly. "I gave them." She began to sob.

"Don't think about that," Wen said. "How is Chao?"

She shook her head. "I have not seen him."

"Jiang, were you working with the authorities?"

That produced a reaction. "No! I believed in what we were doing." She hesitated. "That's not entirely true. I . . . I somewhat believed."

"What do you mean?"

"I . . . was not successful in my career, Wen. No one bought my pictures of workers, of their lives. So . . . I gave the media a reason. I succeeded! Around the world!"

It was not an admirable confession yet Wen could not help but admire the business acumen of it. Still, while her not-entirely-true enthusiasm had uplifted many of the group's members and gave focus to students and aging activists, it would ultimately land many of them here.

"You didn't give them my name," Wen said. "That's not why I'm here. Why did they bring you to me? Why *you*?"

"Because . . . I don't want to spend my life here."

"What do they expect you to do?" Wen asked, even though he knew the answer.

Jiang turned her defeated eyes toward her companion. It was not an act. This woman who had behaved so dynamically, so courageously at protests had been broken. With her confession, Wen was saddened how most of that, maybe all of it, had been an act. Jiang Yiwu was a director shouting instructions, not an organizer encouraging protest. Her husband had probably told *that* to the authorities so they would not arrest her.

"What do they expect?" Jiang said. "They want you to tell them everything . . . about your father."

"I have," Wen answered truthfully.

The woman's lips twisted into something that resembled a grin. "They want you to tell them . . . what they wish to hear."

"Did you tell only the truth about the Counterrevolutionaries, that they were mostly idealists with no focus—until you gave them one?"

Her silence was acknowledgement that Jiang had, in fact, implicated everyone in the group of sedition. Wen had read on the website about what others called "fishnets," hauling in people on inflated charges in the hope that some of them would furnish the names of true anarchists. They were object lessons. Word of these tactics, rippling through friends and relatives, enforced compliant behavior.

"You will have to live with that lie forever," Wen said.

"I will . . . get to live . . . outside of here," she said. She tapped Wen on the back of his wrist. "Let me tell you something. Those slogans we shouted. They were empty. Empty as hope usually is. Our people will see that and go free."

"And if they fight back, the way you did not?"

"Then they will suffer. You will discover, very soon . . . that when you are resting . . . on a dislocated shoulder . . . your mouth has its own urgent agenda."

Wen looked away and rose.

"My father is a patriot and innocent of wrongdoing," he affirmed.

"Perhaps yes. Perhaps no. It is . . . his life for three lives," Jiang went on. "You . . . me . . . Chao. If we give them what they want, we go free.

"Yes, what they tell me could be a lie. But why keep us . . . keep anyone here when the fight . . . has been proven futile? Not just in the streets but here. If you are not broken . . . today, it will happen tomorrow . . . or in a week, a month. A year. Ten years. Those dissidents . . . who have been freed. They will never be free of terror."

Wen turned back to her. "Your husband was working with these people the entire time, did you know that?"

"I did not until they told me."

"What kind of life are you going back to?"

The grin came back. "I do not know. I do not . . . care. As long as it is not this."

Wen had been here just long enough to believe her. His roommate, Kong, had broken with far less pressure. The reality of incarceration without end *was* terrifying. And the pressure would not end with Wen. For all he knew his mother and sister were being subjected to it right now. Would his mother lie about his father to save Wen's sister? Would she confess to sins she herself had never committed?

She might, he told himself. *God in heaven, she might.*

And so might he, to save Ushi. To save himself? Wen did not know—yet. It was a confession that he found dismal and contemptible. There should *be* no question. Yet there it was.

Wen regarded the shattered woman on the cot.

"Jiang, I cannot do what you ask."

Her expression broke. She tried to rise but fell back. "Wen . . . you must! I implore you!"

"When we marched you always used to remind us, 'One step at a time!' You may have been insincere but that did not make you wrong. I will face each of those days, weeks, months, one at a time."

"You will not survive," she announced.

"Others have."

"As what? Shells? You will question . . . *everything* when—*if*—you leave here! Do I really like that food . . . that photograph . . . that person? Are they acceptable? Life will have lost all purpose!"

"Your new motto," Wen said. "Capitulate early."

"No . . . inevitably. They will take you to your mother. You will see her . . . twisted."

There it was again, his family. The most vulnerable point of entry.

"Did they instruct you to say that?" Wen asked.

"They did not have to! I lied when I said I did not see my husband."

"Lied . . . why?"

"Because it would only have encouraged you to foolish, futile action." She swallowed sobs before continuing. "They brought Chao to me as I was brought to you. No . . . ," she said as she saw it again in her dulled memory, "they dragged him in because he could not see. He was beaten, bloodied, his eyes swollen shut . . . to make *me* talk. I didn't, then, so I was bound and left like a sheep, thirsty, hungry, sleepless, and in constant pain. Do not let your family suffer that, or worse."

"You don't know they will do any of this," Wen said, though without much conviction.

"I know this, Wen. In a day or so . . . you will give them what they want." She inhaled, weeping again. "I was bound and in pain and unable to do anything except shout, then scream, while my husband was beaten in the next cell. And he had already given them names, freely. His beating was a warning to me. Maybe yours will be a warning to your father . . . or mother."

The guard came in then and roughly removed the photographer. Jiang was yanked so hard she practically fell against the door. The guard wrapped one strong arm around Jiang, lifted her out, then shut and locked the door.

That last, ugly display was also for Wen.

He stood where he was, numb and searching for some solution that did not cause harm to anyone he loved. Even his suicide, if such were possible, would not do that. His family would mourn and the authorities would turn on a different Dàyóu.

Even in his emotional and aggrieved state, Wen realized that Dr. Yang Dàyóu was the obvious sacrifice. And he had to be the one to make it.

But not yet, he thought.

He would wait until events left him no alternative. Until then he would hold on to what Jiang had said was false.

Hope.

Two hundred and fifty miles to the southwest, Yang Dàyóu had been kept waiting.

General Zhou Chang had waited until Jiang Yiwu had seen Wen Dàyóu before deciding on his own next move. The delay would not only weigh on Yang, but there was always the chance that the boy would capitulate and there would be no need for further maneuvering. If Wen agreed that his father was a traitor, the matter was ended.

That had not proven to be the case, not yet, according to the guard who had listened to the conversation.

Chang did not dislike Dr. Dàyóu. To the contrary, he believed the man to be a patriot. But belief does not matter; what matters is need. The failure of the hypersonic missile had resonated at the highest seat of power and the fallout had to land on someone. That person would not be Zhou Chang. He had spent his adult lifetime in uniform and would not lose everything because a scientist had failed to foresee a problem. Yang was being aggressively stubborn. Had he cooperated without remonstration there would have been a public display of discipline and denunciation but the Dàyóu family would have survived.

Now, what hope is there? Chang thought—with slight sadness but not a trace of personal remonstration.

The phone rang. Chang's adjutant announced on the intercom that it was Dr. Xue Weiping. The general picked up.

"What is it, doctor?"

"General, is Dr. Dàyóu available for consultation?"

"He is not. What is the problem?"

"General, I have looked back at Dr. Dàyóu's original design for the 19. If, as you say, the eleven parts from the 18 were tampered with, can we trust his numbers on the original schematics?"

"You can."

Xue was silent for a moment. "Will you submit a work order to that effect, sir?"

"I am the military commander, Dr. Weiping. You are the project manager. What is your judgment?"

There was another hesitation. "I trust . . . I *trusted* Dr. Dàyóu. To test these designs of his will take—"

"Don't talk to me about time, we have wasted enough of that already! Make your determination and move this along or you will be replaced."

"I understand," the caller said. "Sorry to have bothered you, General."

Chang hung up. He trusted that the scientist *did* understand, the way his predecessor had understood. The *Qi* project was urgent and there was no time for unnecessary caution. Con cerns were not to become delays. They had to be rapidly settled or worked around. The general already missed having Yang Dàyóu on the other end of the telephone. That man had knowledge, he understood the stakes and the challenges, and he had a spine.

It was too bad he had stumbled into the fiery holocaust that had consumed the *Qi*-19.

Chang rose. Distracted and angry, it was time to be rid of the problem of Yang Dàyóu. The general left his office in the military block of the launch center. The bulk of the facility was underground, as much to control security as to protect personnel in the event of an explosion. It was also easier to expand TSLC if the work did not occur on the surface. Already, plans were in the works to expand both the subterranean silos and control centers well beyond the existing perimeter. Workers and materials used to construct the Greenbelt Project were also being used to excavate and pour concrete using underground tunnels.

The general's driver took him to the residential block where Dr. Dàyóu was being held. Chang emerged from the olive-green BJ2022 SUV and went to the room where the engineer was kept. The guard was not at his post. Chang tried the door; it opened and the general stopped in.

The guard was there. He was lying on the wood floor, in his underwear, his gun beside him, still in its holster. He was breathing—unevenly, loudly—but not stirring. There was a large, ugly stain of blood on his left side by his ribs, and a length of lead pipe lying beside him. The lavatory door was open and the chamber was empty; the sink had been partly dismantled. Chang walked over. The meal knife was on the floor, its rounded point rutted, screws beside it. There was a torn, wet pillowcase under the sink. It was grease-blackened and stained with blood. The connecting joints had been turned by Yang's strong, determined engineer's hands, the rent, dampened fabric affording traction and some protection for Yang's flesh.

He improvised with a pipe, Chang thought. Two powerful blows had been struck with one makeshift weapon.

Fire rising in him, Chang turned into the corridor, shouting for the commander of security.

It had been an easy scientific equation.

When Yang Dàyóu was a boy, he had been fascinated by legendary creatures that flew, particularly the dragon and the phoenix. His grandfather, who had marched with Mao Zedong, had been a revered hero of the Long March—a code breaker who translated intercepted communications from the enemies of the nascent Chinese Soviet Republic, the Nationalists under Chiang Kai-shek.

Li Dàyóu told his grandson tales of survival but also fables about China. Spreading his arms and puffing his chest as he sat on his favorite chair, and blowing smoke from his ever-present cigarette, the elder Dàyóu described big billowing leathery wings as he said, *"The dragon is the symbol of water, of rain, and a bringer of good luck."* Then, shrinking into himself, stretching his arms out straight, and turning his narrow face to the sky, he said, *"Fenghuang, the phoenix, the magical rooster, is the union of sky and earth, the product of yang and yin. It stands for honor, great morality—the ultimate physical and spiritual grace."*

Throughout his life, Yang had vacillated between wanting to be one or the other of the legendary creatures. Li Dàyóu died in 1967, when Yang was just eight. Without Li's stories to sustain him, the boy asked his father to tell him about magical things. Gao Dàyóu was not a dreamer. He was a different kind of visionary: he had served in the People's Liberation Army Air Force and become an aeronautical engineer, designing new aircraft based on Soviet designs. He talked to his son about the "real" dragons and phoenixes, the rockets designed to lift satellites and humans into space.

That was it for the boy. He wanted to build things that flew like the dragon and the phoenix. Not just flew but ruled over all birds, like his beloved creatures of mythology.

Yang had worked hard, as his father and grandfather had worked hard, and he had carried their ideas, their inspiration to the skies, merged with his own passion for Chinese flight. The idea that he would betray that for any reason was not just repugnant but impossible. Even for the safety of his son, who had drawn on his own interests, made his own way.

General Chang's proposals were impossible, if for no other reason than that Yang was not a nightingale, a real and submissive bird whose nature was just to sing, to maintain the harmony of the day for its owner. Neither the dragon nor the phoenix would accept incarceration. Like the latter, Yang intended to soar from the ashes—with one key distinction.

He did not intend to die first.

If the engineer had remained in the room he would have been taken to Taiyuan No. 3 prison in Shanxi. He would have remained there incommunicado until the political works commander had rendered a foregone verdict on one of two charges. Had Yang confessed to the false charge of criminal negligence, he would have been sentenced to life in prison. Had Yang confessed to nothing he would have been charged with treason and executed within the month.

Two impossible fates had brought him to remove the pipe, stain his hands with his own blood and the blood of the guard, and leave wearing the man's uniform. Yang's immediate goal had been to get out. He had achieved that, and was crouching in an elevator shaft. The massive carriage was used to transport only large missile parts and none of those were scheduled to be completed, let alone moved, for weeks. He had his ear to the cold iron wall, listening for muffled voices and the drumbeat of running feet. The general would call out every available man to search for him, and that search would expand, like ripples on a pond, from this building to the outer perimeter.

He would wait until there were fewer sounds here before making his next move. Indeed, he had not yet considered what that would be though he knew two things: he would have to get through layers of fence and do so quickly and quietly. He was not a large or powerful man; something else would have to do the work for him and he believed he knew what that was.

Once out, his equally unformed plan was to get to someone who would hear him, someone in a position higher than that of Zhou Chang. If Yang managed to remain hidden for two or three days, Beijing was sure to send a senior general to investigate what had happened here. The engineer could approach such a man. The very fact of Yang's willing surrender would put a torch to the lies of General Chang. Or perhaps Yang could reach the private residence of a cabinet minister, someone who had sworn an oath on the Constitution and might hear the voice of a proven patriot. He knew that Wang Lifeng, Minister of Science and Technology, had an office and apartment in Shanxi.

There were possibilities, options.

But first, you have to get out of here, Yang reminded himself. And even before that, there was something he had to do: rest. He had not slept very much since this madness had begun and, with reluctance, curled on his side on the top of the elevator and shut his eyes. It was quite chilly there and he chuckled. *You, the brilliant engineer—why did you not think to bring a blanket?*

He forgot, for the moment, his own danger and challenges and thought about his family. He did not think that Chang would move against them. Not knowing where Yang was, there was no way to threaten him with prize hostages. And there were high-ranking women in both Military Intelligence and Space Warfare Development. They might object to the debatable sins of a father and son being visited upon a mother and daughter.

Nonetheless, as rest overtook him, Yang found himself thinking not of his family or himself but of his grandfather telling tales of the Chinese dragon and the luck it brought to the true believer. . . .

CHAPTER NINETEEN

The Defense Logistics Agency, Fort Belvoir, Virginia
February 17, 6:31 P.M.

Chase Williams had decided that there is no rush to call January Dow.

For the first time since he had taken over the directorship of Op-Center, Williams felt something calming. He was not sure that was exactly the word; what he felt was the opposite of urgency. It was not patience or caution, more like a tactical stall. That was nothing he had ever encountered in the military, now that he thought of it.

At first, he had waited until the Mongolian cargo plane was out of the reach of an immediate turnaround. As commander-in-chief, Wright could have ordered that, though it would have provided a diplomatic problem for the new president.

Then he waited until the aircraft had landed at England's Gatwick Airport for refueling and was in the air again, watching on NORAD's tracking site until the aircraft had passed over Eastern Europe.

During that time, the admiral had sat in his office reviewing files on Taiyuan and Mongolia, isolating documents, maps, and images that he thought would help both teams. This was not Yemen or South Africa they were tweaking. It was the People's Republic of China. The key was to keep from making a big noise. If Grace adhered to what he told her at the briefing and followed the assignment, that was a manageable ambition. If the lieutenant made it back to the embassy without difficulty, then the rest of Black Wasp would not be required to make any noise.

He did not conduct a mental review of what he intended to tell the assistant to the president for national security affairs. It was just a line or two, after which he would let her indignation and outrage direct the talk. Williams scheduled the videoconference for the end of the day. Logged topic: *Mission Status Briefing*.

Williams signed in just after six. January did not show up until six twenty.

She was still talking to someone off camera as she logged on. When that was done, she studied her phone for a few moments before finally looking up at the screen. Williams watched her as she watched him; small eye movements showed that she was quickly scrutinizing his surroundings.

"Rather spartan, Admiral," she said. "No natural light?"

"I find it warm and familiar. It's a little like being in a submarine," he added with a chuckle.

She smiled quickly, politely, then it was down to business. "How is everything in your AOR?"

"Everything in my Area of Responsibility is OTT," he

replied. He waited as she tried to puzzle that one out, then added, "On time and on target. Lieutenant Lee is on the ground in Shanxi near Taiyuan, at her uncle's home. She should have gone to surveil the launch center by now. She will text her observations when she's done."

"Very good."

"I did make one adjustment, however."

January looked down at her phone again. "What's that?"

"I sent the rest of Black Wasp over as backup."

The woman's eyes jumped from the phone to the screen. She took a moment to try to ascertain whether Williams was serious.

"If this is a joke on the West Wing frosh, it's *not* funny."

"It's no joke, January. Major Breen and Lance Corporal Rivette are en route to their staging area."

"I want details and I want your resignation," she snapped. "In that order, at once."

"You don't have the authority to demand either, January."

"I'm going to get it at once, Admiral Williams. You are through!"

January was looking at her phone again, this time texting.

"Before you do anything, take a moment to consider—"

"I'll consider *nothing*! You wanted that woman from Naval Support Activity Philadelphia? I'll have her there in the morning!"

"To do what? Recall Black Wasp? Learn this about the military, January. Those men—no soldier—will leave their comrade in enemy territory without support. Whether Captain Mann or someone else comes in, Major Breen and Lance Corporal Rivette will not return without completing their mission."

"The president made that determination and it was not, *is* not up to you to second-guess him!"

"The president ordered Lieutenant Lee to China, and she is there. He placed no restrictions on the disposition of her teammates. By my authority as the director of Op-Center, under the JSOC Provision in the charter, I have the power to field support personnel in, I quote, 'a situation where the lives of soldiers are facing clear and present danger.' I also have the right to send JSOC members on tactical training missions, so you can call this that, if you like."

"I do *not* like! Do you have the permission of the host nation for this rogue operation?"

"Sorry, that information is for the president's ears only, January. I suggest you ask the president to request them and, at the same time, ask him to remove and replace me. Until then, this mission proceeds as I've outlined it to Black Wasp. And before you attempt to undo that, January, recognize that reversing an operation in motion is hellishly more difficult than launching it."

She glared at him. "You are finished, Chase. Done."

The call ended and the West Wing videoconference screen returned. The discussion had achieved what Williams had intended. Either he fought for Op-Center or he waited for the administration to attenuate and eventually kill it. Better to have that out now before putting Black Wasp in situations that were less localized and specific than this one.

It had been a long day and Williams felt he could use both

fresh air and dinner. He would need both before seeing the political angle, at least, to an end.

The Ilyushin Il-76 did not so much land as stop flying.

The cargo jet touched down at seven twenty-two ULAT—Ulaanbaatar Time. Rivette felt the jarring, thudding impact of the wheels on the tarmac go up his spine to the base of his skull as it thrust him against his shoulder harness.

The lance corporal thought he had been cold 37,000 feet up. He was wrong. When the side cargo bay door was opened, Rivette hung back a few paces. He remembered this much from science class: heat rose. And it rose from here, leaving nothing but the bitterest iced air he had ever experienced. He rolled his shoulders forward in a futile effort to hug some heat to himself.

"We got a return ticket, Major?" Rivette asked.

"You knew it would be really cold."

"Major, 'really cold' is when I wore a sweatshirt to Cabrillo Beach back home. Being here is what my grandma would call 'unintelligent.'"

The men remained in the open hatch as the crew came back and a ramp was unfolded.

Breen looked out. Buyant-Ukhaa International Airport—formerly Chinggis Khaan International Airport—was clean and modern, a long, low, rectangular structure that rested entirely on slender, white columns. There was a flat white roof atop walls of green glass opening onto an endless concrete field. The rising sun revealed a modern urban landscape of six-to-ten-story-tall offices, hotels, and apartments.

"We're not going inside, right?" Rivette asked.

"We don't have papers."

"That's what I thought," Rivette said.

Breen looked around. He was seeking any sign of the for-hire men Williams said would be there. He saw a clutch of workers coming from the hangar with dollies and handcarts. They were dressed in an array of clothes, from shearling flight jackets to heavy coats made of fur—yak and rabbit, it looked like. Several wore wool-lined Sherpa-style hats with long, narrow ear flaps. They did look like nomads, many of them; they did not look like the kind of men who could transport them quickly to the Gobi Desert.

Breen found himself growing tense, annoyed. The major was becoming resigned to the fact that nothing ever went the way Black Wasp drilled it or he laid it out at Fort Belvoir. As Rivette had put it, "Quick and dirty is our brand." But it was always Williams who took the lead on these makeshift missions. This was the first time the major had to wing it, and he was not happy.

Pel Dogsom went down first; the two Americans deplaned before the crates of stove parts were unloaded. Breen approached the captain, who lit a cigar; it, and the silent engine behind them, were throwing out the only heat on the tarmac.

"*Bayarlalaa*," the major said, adding, "Thank you."

Dogsom nodded and Breen took out a map with three hundred thousand tögrög paper-clipped to it. The major pointed to Tavan Tolgoi Airport.

"Tsogttsetsii?" Dogsom asked.

"Yes, Tsogttsetsii in Ömnögovi Province."

"Dalanzadgad," Dogsom said. "That is for Tavan Tolgoi Airport."

Breen recalled that from the map. "All right—Dalanzadgad," he said. They would have to make their way south from there.

Dogsom took the money then gripped Breen by the elbow and led him around the hangar to a row of airplanes. They sat in the growing shadow of the hangar, suggesting most would be engaging in unsanctioned shipments before long.

"They look like rats in a cellar," Rivette observed.

"They go," Dogsom said.

"They'll take us now?" Breen clarified.

"*Tiym,*" the man said, nodding. "Yass."

Breen's uneasiness was dispelled—a little. They were still about to leave a mostly legal operation for an illegal one.

"*Bayarlalaa,*" he said, again, smiling. "*Bayartai.*"

"*Sain suuj baigaarai!*" Dogsom replied.

Rivette just smiled back and bowed his head as the men walked off.

"What did you guys say?" he asked.

"Pretty sure I said 'thank you and good luck,' but I'm not sure what he said."

"Probably, 'You better keep some of that luck, men. You're gonna need it.'"

Breen did not dispute that.

As they neared, the major saw that five of the eleven planes had pilots in the cockpits.

"They won't come up," Rivette suggested.

"Why do you say that?"

"Like drug deals in a car. You sell, it's 'x' number of years. You solicit and sell, it's 'x-plus-your-ass-will-be-dragging' before you get out of jail. You gotta knock on the window."

"Or they could just be staying warm."

Rivette jerked a gloved thumb toward the hangar. "Guys in the dirty window there, see 'em? They're just staying warm. Guessing they're waiting for legal cargo."

Rivette made sense. Breen had spent too long in white-glove courtrooms. Yet aspects of those years came back to him as they crossed the tarmac. In particular, the number of undercover and secret internal investigations he had arranged through the Office of the Special Assistant for Strategic Planning. Stings were frowned upon though not illegal. Here, where there were no rules, he asked himself whether one of these pilots would just as likely kidnap and ransom a pair of Americans as do an illegitimate deal with them.

"Major, looks like one of them is a woman," Rivette said.

"Yeah, I saw."

The woman was at the far end of the row—a rear position that was no doubt a holdover from centuries-old male domination. She was the only one who opened the door and stepped out. She was a big, broad-shouldered woman who looked about forty. She had on a Cossack hat and a fleece-lined long coat made of what appeared to be reindeer. The woman stood boldly, almost impertinently beside the open door of the cockpit. She was frowning, though Breen suspected that was her natural expression and not a show of disapproval. None of the men moved.

"Lady is inviting business," Rivette said.

Breen looked back at the hangar. "And we have a new addition."

"Huh?"

Rivette followed Breen's gaze. A man in a uniform had joined the others.

"What do you think?" the major asked. "Is he there to intimidate us or the pilots?"

"Can't make out his expression, but my guess? He's there to see who to touch for his cut."

Once again, Breen decided to rely on the lance corporal's instincts. They had to get south in a hurry and this was the only means they had.

The men made for the single-prop Cessna 172 Skyhawk, a four-seater with a beat-up paint job. Breen thought he saw a trio of bullet holes, crudely patched, in the tail section. Unlike the other aircraft hidden in the semi-darkness, the cockpit did not have a faint, green glow from panel lights. That suggested old-school dials and gauges instead of digital avionics.

"Hello," Breen said when they were just a few yards away.

The woman nodded though the scowl remained.

"English?" he asked.

The woman nodded again. "Also Chinese and Russian. You're American?" she asked.

Breen nodded and stopped at the nose of the aircraft.

"At this rate, we'll be here all day," Rivette said.

"Where do you want to be instead?" the woman asked.

At least she has some kind of sense of humor, Breen thought.

"Dalanzadgad," the major answered. "Tavan Tolgoi Airport."

"Three hundred miles," she said. "Two hours. Coming back?"

Breen took a chance and replied, "Hopefully. But I won't need you to wait."

The woman nodded. "Let's go."

CHAPTER TWENTY

Jinzhou, Shanxi Province, China
February 18, 6:02 P.M., CST

It had been a disappointing afternoon for Grace Lee, and it had threatened to get much worse.

She had pedaled back to Ho's Market, discouraged by the apparent impenetrability of the Taiyuan Satellite Launch Center and the lack of any other obvious opportunities for intelligence gathering.

That's not it, she told herself as she rode back along the Greenbelt. What gnawed at her was the lack of immediate satisfaction. She had never had to wait, really. Training, schooling, exercising—the results were immediate. Kung fu taught that "nature does not struggle." Wind blows, water flows, and humans must do the same. *You don't stop to fight, you go around a conflict . . . or through it.*

Here she was, heading toward Ho's Market to pick up dinner and hopefully find a few men from the launch compound to talk to. She wanted to be there, doing it.

The ride back took over two hours. Once Grace was off

the flat, newly paved Greenbelt, the main road offered winter-bare trees, the distinctive and immediately familiar shacks and homes, all of it dusted in the deepening orange of the sinking sun.

Ho's Market was busy with people doing what she was doing, picking up dinner. Grace parked her bike where motorcycles, a few cars, and one Jeep parked behind the shed. The fire pits were ablaze and many young men and women sat outside—some of them in uniform. Many of them were still drinking or eating. There was time to go inside and pick up her package without seeming overanxious to talk.

Chu Hua was still at her post beneath the *Lycoptera muroii* and retrieved both Grace's package and a complimentary cup of tea.

"Tell your bachelor uncle his beloved *hétún* sends her love." The older woman winked.

"Oh?" Grace said, feigning shock. She had never heard "blowfish" as an endearment, but was grateful for the connection—and the tea. It was reason to sit and she was annoyed she had not thought of it.

Because you're overeager to get something, she told herself.

Grace went back outside and chose a small, empty table. The spot shared a fire pit with two young military men. One of the men, a lanky NCO corporal first class, made it easy by pulling out a stool for the new arrival. American gender independence had not penetrated to Shanxi, apparently.

"Thank you," she said, sitting.

He helped her steady her lopsided plastic dinner bag on the

table. Now that she had stopped moving a chill had settled upon her. The fire felt good.

"I am Shen and this fellow, whom you need not know, is Yat-sen."

"As in Sun Yat-sen?" Grace asked as she sat.

The other man, a private first class, shrugged. "My parents chose the name of a controversial man so I would learn to fight."

"And they obviously succeeded," Grace said cheerfully.

"I have not seen you before," Shen said, easing his own stool over a little.

"He would have remembered," Yat-sen said. "He is locally infamous as a ladies' man."

"I am friendly," Shen corrected.

Grace sipped tea as she explained that she was visiting a relative—though she did not say who. It occurred to her now that it was bad enough Chu Hua knew; she did not need to include the military.

"You are stationed nearby?" she asked.

"At the launch center, north of here," Shen said.

"Is that what I saw?" Grace said. "I just rode the Greenbelt to the end."

"That was it," Shen said, boasting.

"It's very secret or I am sure my friend would offer a tour," Yat-sen added.

"That would have been fun. It must be an exciting place—a 'launch center.'"

"Always," Shen said, but he did not elaborate.

The NCO was loose with charm, tight with information.

Grace fought the discouragement that threatened to settle in. She did not ask *what* was launched, deciding it was too much, too pushy.

"Do you live on the base or are you headed home somewhere?"

"Here is some information for you," Yat-sen said. "A base is a place occupied by troops and fortified with arms and barricades. This is a research and development range and we are a *detachment*."

"But it was an adorable error," Shen said, winking.

Grace played the part of wide-eyed naïf though what she really wanted to do was put a leopard paw into the winked eye. She was considering how to follow up the last statement when there were dual beeps from the shirt pocket of each soldier. Their demeanor changed from flirtatious to professional in an instant.

Both men read the text message in silence before Shen turned to Grace. "We are recalled," he informed her.

"Is everything all right? It sounds—sudden. A fire or something?"

"No, someone—" Shen began, then stopped himself. "It will be fine. I hope I may see you again?"

"Of course, I would like that." She added, "Tomorrow morning?"

Shen wagged his phone before he put it away and rose. "That depends. Hopefully, our work will be done by then."

"Be safe," she added.

"We will be." Shen turned back and smiled at her as they hurried to their motorcycles.

Grace watched as the two men roared off. They took up positions on opposite sides of the road, both of them constantly turning their heads to the side as they sped into the distance.

They are looking for something, she thought. *It could be that "someone" escaped.*

Grace grabbed her satchel and walked to her bike. She paused behind the shed to text Chase Williams.

> Soldiers looking for someone possibly escaped
> Taiyuan. Must know if it's our man. Please find him
> for me.

Washington was twelve hours behind but Williams responded at once.

> Will do.

CHAPTER TWENTY-ONE

The Watergate Apartments, Washington, D.C.
February 18, 6:40 A.M.

The night had passed with cemetery silence.

Williams rose with the sun, dressed in sweats, and ate breakfast in his small eastward-facing condo. There was no reason to go to his basement office. Not when he was likely to be called to the White House at any moment for an upbraiding and dismissal. He sat at the small butcher-block table, facing the window, waiting to hear from either Grace or Angie Brunner.

The room seemed uncommonly empty as he faced his own future.

You need a woman in your life who is not connected to work, he told himself as he sat with his second cup of coffee and checked several news sites. He had seen too many single military men take their pensions and travel for a while, fish or hunt or boat for a while, write and never finish their memoirs, then seek out a position somewhere, anywhere, that drew on a lifetime of skills. Too often that search failed, leaving an embittered figure in its wake.

He reminded himself, too, that he was anticipating a termination that was still poorly defined; defined, in fact, only by supposition. Events had a way of overtaking anticipation, the paranoia that made any career federal employee intuit that forces were moving behind their backs—never for them, always to bring them down.

What Williams knew was that after the videoconference with January Dow, she would have gone directly to Angie Brunner. Through their own sources, they would try to find out where the rest of Black Wasp was headed, probably by leaning on Matt Berry; failing that, they would have looked into it through staff at Fort Belvoir—tricky, since they did not know anything about Williams' activities there—as well as highway surveillance footage and emails.

They would find nothing.

Perhaps Dow had made good her threat and Captain Mann was in the process of being brought up from Philadelphia. If so, and even if Mann had been told not to contact Williams, she would have let him know. Regardless, that was fine with Williams. Op-Center would be in good hands.

Or it could be that Op-Center was being shut down altogether. In that case, Ambassador Simon would be told to turn Lieutenant Lee around—though she would have to confess that she had no idea where Grace had gone.

As for the rest of Black Wasp, once found, those experienced assets might be passed to another organization—one of the military intelligence arms, Williams suspected, given the battle-seasoned personnel of Black Wasp. If the three-member team were passed off intact then their hard work and his legacy at least would live on—

The pinging text notification startled Williams. He slid the phone in front of him, saw there was a message from Grace Lee, and read it. In that moment, whatever Angie and the president had been planning or thinking became moot. Williams did a quick check of the Pentagon's recently launched Space Development Agency which tracked and coordinated intelligence from thousands of spy, climate, and communications satellites and Department of Defense robotic space planes. He highlighted data and, without hesitation, called Angie. Whether or not she took the call would depend on how much her sense of Hollywood entitlement remained. Not answering would put Williams in his place; it could also endanger national security.

She answered.

"Are you calling to tell me you have re—"

"Forgive the interruption but we have a situation in China."

Williams could almost feel the woman's disposition changing before she spoke.

"Go on," she said, thick concern replacing scorn.

"Lieutenant Lee believes that someone has just escaped from the Taiyuan facility. It appears that a massive manhunt is just now being organized. SPAFCOMM has the Project Blackjack satellite Asia-3 and the Pit Boss satellite Flyover-11 over Taiyuan. The F-11 can take thermal scans. Turn it loose on the perimeter around the satellite launch center."

Project Blackjack was the MSA—Miniature Satellite Array—managed by Space Force Command. It was designed to create a visual and data-impulse spy web across the entire planet. The original system, completed in 2021, worked only in daytime environments. The most recent upgrade—completed during the final weeks of the Midkiff administration—was a TARS, a Thermal Asset Reading System, which made it possible for satellites to search moving images in nighttime environments. Orbiting at a low altitude of 175 miles and employing a 100-megapixel sensor, each mini-satellite covered five yards with resolution of four inches per pixel. To see more of the surface with a limited number of cameras, you need to fly higher.

An added drawback of low orbits is that they are fast: the speed of the ground track is approximately 6 to 7 Km/s (an area of 100m is crossed in 14 milliseconds).

The Pit Boss program was a complementary system that connected every soldier to Project Blackjack and made it possible to receive real-time data on the movement of enemy troops and vehicles, as well as to follow any electronic signals that passed between them. It was virtually impossible for an enemy to organize an ambush on-the-go since the location of opposition players was instantly known.

The beauty—and controversy—of both systems is that while the programming concentrated on enemy installations and conveyances, the effective perimeter went from one to five miles beyond. While the Department of Defense could watch supply lines and other logistics, they could also spy on any civilian who happened to be within the radius.

"If Lieutenant Lee is correct and there are troops already

fielded," Angie said, "how will we know who might or might not be—"

"Troops will be in pairs at a minimum," Williams interrupted her again. "We will look for someone who's traveling alone and likely at an inconstant speed, either racing or hunkering down."

Angie was silent.

"This is not about politics and job security," Williams said impatiently. "You will have my resignation when this is done. At this moment we have a potential prime target in play and a lone asset—emphasis on 'lone'—who is willing to put herself at grave risk to intercept. You're new at this, Angie, and I urge you to decide now what is more important: January Dow's hurt feelings or the security of the nation?"

"This is all based on 'ifs,' Admiral. The lieutenant 'believes,' 'it appears.'"

"If you're going to suggest that we wait for firmer intel, that is not how this works. Op-Center does not have drones for quick confirmation flights. The Chinese would shoot them down anyway. And if we do not act, they may soon have a drone that is far worse. Please. Get me the imaging."

"What will Lieutenant Lee be doing?"

"I believe she is still on a bicycle," Williams said. "I am going to suggest that she find herself a vehicle and get in position for a rescue mission."

"What if it's not Dr. Dàyóu, or he won't come?"

"It's still intelligence gathering. Angie—we can discuss that later."

Williams' firm insistence shut down further debate.

"All right. I'll tell the pres—"

"I don't want to explain this again," he said, adamant. "Get it done."

"Don't push," Angie warned and hung up.

Williams tapped the messaging icon. Angie had some brass, he had always known that, but it flowed downhill. Would it also flow up?

That will reveal itself, he thought. Right now, he had to reply to Grace. He typed:

Satellite surveillance demanded. Can you secure
vehicle?

Grace wrote back immediately:

Have several-hours bike trip to go in dark. Will
take Sun pickup. Can be on-site by ten pm CST.

Williams responded:

Affirmative. Stay safe.

Before doing anything else, Grace would erase that data; the phone itself would take care of expunging any trace of the communication.

The lieutenant had guts. Williams felt guilty for being safe at home while she was in what the navy euphemistically called Jeopardy Status in the field; but he could not be prouder of her.

His last communication from the rest of Black Wasp had been late the night before when they were en route to Tsogtt-setsii. Williams had said he would not contact Breen but would wait to hear that they were in position.

He would wait until then to inform him of the latest developments since there was nothing he could do en route. But Williams had a sense that was even stronger than his Washington intuition. That was his military instinct, something he first acquired during his years at the Naval Academy in Annapolis. Strong now, it told him that his message to Breen would be simple:

Hit the ground running.

Angie Brunner sat in her office in the West Wing.

The chief of staff did not miss Hollywood. Virtually everything she had learned and experienced there could be found in Washington, D.C. It was an industry town with vast egos and untrustworthy players. Angie herself was not immune. When she was successful, others wanted to see her fail. They did not say it but she knew it. If others were successful she quietly celebrated when their latest film or series belly flopped—the bigger the chaotic splash, the better.

The one big difference between Hollywood and the nation's capital was that only careers and marriages were destroyed. Sudden death, when it came, was either an accident or a suicide driven by failure, depression, or addiction. Angie had never directly experienced something like that. To her knowledge, she had never been responsible for an actor or director making such a choice.

Regardless of her feelings about Chase Williams—and right now they were hostile and vindictive—he was not wrong about a young officer having put her life in jeopardy for something the president needed. Yes, that was the lieutenant's job. Yes, Grace Lee was trained. What Angie had to do was ignore her dislike of Chase Williams and the reckless thing he had done and get him what he asked.

The president was having a working breakfast with the Joint Chiefs of Staff. If she interrupted with this, he would tell her it would have to wait. She did not expect Williams to be running Op-Center for very much longer; any request he made would come under scrutiny. Since there was no time to lose, placing this Top Priority Surveillance Order—in the president's name—meant putting her job and her reputation on the line.

To: Intelligence Commander, SPAFCOMM
From: POTUS
Authorization: P-191

Angie's eyes were on the notes she had taken in longhand when she spoke with Williams—a page that could be shredded when she was done. Even as she began to type the instructions, it felt as if they were someone else's fingers moving across the keyboard.

When she was finished, Angie brought up the checklist for

sending military orders. This was the fourth one she had written but the first she had composed. Everything seemed right.

Angie hesitated. Then she reminded herself that this was not for Chase Williams but for Grace Lee and, without further delay, pressed SEND.

CHAPTER TWENTY-TWO

Dalanzadgad, Mongolia
February 18, 8:33 A.M., CST

Neither Hamilton Breen nor Jaz Rivette had trained for this kind of trip.

The pilot's name, Breen had learned, was Odval Bayar. He found this out not because she had introduced herself when they paid her eight hundred thousand tögrög up front, but because she had called the tower before takeoff. The first thing the air traffic controller had said was:

"*Öglöönii mend, Odval Bayar.*"

Breen knew that *öglöönii mend* meant "good morning."

The woman taxied at once, even as the men were still stowing their bedrolls and backpacks and buckling themselves tight into the two thinly cushioned back seats. The leather was worn through and the seats no longer reclined. Once they were airborne, the bucket contour and the high back of the seats communicated every bump, burst of acceleration, and drop caused by the turbulent air. The wing flaps squeaked loudly and the low voltage warning light was perpetually lit. As they climbed to ten thousand feet, the temperature fell and the loud rush of the air rose. The marginal warmth from the heater did not reach the rear seat air vents as anything but cold air, and both men shivered while they braced their feet and lower back against the seat to minimize the jolts.

Breen kept himself busy—or at least distracted—by reviewing maps on his tablet and finding out where they could hire a Hanma—a Chinese Humvee knockoff—at Tavan Tolgoi Airport. If Grace had held to the schedule Williams had laid out, they still had a day or so to get where they were going. She would spend a day settling in and getting the lay of the land before making any kind of move toward Taiyuan.

Rivette sat with his backpack on his lap feeling the weight and contour of the guns on his knees. It afforded solace, even though there was no one and nothing to shoot up here. Now and then Breen would watch the pilot. Odval was impressive, outwardly unperturbed even as they passed over low mountains and she had to muscle the controls to keep the airplane steady in the updrafts. Breen was glad that the taller mountains of the Khentii and Khangai Ranges were to the north. The Cessna could not have crossed them and Rivette might have gotten his wish to scale a high peak.

After nearly two hours in the air, the Cessna neared Tavan Tolgoi Airport. The field was some fifty miles northeast of Dalanzadgad and they flew over the town to make their approach. The capital of the Ömnögovi Province reminded him of remote towns he had seen in Alaska. It was about one-third the size of Manhattan and consisted of red-roofed, one- and two-story structures.

There were rows of Chinese coal trucks parked in open lots, announcing both the leading industry and its largest consumer.

The trucks were a warning sign to Breen. So were the Chinese planes they saw as they landed. It was a reminder that being in southern Mongolia was not significantly less risky than being in China. Odval taxied toward a spot on the edge of the field where small planes were parked, as in Ulaanbaatar.

Looking around, Rivette said, "We are way out in nowhere."

"This is civilization compared to where we're headed," Breen replied.

"How are you getting where you are headed?" Odval asked.

"We planned on renting a Hanma to drive toward the Gobi," Breen said—as his phone beeped. The message was from Williams. Breen opened the text, expecting a routine report. As he read the message his expression darkened.

"What is it?" Rivette asked. "We've been recalled? We're going home?"

The major shook his head. He felt a sudden and familiar urgency, as on previous missions. "Someone exceeded expectations and may need imminent support. We have to leave here asap."

"For Gobi?" Odval asked as she pivoted, braked, and shut the engine.

"Yes," Breen said.

"Where?"

There was no point being secretive; not now. "As close to the border as possible."

Odval nodded. "You don't want Hanma."

"Why?" the major asked.

"Chinese built, sand clogs intake, sticks to cheap aluminum. Won't get you back. You need motorcycles."

Rivette looked at Breen. "You're on, Major."

Rivette was not wrong. Breen had moved to Fort Belvoir from the University of Virginia where, as part of his duties for the Judge Advocate General's Corps, he taught military law. Since making the move, Breen had missed regular visits with his lady Inez Levey . . . and time to ride his big, transcontinental Yamaha Star Eluder.

"You ever ride?" the major asked. He was running the map in his memory, starting to tick off the impediments they might face on two wheels.

"A couple times, and on the beach. So I'm set."

"We'd need extra gas," he said to Odval after calculating distances.

"Easy."

"All right," Breen said. "Where can we get them?"

The pilot popped the cabin door and cocked her head. "Come with me."

Odval walked the men to the small parking lot just a hundred yards away. "My cousins Ganzorig run tours. Not so busy in the winter. You can buy from him."

Ganzorigs senior and junior did not speak English, and Odval negotiated a deal for a pair of compact, powerful four-stroke KTM 450 EXCs. Breen bought a basket to carry extra gasoline and bottled water, which the Ganzorigs furnished.

The men helped him fix it to the upswept rear fender, making sure the bottom of the basket did not scrape the top of the wheel. They threw in two pair of goggles, a wrench, and a high-pressure mini-pump. Those went in a smaller basket they put on Rivette's handlebars.

"They're like helpful elves," the lance corporal said.

"They like you," Odval told Rivette.

As they were strapping their gear to the bikes, Rivette asked the major, "What do we do with passengers, if any?"

"The assets leave, we stay."

"I can carry more," Odval said.

"How?"

"My other cousin, Bat Erdene, has six-seat Piper."

"I'm loving this," Rivette said. "She's like the leader of the Santa Cruzer Gang back home, Rodrigo Cruz. They were all brothers and half brothers."

Breen asked Odval for her cell number in case they needed her.

"You think we can trust them?" Rivette asked.

"I do. Like you said about Genghis Khan Jones, they have a reputation to uphold."

"Go home and tell your friends about us," Rivette said.

Breen finished and checked the compass on his phone. They were now headed for the border, or as close as they could get to it, with as direct a line to Tiyuan as they could manage. The spot he chose was two hundred and twenty-two miles to the south. It had no name on the map; nothing had a name below where they were right now. The major was glad for that; lawlessness worked for them.

Walking over to Odval, Breen thanked her and gave her twice what he had paid her for ferrying them down.

"That's about all I have," he said. "You'll wait?"

"I'll wait." She smiled for the first time. "I like your—" She sought a word, failed to find it, beat her chest twice.

"Thanks. Coming from the woman who wrestled a Cessna, that means a lot." Breen threw a soft salute at the cousins. "Tell them we appreciate their help. When we get back, they can have the bikes—no refund necessary."

"They will be very pleased."

The cousins watched and Odval returned to her plane while Breen took a moment to make sure he—then Rivette— understood the controls. The EXC was a European model with a small headlight and taillight, which was good for surreptitious night travel, though the older PDS rear suspension would be unkind on rugged terrain.

"If we need to pad the seat, we'll cut up the bedrolls," Breen said.

With a final wave, the men were off, following the road in front of the airport to a field that led south.

And ran into a convoy of ten trucks belonging to the general purpose Ground Forces of Mongolia.

"Ease to a stop!" Breen shouted over the roar of the bike.

Rivette nodded and did as he was instructed. "Cut the engines?"

"No. Be ready to turn back!"

Rivette watched as the convoy crossed some three hundred yards ahead. "What do you think they're doing here?"

"Border patrols, I suspect, to keep Chinese profiteers from raiding the coal and copper mining regions."

"Which we are in, of course," Rivette said. "Tourists would wave, probably take pictures."

"Not the time or place for selfies, Lance Corporal."

"I am suddenly not so cold," Rivette said, bending by the front wheel as Breen watched the convoy. It was a combination of canvas-backed trucks and Russian-made BTR-60 personnel carriers. They were headed north, away from the border; they had probably been on training exercises. Though the troops were descended from centuries of proud fighting men, their forces were mostly peacekeepers now, participating in missions that ranged from Afghanistan to the Congo.

"I didn't see any military aircraft on the field," Breen said. "They are probably just passing through."

The rear vehicle stopped and the others went on. It turned toward the airport.

"They looking for us or making a coffee run?" Rivette asked. "Or maybe they want to steal our bikes."

"Get back in the seat," the major said. "Throttle up and be prepared to make a run to the west—left," he added.

Rivette looked out at the hulking eight-wheeler. There was a turreted machine gun on top, angled up but facing in their direction.

"That's a 14.5 mm KPVT heavy machine gun, five hundred

rounds," the lance corporal said. "Won't do them much good at this range but they're sure to have guns in there."

"More than we do. Keep the backpack on. Let's do what you said, wave, then head off. They may not be interested in us—"

Just then, the men heard a hum above and behind them. They turned to see the Cessna approaching—low and then lower. The aircraft passed over them, surrounding them in swirling dead grasses and dust, sweeping the cloud south. It grew and engulfed the BTR-60.

"God bless you Odval," Rivette said as he spit dirt. "I think I may marry that lady."

"You'll have to wait in line," Breen said. "Let's go around it, straight ahead."

Rivette nodded and the two roared ahead, following the small plane as if they were being towed. As they crossed the field and left the armored vehicle behind, Breen updated Williams via text and grinned. He had settled at least one curiosity:

Those were definitely bullet holes in Odval's tail section.

The freight area of the building was heavy with silence.

Yang Dàyóu woke suddenly and, for a moment, he did not realize where he was. The airlessness of the space and its oily smell hit him at the same time, and then he remembered. He was on top of the large service elevator.

Despite the fact that he had been curled up on an iron panel, he had slept well and was alert. Shouts from outside had startled him awake three or four times but they were short-lived and he was able to resume his rest. The airmen were searching

for him. He knew many of them by name and did not wish them
ill. He wished them only a lack of success.

Shielding his phone, Yang checked the time. It was
nearly 3:00 P.M. Less than two hours of good light remained;
he had to use them to make his way from the elevator shaft to
somewhere—anywhere—outside the building. Somewhere he
could wait for dark in order to leave the launch center. From his
current position the "scrap pile" would be his best bet for access
and concealment. That was where the remnants of the *Qi*-19
mobile launcher, exploded tires, and other non-missile components would have been taken, piled upon the detritus of other
failed tests.

Some of that was the natural attrition of testing new technology. Some of it, he thought bitterly, was the haste of those in
command.

Rest had given Yang the energy to be anxious. Breathing
through his teeth to keep from hyperventilating, Yang raised the
access panel in the top of the elevator. He had used a stepladder
to get up and then pulled it in after him; he would not need it to
get down. He listened then eased through the square hatch and
dropped to the carriage floor. Again, he listened; again it was
silent. He pressed the button to open the door and eased into the
dark, industrial-sized corridor.

The hall was deserted; nothing was being assembled or
transported. Until the "cause" of the explosion was determined
absolutely, and any of Yang's "accomplices" rooted out, Chang
would not start building another missile. A smell of chemicals
and the hiss of acetylene torches could be heard from behind a

closed door; no doubt technicians performing forensics on the *Qi*-19. A bastard hybrid of science and politics to produce a desired finding.

Yang walked briskly toward a T-shaped turn. To the right were the large factory areas with cranes and treaded platforms to move assembled components. To the left was the research and Small Construction Works, where those parts were made and fitted together.

The left turn also led to the exit.

Yang stopped at a workstation and went to the refrigerated storage cabinet to secure what he needed for his evolving escape plan: peroxymonosulfuric acid. Yang's team of chemists employed it as an oxidizing reagent in rocket fuel. But that was not its only use. The syrupy compound was also known as "piranha solution" due to its rapid and complete consumption of whatever it touched. The engineer decided that applying it to the support posts, he would be able to push them over silently and almost instantly. The risk was that if the acid came into contact with a high concentration of organic matter, the mixture had a tendency to explode.

At least there's always a bomb handy, he thought, though an uncontrolled explosion would be as dangerous to him as to a wall or jeep.

It was stored in pint-sized polymethylpentene bottles; Yang took one and also grabbed a pair of thirteen-inch ten-gauge gloves from a lab table to handle the container. He emptied a spill kit and put the items in the flexible, non-fiber shoulder bag.

Before leaving, Yang used scissors to adjust the stolen

uniform; the pant legs were long and he cut them to keep from
tripping. He set the shears back in the wall rack and threw the
fabric down the incinerator chute. It was strange. His right hand
had felt empty until now. He usually had a phone or a tablet
or a clipboard when missiles were being assembled here. Yang
did not, however, regret leaving the pipe behind. The engineer
hoped he never had to turn a violent hand on any human being
again.

He saw a few other technicians in offices, reviewing sup-
plies and blueprints. They were focused on their work and barely
looked up. Men in uniform were a common sight in this building, enforcing security protocols and occasionally checking IDs.
The workers ignored them unless approached.

Reaching the door beside a massive hangar entrance, Yang
disabled the alarm code on the lock and stepped outside. The
ruins of the MA3-7917 lay a dozen yards to the side. It looked
like the remains of some prehistoric beast, girders and rubber
taking the place of bone and flesh. The noxious smell of the rubber clung to it like a heavy mist.

He walked out quickly as he made for the wreckage. He
stopped on the far side, hunkering down and looking past one
of the blocky storehouses. The fence had high spotlights every
thirty feet and a large double gate that admitted large tractors
into the Heavy Assembly Building, roughly one hundred yards
away. That was closer than he would have liked but he selected a
spot away from the nearest of the spotlights. There he would attempt to burn through the multiple fences. His best opportunity
would come at dusk. The dog shifts changed at five thirty, and the

guards let the animals snap and growl at one another for several minutes, keeping them feral.

Yang found concealment inside one of the two five-foot-diameter tires that had not melted. The rims had been blown out during the explosion; the partly melted, warped rubber was held in place by the massive mesh chains that had given them traction. The tires were sitting upright, side by side, leaning against the bent and detached "dead axle," a seventh rod that was not used to drive the launcher but to help support the load borne by the other six axles.

The engineer sat deep inside the empty barrel of the wheel, his knees up, legs spread. As a child he had been fascinated by the biological engineering of the ungainly looking yet perfectly balanced praying mantis, limbs akimbo and blending into its environment. He felt like that now.

Yang set the carrying case on the ground before him. He unzipped the top flap, put on the gloves, and removed the acid.

His engineer's mind screamed, *This is madness*. He was a man who had reached for the stratosphere time after time; yet here he was huddled in ruins, on the cold ground, hiding until sundown, preparing to dissolve his way to freedom. Yang's very precise calculations had always pushed his creations higher and faster, yet here he was, regressed to a primitive insect. He fought tears not from pride but because he needed clear eyes to study and memorize the terrain before him and the location of the fence posts. The next time he moved it would be dark.

Yang left the gloves on for the slight warmth they provided. This was a good spot, albeit chilly, especially as the hours passed and the sun dropped lower and the shadows increased. He could still see directly ahead and the rubber was like an architectural whispering arch, amplifying the sounds around him.

Which was why, shortly before sundown, with only the dim edges of a spotlight reaching this untraveled area, Yang heard voices and footfalls coming toward him.

CHAPTER TWENTY-THREE

The Oval Office, Washington, D.C.
February 18, 9:22 A.M.

The Joint Chiefs of Staff rose as the president abruptly announced a five-minute recess. He left the cabinet room, strode through his small, private study, and entered the Oval Office.

His executive secretary was standing in the open doorway.

"Send them in, Mr. Deerfoot," John Wright said as he sat heavily behind the desk. The president did not look up as Angie Brunner and January Dow walked in. He was rereading the text he had just received from his national security assistant.

Neither woman sat. Running the Wright campaign, Angie had gotten to know the president well enough to know that this would not take long. What she did not know was which way it would go.

"Chase Williams has sent Black Wasp overseas in support of Lieutenant Lee," the president read. "The chief of staff has ordered an intelligence support." He finally looked up. "What the hell is going on, Angie?"

"Admiral Williams sent the rest of Black Wasp to an unspecified location in a support function for the mission," she said. "That authority is given to him in the Op-Center charter."

"Where did they go?"

"He will not say," January Dow answered. She held up her tablet. "Withholding information is *not* permitted by charter."

"Withholding information from the commander-in-chief," Angie corrected her. "The commander-in-chief has not asked. As to the second and more urgent matter, Lieutenant Lee has reason to believe that a detainee has fled captivity at the Taiyuan Satellite Launch Center. Admiral Williams believes it may be someone involved with the *Qi*-19 mishap and requested surveillance. I made that request."

"In your name, sir," January added. "*That* is beyond the scope of the duties of the chief of staff."

"Lieutenant Lee is operating under the assumption that this escapee fits the parameters of Op-Center's assignment, which is to gather intelligence on a dangerous new Chinese weapons system," Angie said. "That means putting eyes on the facility with troops of the People's Liberation Army fanning out through the region. She requires—she *deserves*—support."

"That is not the judgment the chief of staff is empowered to make," January stated flatly.

"No, it is not," the president agreed.

"Chase Williams has also overstepped his authority using the inverse orders theory, that if something is not directly proscribed, it is tacitly approved. The relocation of Black Wasp assets from Fort Belvoir is a provocative, dangerous move."

Wright regarded Angie. "You have no idea where? No thoughts?"

January said, "Wherever it was he snuck them out. The DoD, the CIA—no one had any knowledge of their departure."

"Angie?" the president pressed.

"I don't know."

"Get him on the phone."

"Mr. President, sir—you want clean hands in this," January cautioned. "If Black Wasp has entered China, or are using another nation as a staging area for military incursion, you will need more than plausible deniability." She raised the tablet again. "As in the past, Op-Center may have broken at least eleven Geneva Convention statutes pertaining to national sovereignty. At a minimum, that exposes the military to global censure. At the worst, we or our interests may face military retaliation. Mr. President, it is one thing for a marine intelligence officer to be attached to the embassy. We all do it and there are avenues of redress for exposure. A military adventure is something else entirely."

The president looked down and was silent for a moment. "Angie? What was the urgency behind your ordering an intelligence support?"

"I did it because the lieutenant's life is at risk—which *is* at the request of this office."

"That's her job, dammit," Wright replied.

"Then what is our job?" Angie asked. "Just sending her out there? I believe—no, I know—that Admiral Williams is looking out for her and therefore safeguarding the 'job' you gave him."

"Chase Williams is a rogue in league with Matt Berry and

his Trigram Institute data-peddlers. I'm sure Berry had a hand in arranging the unauthorized Black Wasp action."

Wright looked at the time on his phone. He rose. "I have a meeting to finish."

The president's two assistants stood silently. It was one thing to pretend not to know about the admiral's actions; it was another thing to be faced with the reality and ramifications of it.

"Do we have anyone to replace Admiral Williams?" the president asked.

"We do," January Dow said. "Williams knows her. He even approves."

"It's *Admiral* Williams," Angie snapped, surprising herself.

January was savvy enough never to shoot back when an opponent showed bias. An advisor who lacked objectivity had an expiration date.

Wright considered the matter as he turned toward the study door. "Angie, get Mr. Williams any intelligence that will assist Lieutenant Lee. January, tell him that I have authorized a lone wolf operation and nothing—emphasize *nothing*—beyond that. We will reconvene this afternoon. Angie, have Mr. Deerfoot put it on the calendar."

"Yes, Mr. President."

January stopped herself from asking if she should bring Captain Mann up to speed. Being overeager would put her position in jeopardy as well.

Wright left the Oval Office and the two women did the same. January departed first—tall, efficient, very official. The national security assistant blew past the president's executive secretary while Angie stopped to pass along Wright's instructions.

"Three o'clock, Ms. Brunner," he said.

"Thank you," Angie replied as she headed to her office.

The chief of staff knew that her fate was now tied directly to that of Chase Williams. She had been there before, betting her career and her studio on the stars and directors of Hollywood blockbusters—a major factor in which, ironically, was how well the movies did in China.

I thought I knew what "stakes" were, she chided herself, feeling proud of not just the tactical decision she had made but of the irrevocable moral choice as well.

As she walked down the busy West Wing corridor, crowded with office-seekers looking to fill a dwindling number of positions, her phone vibrated.

She stopped and looked down and did not wait to get to her office before taking action.

CHAPTER TWENTY-FOUR

Jinzhou, Shanxi Province, China
February 18, 9:08 P.M., CST

Grace pushed herself and the bike hard.

Her uncle had texted at 8:15, making sure she was all right. She told him she was, had met some nice men at Ho's Market, and was on her way back.

Even her well-exercised legs were tired by the time she reached the city and near exhaustion when she reached the home of Uncle Sun. But that was not what weighed on her as she put the bicycle in the shed and grabbed the sack with their dinner. She was thinking about what to tell Uncle Sun if Williams found the fugitive from Taiyuan.

She came in to find the wood stove bright and warm and the frying pan and utensils laid out on a Formica counter beside the gas range. Showing none of the distractions she felt, Grace told her uncle about her day as she prepared dinner. The lieutenant did not fancy herself a cook, but she remembered watching her mother grill fish and made a good show of it.

The two sat down to eat, Sun enjoying the company of his

niece and hearing of her life in America. Grace showed no tension or expectation as they chatted, laughed, and traded stories about her mother. They were nearly finished when the lieutenant's phone signaled a text. She excused herself, rose, and turned her back to the table as she read.

> Forty-plus men searching Taiyuan. Thermal reading
> shows lone figure in junk heap near northeast
> perimeter. Possibly waiting for dark.

Grace waited while the image downloaded, green-tinted like night-vision goggles with a red heat signature coming from the fringe of the mound. It was humbling as always to see with the eyes of an eagle. She texted back:

> I'll get out there asap.

Williams replied:

> *Do not enter.* Dangerous and may not be our subject.

To which she responded:

> Understood.

That was the truth; she did understand. Grace turned back to her uncle, who was still picking at the fish. With effort, she smiled.

"Uncle, might I borrow the truck?"

Sun pulled a bone from his tongue and rubbed it from his fingers. "That was delicious," he said. "I haven't eaten so well in years."

"Uncle?"

He looked up slyly. "Borrow my truck to go where? Or should I ask, to see whom?'"

"One of the men I met at Ho's Market."

"But they're closed," Sun said—then nodded. "Forgive your mother's fool of a brother. Yes, of course." He went over to an ashtray and collected his household key ring. "The black one is the truck, the square top is the front door. In case you come in late."

"Thank you," she said, putting them in her pocket. "I'll try not to wake you."

"Don't bother pulling into the shed. Park on the garden side, away from my room, and I won't hear a thing. Don't bother with the dishes," he added. "I'm used to cleaning up here."

Grace kissed her uncle on the cheek and, a contrived bounce in her step, she went out the door and headed for the shed. Climbing into the truck, she programmed the photo into her Op-Center GPS system, which contained overlay maps of Taiyuan. The trip was estimated to take forty-three minutes. The phone would automatically update the route if and when additional images arrived from Williams.

The vehicle did not have a smartphone holder so Grace put it on the seat beside her, first dimming the screen so that it did not catch the eye of anyone on the outside. Smash-and-grab crimes at traffic lights were noted in the briefing kit Williams had provided.

After familiarizing herself with the dashboard, Grace drove out of the yard and into Jinzhou.

Because of his position inside the tire, Yang was unable to hear what the newcomers were saying. It seemed conversational—and there were no grunts. They were not adding discarded material to the pile. They were not hurrying, which suggested they were not soldiers.

Or were they looking? He thought he heard the crunch of boots.

The question was whether they would pass by him. For all he knew they were metalworkers who had come out for a smoke.

Yang did not want to be caught hiding but he could not think of a reason to suddenly step out. These men might not even know about his arrest or his escape. He tried to think of an excuse a solitary soldier could give for being here—but if they knew him, what excuse could he give for being in a People's Liberation Army Air Force uniform?

"What are you doing out here?"

It was a voice from the other direction. Yang tensed, shrank, wondering how he could have been seen.

"Lieutenant Colonel Kun, one of the reclamation engineers thought he saw Dr. Dàyóu in the Small Construction Works. He reported to General Chang and we were sent to investigate. He was not inside so we came out here."

"Go back to the perimeter search," Kun said. "We do not want him getting outside the fence."

"Yes, sir," the men said.

"Wait!" Kun said suddenly. "Where was Yang reportedly seen? Exactly?"

"In the metalworking area, sir."

"Go there," the lieutenant colonel said. "See what he might have been after. Have everyone stop what they are doing and help. Report personally to me anything you find, however minor. I'll be here."

The two acknowledged the order and departed but Kun remained.

Yang relaxed himself so he would not shiver and he barely breathed. The lieutenant colonel had the instincts of an alligator. He knew when things were not right.

Time crept by. There was no rush and Yang was a patient man. This was just another countdown to him. Instead of numbers the seconds were measured by the hollow sound of Kun's boots on the hard earth and, now and then, by his fingers drumming his holster or the walkie-talkie that hung from his belt. It was not anxiety but an eagerness to act.

After a half hour or so Yang heard a single pair of footsteps. They were approaching quickly.

"Lieutenant Colonel Kun, sir," a young voice said. "Someone was definitely there who should not have been. Rubber gloves were taken and, upon examination, the chief chemist discovered that a bottle of acid had been removed as well."

Yang felt sick. He thought he had been so careful.

"Remain here," Kun told him. The lieutenant colonel got on his radio and contacted General Chang and briefed him.

"Bring men inside," the general ordered. "The traitor must be found! I want every building searched and bring out the portable spotlights. I want the perimeter fully illuminated."

"At once, General," Kun replied.

Traitor.

The word was a knife to Yang and it cut very deep. The engineer knew that everything he did now in support of flight would reinforce that view. He was tortured by the thought of not just leaving the lie unchallenged but by reinforcing it with everything he did.

The lieutenant colonel switched channels on his walkie-talkie and gave Chang's instructions to the captain in charge of deployment. When he was finished, Kun turned to the soldier at his side.

"Search through the pile. He may have crawled inside."

The soldier switched on his flashlight and turned toward a portion of the mound that offered the best point to scale to the top.

The flashlight poked and probed to Yang's far right. He heard materials grate and shift as the soldier made his way up and along the pile. Very shortly, the flashlight would stab through and uncover Yang.

The engineer felt a sense of unreality wrap around him in the darkness. His situation and his choices were equally unfamiliar. There was no time to consider options. His actions must be directed by his instinct to survive and escape.

Yang did not want to lay violent hands on another human being, not even Kun. But he would act if it became necessary.

Unscrewing the cap and holding the bottle of acid, Yang stood, bent forward, and emerged from the tire in a cramped and awkward movement. The noise had attracted the soldier's attention and the flashlight swung toward Yang and Kun who stood just yards apart. Kun's expression registered delight. Slowly, without menace, Yang extended the bottle with one arm so the fumes did not scald and poison him.

The lieutenant colonel unholstered his firearm but kept it pointed down. The soldier on the pile started over but Kun raised a hand to stop him. Except for the distant sound of men and dogs, the area around the scrap pile was quiet.

"Inspired, Dr. Dàyóu."

The engineer was silent as Kun got back on the radio and ordered a jeep to transport himself and the prisoner.

That last word, too, struck hard.

"Lieutenant Colonel Kun, I am innocent of treason and will not be a *Tìzuìyáng* for General Chang."

"The sacrifices in ancient Yinxu were innocent. You are not." With his free hand, Kun reached for his radio.

"Do not call Chang," the engineer warned.

"Do not dictate terms, Engineer." Kun raised his weapon. "Cap the bottle or you will perish here, now."

"What does it matter how or when I die?"

"You solve the philosophy. My job is much simpler."

Yang hesitated. He knew the young soldier had a sidearm

and assumed he had drawn it. Even if he attacked Kun, he would die—and with a death on his hands.

It seemed foolish, now that he thought of it. The entire plan. Slowly and with resignation, the engineer capped the bottle.

"Put it on the ground and leave the gloves," Kun said.

Yang hesitated.

"Put the container on the ground, Doctor, and step away or my report will state that you died trying to escape."

The engineer obeyed just as the jeep pulled up. Inside were the two men who had taken Yang into custody. The exited to collect the prisoner.

The lieutenant colonel addressed them without taking his eyes from his prisoner. "Take Dr. Dàyóu to the *Qi* project blockhouse," he said. "Remain inside with him until transport to Beijing has been arranged."

One of the two occupants got out. He was about to lead the engineer to the vehicle when they heard shouts from the double gates that opened to the Heavy Assembly Building.

Grace was glad that the road to the Greenbelt—the northward-running S209—and then the so-called Old Road to the Greenbelt itself were straight. The lieutenant was constantly checking the phone and was glad not to have to think about directions. Growing up in Manhattan, she was not an enthusiastic driver to begin with and was also glad that Sun's truck lacked the fancy electronics of cars she had seen since enlisting.

The Project Blackjack–linked phone was refreshing at a

pace that made the images seem like the flickering old nick-
elodeon movies she had once seen in an antiques store. That
technology was welcome, though the night-vision aspect was
overdue for a next generation. The view was almost directly
overhead, the greens and reds showing what looked like a man
standing outside a structure, another man coming and going.
That was likely a security guard, not the escapee. The latter had
disappeared into a structure of some kind. The overlay of the
map provided little help; the image was as tight as the satellite
could provide and the diagram of the compound had been thin
on details to begin with.

There was very little traffic outside the city and as Grace
passed Ho's Market on her way to the Greenbelt she thumbed on
the voice recognition system. The PUT technology—Personal
Use Transcription—was programmed to respond only to Grace's
normal speaking voice. If she were captured and drugged, the
device would not acknowledge her commands.

She voice-texted Williams:

Guards at last known target position?

He answered:

Likely.

The lieutenant asked for a pullback image in real time of the
surrounding area. Within a minute, the tight picture of the escapee's last known position had expanded to show the unknown

structure, a square section on the left and top that looked like a building, and a severely washed-out section along the right side of the image.

Williams wrote:

Building and brightly lit fence with target between.

Grace glanced at the superimposed map. Based on previous satellite surveillance, a gate was indicated not far from where the men were standing. More red shapes on the ground put the number of security personnel at two.

Everyone else is in the field, looking for the escapee, she thought. *It has to be Dr. Dàyóu.*

There was no guard tower as such, which did not surprise her. The compound had been laid out before spy satellites were the norm, large sections of it built underground and designed to present a low profile above ground. That accounted for the number of surrounding trees.

She texted:

Pull back further. Surrounding terrain. Access to fence.

Williams sent a higher image. Grace noted the location of search clusters, fanning out in a widening pattern. She was going to have to leave the truck about a quarter mile from the fence and hope it was not seen.

It occurred to her, then, that if the truck was spotted and recovered, it would wrongly implicate Uncle Sun in this action.

That meant deciding now whether she was going to the fence, possibly to the gate, or not.

She texted:

If asset is present do I attempt recovery?

There was an uncommon delay in Williams' response.

Risk assessment at top ceiling. Escape with burden unlikely.

As a civilian, Williams did not have the authority to "order" a member of Black Wasp in a go/no-go situation. The limit of his command was to put the team in the field and execute the orders of the president. That was one reason the retired admiral went with them: to lend wisdom if not command to critical junctures like this.

She asked:

What would you do?

To which he replied:

Surveil for next opportunity.

Grace considered that as she entered the Greenbelt. She had trained with *sifus* who taught her to be like water and the wind, to move constantly. More than once her teachers had cautioned the young woman that she had brilliantly mastered the tsunami and cyclone but must also learn to ripple.

Was this the time for that?

Why did the Universe align my sifus and the admiral on the same side and then give me a solo mission?

Grace shut down the internal conflict as she faced the outer one. The woods loomed and the question of the truck loomed larger. If it were found, Uncle Sun would be implicated in whatever she did—even if it was just observing. She checked the location of the patrols and pulled up in a spot they appeared to have already cleared. Pulling up behind a tree, she killed the lights and shut the engine. The lights of the compound showed her where to go.

After stowing the phone, Grace slipped from the car. She was instantly in motion, moving from tree to tree, waiting a moment behind each to listen. When she was certain no one was near she moved on. It took her ten minutes to reach the tree nearest the gate. She went to the ground using a leopard stance, a low, crouching posture that reduced her profile and adjusted her balance in a way that was unique to the form. Her hands faced down, fingers curled tight against her upper palm, her thumb bent in—a slim fist designed to jab soft tissue like eye sockets, the throat, and the gut. She felt feral, hyperalert, at home in this environment.

Nearing the gate, she saw a chicken-wire door that opened to a guardhouse; inside that small post was a door to the compound. The shack was empty; the two men were outside, watching the interior. To her right, northwest, she saw that the "structure" she had seen in the photos was a debris pile. The blackened contours suggested a mobile launcher and possible projectile.

Beyond it was a figure holding a gun on another, both in uniform. A third figure was watching from atop the mound.

Grace had expected Dr. Dàyóu, if this were he, to be in civilian dress or a lab coat—not uniform. Withdrawing her binoculars and lying on her belly, she turned the range finding reticle on the man at gunpoint. He was wearing rubber gloves and holding a container of some kind.

This could have nothing to do with Yang Dàyóu, she thought.

The man might have been spying on the debris or using some caustic material to collect samples or analysis for some other government. Even if she had a photo of the engineer, she could not see this man's face.

It is not worth going in, she decided.

Then she heard a voice say, "Take Dr. Dàyóu to the *Qi* project blockhouse . . ." and, without hesitation, she returned to leopard stance and ran at the guardhouse.

CHAPTER TWENTY-FIVE

The Defense Logistics Agency, Fort Belvoir, Virginia
February 18, 9:30 A.M.

Chase Williams was in his office, looking at his desktop, when a new figure appeared on the Project Blackjack feed. The details were not clear on the high, wide view; they did not need to be. From the location and speed, Williams knew it was Lieutenant Lee.

She went in.

The first thing Williams did was to notify the rest of Black Wasp that Grace had apparently gone into the Taiyuan compound. The admiral had been able to track the progress of Breen and Rivette through the Pit Boss link. He was charting their location on a tablet; they showed up as black dots on a geophysical map of the terrain.

After stopping—presumably to refuel—the two men had headed south through the Gobi Desert on their KTM 450 EXC motorcycles. Williams had felt better about their part of the mission after receiving Breen's one and only text; the major knew his way around that mode of transport. Though it was night now in Mongolia, the men had not stopped. Williams knew they would not rest until they reached the Chinese border.

Breen did not acknowledge the update. Williams had not expected him to. The device indicated the message had been received. It would be up to the two men to decide whether to wait for an update or get in position closer to Taiyuan. Breen would not have to inform Williams of that either; the Pit Boss stream would tell him that.

Williams was not even aware that he had moved the tablet aside after sending the message to Breen. His eyes were on the desktop monitor. A phrase jumped into his head. It was uttered by Senator Sam Ervin during the investigation of the Watergate break-in during the Nixon administration. Ervin asked, *"What did the president know and when did he know it?"*

The admiral posed that same question to himself. It was not inconsequential; it spoke to the root of his method of command. As he watched the screen he asked himself, *What did you expect when the president sent Grace Lee on this mission, and when did you expect it?*

He expected from the start that the lieutenant would do just what she did. If Dr. Yang Dàyóu was in the complex, she was going to try to get to him—for intel if nothing else. There was no way Grace would come back empty-handed.

A third device made a sound. Williams looked over at his phone. January Dow was calling by phone, not videoconference. He thought—with sadness, not with satisfaction—*Either she is recording the call, can't deal with a stoic countenance resolutely blocking her, or both.*

He poked the speaker button. January charged into him.

"Where are they, the rest of Black Wasp?" she demanded. "The president wants to know."

"Then he will have to ask," Williams answered evenly. "You can be in the room, of course. That's up to the president. But the charter is very specific about the chain of intelligence service. It goes from me to the president, not to the national security advisor to the president."

"I don't understand this obstinacy, but you know you're finished at Op-Center, yes?"

"I acknowledge the will of the president, not the threats of his national security advisor."

"This is no empty threat, Mr. Williams. When it happens, will you brief your replacement?"

"Deployment and operational status of Black Wasp is need-to-know. The director of Op-Center would need to know."

There was a short silence. "I have other agencies looking for Major Breen and Lance Corporal Rivette."

Williams was not surprised by that, nor did it matter. Finding the men, then acting, would only call attention to the unauthorized incursion and embarrass Wright. He made no comment. His gaze was on the desktop monitor. The red shapes were all moving; it was difficult to be sure which one was Grace.

January sighed. "What a pointless way to end a career."

"If you mean me, be careful. You've been in the game long enough to know that results are what matter. Black Wasp may overperform."

The conversation was ended but it was a few moments before January said, "Goodbye, Mr. Williams," and hung up.

The admiral immediately put January's call from his mind. He had a mission to oversee and, with luck, a dual extraction to organize.

Quickly.

Jaz Rivette was disappointed.

In all the old movies his grandmother used to watch, the Gobi Desert was depicted as exotic, rippled dunes, blazing sunlight, and camels in festively colored Uyghur blankets. Parts of it might be, but not the part they were crossing. This desert was endless flat scrub dotted with drought-resistant shrubs and sagebrush with occasional ATVs, jeeps, vans, and horses instead of camels. Most were tourists, judging from their Western garb and noisy enthusiasm. The locals were easy to spot by their wooly, traditional garb, sacks of goods, and proximity to huts that had trails of black smoke curling from thatched roofs. The two men occasionally saw corrals of livestock and herders on horseback. For Breen, the journey was a microcosm of a shrinking way of life.

For the most part, the journey had been uneventful. Although Rivette had expected it, the desert was cold. The sound of the motorcycles prohibited conversation nor was there any need for talk. Both men simultaneously received updates from Williams as well as course corrections from Pit Boss. They ate and drank without stopping, pausing only once to fill their tanks. They were able to fill the gas tanks at a market in a small *ger*, a circular settlement of yurts that catered to tourists.

The border between Mongolia and China stretched 2,880 miles, the majority of it in the Gobi Desert. Homeland Security considered the region Extremely Low Interest. Most of the unrecorded crossings involved human trafficking; shipments of "donor" organs, corneas, and other body parts; and drugs bound for Europe. China enforced border security haphazardly, using powerful anti-vehicle mines and rocket-launched barrel-missiles containing clusters of explosives. The former were buried; the latter were quickly covered with windblown debris until unwary travelers triggered a chain of explosions. The locations of all were provided to any black marketer who paid for that information. For its part, Mongolia stationed troops around its coal mining regions, ignoring the rest. Except during the COVID pandemic, when military convoys deposited thousands of militias to shut and patrol the crossing, it was an otherwise ungoverned region.

As they drew to within one hundred miles of the border, both men noticed a marked change in the nature of traffic. The vehicles were mostly trucks, and Rivette's instincts told him they were carrying or seeking contraband. This was confirmed when he diverted to pass close beside a canvas-backed civilian truck traveling toward them from the south. It was traveling slow and heavy. Raising his sand-glazed goggles, he saw a rifle in the hands of the civilian passenger. The man glared out threateningly at Rivette as they passed. The lance corporal stopped and Breen braked.

"What is it, Jaz?"

"That truck is bad, and everyone who sees it knows it."

"I don't follow."

"We take it, we have a hall pass. No one will think twice about what we're doing here. And if we hook up with the lieutenant—"

"No one left behind." Breen studied the retreating vehicle. "What's your plan?"

Rivette answered by removing his backpack. He took out the M4 assault carbine, handed it to Breen, and kept the M1911 semiautomatic handgun for himself. This was the kind of unplanned, reckless play Breen favored, the very definition of what he always cautioned against in training: self-inflicted risk. But he could not argue with the logic of it.

"Driver isn't armed," Rivette said. "I'm going to approach on that side. You watch the back flap."

"They'll be out of range in—"

"Nope," Rivette said. "Just cover the back."

The lance corporal swung the motorcycle around and, bending low, pushed the four-stroke engine hard. Dirt and grass flew in his wake as he raced to catch the truck. Breen dropped his goggles, put the buttstock to his shoulder, and aligned the rear and front sights. The truck bounced on the uneven ground and Breen stayed focused on the area around the flap. He would not shoot if someone simply looked out; he had to see a weapon, and even then he would not shoot to kill. There was a sharp legal line between homicide and self-defense; the major drew moral lines against murder as well.

Ahead, and gaining swiftly on the truck, Rivette was grateful for the damping power of the shock absorbers. The gauges were all below the handlebar, giving him a clean shot along the center. His left hand on the throttle and clutch lever, Rivette held the semiautomatic straight ahead, closed one eye, and picked a target that would not disable the truck.

The driver glowered into the sideview mirror; as he did, the lance corporal put a pair of bullets in the glass. Shards flew in a glittering blossom, causing the driver to duck right and swerve. Two more shots knocked the mirror frame forward, which left it dangling and banging on the door.

The driver floored the gas and the truck picked up modest speed; Rivette matched it and pulled away slightly so he had a clear shot at the driver through the side window. Rivette motioned for the man to get out.

The truck swerved to the right, spitting pebbles and grit and nearly causing Rivette to fall. He managed to push off the ground with his left foot and spin after the vehicle. Revving, he shot forward to get ahead of the truck. He remained on the driver's side so the passenger would not have a shot.

This time Rivette paced the truck, which afforded him a view of the driver only from the elbows up. He made himself an easy target, not for shooting but for ramming. The driver took the bait, turning the wheel with the intention of butting the motorcycle.

He never got the chance. As soon as the driver's hands moved, Rivette put a bullet in his left shoulder. Glass blew in, blood blew out, and the man fell onto his companion. The truck turned at a sharp right angle to the left. Rivette braked hard as the truck barreled in front of him.

While all of this had been going on, Breen had kept his weapon trained on the back flap. When the truck stopped, it finally opened and two men jumped out holding rifles. Breen shot at the ground in front of them and the men dove to opposite sides, hitting the hard earth. The major did not come forward but kept the assault carbine trained on them. Neither man raised his weapon, only their hands.

Rivette, meanwhile, had jumped from the motorcycle and ran around the front of the truck, crouching close and low. The gunman inside could not see him and finally popped the door. When he did, Rivette came around that side with the semiautomatic trained on the man.

The rifle of the shotgun-rider was pointed up so he could exit; it remained up as he stared down the muzzle of the handgun.

Rivette motioned for the man to toss the rifle. The passenger obliged. Then Rivette motioned him from the cab. The man stepped away and, cautiously, Rivette came around to check on the driver. He could hear the man moaning but that did not mean he should abandon caution.

Rivette bent before coming around the door. He pulled a shrub from the ground, earth frozen to its roots, and hooked it into the cab. Three shots cracked from inside as the driver, lying across the seat, fired out the open passenger's door.

Only two shots emerged. The driver screamed as one of the bullets ricocheted from the iron door frame and grazed his neck. The sound of pain was genuine and—without lowering his gun, which remained on the other man—Rivette stepped around the door, aimed at the twice-wounded man, and snatched his Type 77 semiautomatic.

"People's Liberation Army," the lance corporal said as he held it on the driver. "You guys are all goddamn whores over here."

Rivette collected the other man's rifle and patted him down as Breen drove over. He took a Swiss Army knife from the man, collected smartphones from each, then went around back and covered the two passengers who were still on the ground. Breen collected their weapons and went over to the flap. He pulled it aside.

There were thirteen girls in the back, chained with hand-cuffs to U-bolts screwed into two wooden benches along the sides. The young women looked to be from twelve to sixteen years old. They were dressed in simple skirts and blouses and were shivering. None had shoes on. The captives were not intended to leave this truck.

Breen's expression darkened.

"What is it?" Rivette asked.

"Girls. Probably for the mine workers."

Breen heard footsteps, a punch, and then saw the shotgun-rider fly backwards.

"You're lucky it wasn't a .45 slug, you garbage!"

Breen motioned for the girls to relax. "English?" he asked.

"I," one said.

"Name?"

"Chingmy," she answered.

"Tell them they are safe," the major told her. "We are going to take you home."

Ten minutes later, after the two motorcycles had been hoisted into the back, Rivette went up front to pull the driver from the cab. He left the man on the ground and found a first aid kit under the dashboard. He threw it at one of the others.

"Fix your wheelman," he said, "then see if you can hitch a ride the hell outta this place. Or use those expensive Nikes you've got on your feet, dirtbag."

The three men spoke imploringly in Chinese but Rivette just waved dismissively as he went back to the truck.

Fishing through the glove compartment, Breen had found the keys to the girls' bonds and removed their shackles. He also found their shoes in a locker. There was suspicion from some of the women, uncertainty as to whether they were freed or simply passed to new traffickers. Breen tried to assuage them by showing them a map of where they were headed. The women were still trembling, huddling close on the benches.

"Hold up," Rivette said. "That's not just fear."

Following Rivette's lead, Breen removed his coat and gloves and handed them to the woman who spoke English. Rivette ran up front and, at gunpoint, roughly pulled the leather jackets and scarves from the Chinese men and brought them back. He passed the garments to the women.

"Share," Rivette said.

Breen took one of the bedrolls to the cab. While he stuffed it in the broken window, Rivette grabbed the other sleeping bag and gave it to Chingmy. He pointed to the smallest of the women.

"For her," Rivette said.

The recipient nodded gratefully; several of the girls began to cry. Rivette shut the flaps.

Breen had brushed the shards of glass from the seat and used the pocketknife to hang one of the open bedrolls in the broken window. They would need it as a buffer against the cold, especially when darkness settled in. Then he texted Williams with an update and turned the truck around.

"That was one helluva traffic stop," Breen said when they were under way.

Rivette was reflective.

"You okay?" Breen asked.

"Yes, sir. Sorry about the sideview mirror."

"Don't be. Makes us look like authentic lowlifes. What else is on your mind?"

"I was thinking . . . we just saved thirteen women from slavery."

Breen did not reply. They had saved people before, and in greater numbers, and Rivette had not been wrong the other day when he complained about the inadequacies of the training scenarios they ran back at Fort Belvoir. This was the kind of experience—the kind of growth and maturing—that no classroom, no dummy car or village could duplicate.

And as he thought that, he found himself wondering how their lone team member was doing in China. . . .

CHAPTER TWENTY-SIX

Taiyuan Satellite Launch Center, Shanxi Province,
China
February 18, 9:19 P.M., CST

Grace Lee had trained extensively with blindfolds. She had to listen. She had to make contact and never release it; each move had to flow into the next while she listened for other opponents—footsteps, breath, the inadvertent knock of a gunstock on a button.

Grace had trained with blinking. She had stood opposite an opponent in her kung fu school. The first one to blink took a palm strike in the chest, gut, or groin from the other. Or a meat grab: when the palm struck the fingers closed, grabbing not just the fabric of the *gi* but the flesh underneath. Even a forearm had skin to grab; it was up to the combatant to find it.

As a woman in a male-dominated martial art, as a shorter fighter than most, Grace had mastered technique. She never used muscle. She used skill and one thing more: movement.

During a fight, motion kept a martial artist safe. Each move manifested qualities of both offense and defense. Making contact with an adversary not only allowed a fighter to neutralize them, it made for a muddled target to other enemies. Aggressive, unrelenting movement also created fear and uncertainty—a localized fog of war. It was momentarily shocking, disorienting to see a comrade upended or cut down, by a strike or throw, knife blade or bullet. That gave the attacker time to execute the next move.

Still a leopard in form and spirit, Grace entered the guardhouse at the gate and leapt through the door that opened to the compound. She had noted that the attention of the guards was on the activity by the scrap heap. There was no need to throw the door open and startle them. She cracked it, slipped through, and attacked both from behind.

She drove a curled leopard fist into the lower back of one man. That caused him to arch back. As he did her fist never lost contact with his back. The hand shot up his spine, her arm hooked around his throat, and Grace slammed him to the ground. Stepping on and over him she kicked the man beside him, her instep in his throat, as he was still turning to see what had just happened. As he fell, she turned back to the first soldier, stomped on the bridge of his nose, then spun and kicked the other man in the temple. With both men incapacitated, she left them and their fallen rifles and moved on—still low, leopard-like, keeping to the shadow outside the bright circle thrown by the spotlight.

After seeing the confrontation between Dr. Dàyóu and the others in night-vision greens and reds, actually being here had a sense of hyperreality. Her Shaolin-trained eagle eyes had become almost feline, missing nothing as she approached. She decided to go for the driver of the jeep first, cut off a quick retreat.

The lieutenant circled wide to the vehicle and crouched low at the driver's side. Dr. Dàyóu—if it was indeed he—remained with the other guard; they went to the back as the driver came around. The soldier on the mound started down and the officer—a lieutenant colonel, standing clear in the sharp headlights—watched the process over his gun barrel.

The driver fell, as though he had slipped on a grease stain. His knees had been kicked from behind, silently dropping him. As soon as he was on his back Grace elbowed his chest hard, cracking ribs and causing him to exhale weakly.

The other men froze, as she knew they would. That was the "blink." Grace charged the officer, knocking him over with a shoulder, grabbing his radio and throwing it, then swatting his gun aside, all of it in a fluid, circling movement. The dust of her swift attack was still in the air as she ran for the soldier on the mound. He was a foot from the ground behind him, and he stopped to bring his rifle around. There was no way Grace could reach him before he fired. Reluctantly, she drew the butterfly knife from the sheath on her right shin and flung it underhand. The knife stuck in his belly. It did not penetrate deeply due to the layers of his winter uniform, but the impact startled the man and he fell on his seat. That bought Grace time to reach him, grab the rifle barrel with her left hand, and drive her right palm up and into his chin. His head snapped up, not enough to break his neck but sufficient to send both the man and the gun falling back. Grace recovered her knife and without hesitation she turned on the man holding Dr. Dàyóu.

The man was frozen not entirely with fear but with determination, holding his charge by the upper arms, half as a prisoner, half as a human shield. She ran at him and, as though rising from a stupor, the private began shouting for assistance.

Dr. Dàyóu did his part, wresting free just as Grace reached the soldier. A side-kick in the gut doubled him over as Grace ran for the driver's side. The jeep was still running and she leapt in.

"Get in!" she shouted.

Dr. Dàyóu hesitated. "Who are you?"

"A friend. Get in and I'll explain," she said, imploringly.

The engineer nodded, pausing only long enough to pick up the bottle of acid and a thick handful of soil and dead grass. As soon as he was inside Grace pushed the gas pedal to the floorboard just as other soldiers began to appear, running from the far side of the compound.

"I have a truck outside the gate," she said. "It may be less conspicuous than a stolen military vehicle."

Grace reached the gate as soldiers were arriving to assist the guards. She was angry she had not taken their radios. She had a few seconds to decide whether to try to make it through the guardhouse with her passenger or ram the gate. The latter was unlikely to get them all the way through and the impact could leave them injured.

"We're going to go through the sentry post," she said. "You go first, I'll cover."

"You go and lead the way to the truck," the engineer instructed as he unscrewed the bottle top.

"What are you going to do?"

"Delay them, I think," Yang Dàyóu replied.

Grace did not argue. They skidded to a stop and she jumped out. Dr. Dàyóu emerged, stepping carefully, and dumped the dirt on the seat. Grace backed into the shack, watching as the soldiers began to draw their weapons.

"Doctor!" she cried.

Yang Dàyóu backed toward the guardhouse and lobbed the bottle onto the pile of dirt and grass. The mixture immediately began to sizzle and smoke. A moment later there was a gurgle and then a loud pop. The jeep was immediately engulfed in noxious white smoke.

The engineer was walking backwards as he watched. Grace grabbed him by the sleeve and pulled him around.

"It was supposed to explode!" he said as they ran through the shed into the field.

"Sir, I don't think anyone will be running through an acid cloud," Grace said.

The man Grace had seen in the floodlight by the scrap heap was a round-shouldered, tired figure. She never let go of her companion lest his strength give out as they ran toward the truck. There was no caution now. The refugees had trees and darkness for cover, but the soldiers had guns. A lot of them. Even a blind, lucky shot could kill.

Grace could still hear the acid hissing. When she turned to check on Dr. Dàyóu she saw the chemical throwing off magnesium-white flakes and driving the troops back. A smell like burnt plastic reached them, and the engineer advised her to hold her breath and narrow her eyes.

As they ran, the dogs barked to announce the presence of

intruders outside the fence. In the midst of their flight, Grace smiled. The animals' well-intentioned inefficiency was almost sweet.

It was a momentary respite from the unrelenting urgency. Dr. Dàyóu's energies were flagging and she swung behind him to urge him along. His ill-fitting military cap fell off; she snatched it up and flung it as far to the left as she could. The dogs would eventually be set loose to find their trail; this might detour them for a vital few moments.

They were beyond the flickering light of the acid fire, but behind them were the sounds of men trying to fight it.

"Sand!" she heard. "Get shovels!"

"Not *sand*!" someone cried. "It's combustible! Get foam from—"

The command was swallowed in the explosion of the jeep. Grace pushed her companion behind a tree as the sound reached them. She hunkered near him as the ground rolled and the air grew warm on their exposed cheeks.

"Let's go!" she urged as the roar still echoed around them. This would block the entrance and it would take the soldiers time to organize a pursuit from the west.

The engineer obeyed with a will that was stronger than his legs, and she threw his arm around her neck to help him through the last few dozen yards. The truck was dully illuminated by the fire, welcoming as a hearth. Grace helped her companion into the passenger's seat, where he deflated and wept.

She hurried around, got behind the wheel, and eased the truck back the way she had come. She kept the lights off in case they were spotted by patrols; she saw a few teams that shined lights, fell short of finding them, and no shots were fired. Foot soldiers were not her concern. As quickly as that lieutenant colonel could organize it, there would be vehicular pursuit with airborne support from the Z-20 she had noted in the surveillance photo of the launch facility.

Grace tore onto and along the Greenbelt. She was not only trying to put distance between herself and the pursuers, she wanted to get to the main road, which had places to conceal the truck. There was no question about taking it to Jinzhou; it would have to be abandoned.

Which left Grace with a guilt-edged decision to make: what to do about Uncle Sun.

While she had the time, and while Dr. Dàyóu rested both body and eyes, she took her phone from its carrying case and called her uncle. She put it on speaker so her companion could hear.

"Let me guess," Sun said when he answered. "You are—"

"Uncle, listen. Neither I nor your truck are coming back. I will make good for your losses. When the authorities contact you, most likely tonight, tell them everything from the time I contacted you, tell them what I just said, and tell them that is *all* I said."

"Grace dear, it's late and I've had my medicinal Tsingtao but I'm not sure I—"

"Uncle Sun: I love you and I am sorry for this."

"For *what*?"

Even as Sun asked the question, Grace realized that her answer was insufficient. If the Chinese military were permitted to find the truck, even a burned husk, they would find Sun Fenghe. Finding him, they would know who she was. The embassy could disavow her but her exposed identity would lead the Chinese to the U.S. Army Special Operations Command, Airborne, to press releases about her on the USASOC website, to the desks of the command at the U.S. Army John F. Kennedy Special Warfare Center and School—

There were two options. One was to make a run for the Mongolian border. But chances were good the military would marshal land and air resources to blanket the region. They might not know what she looked like but they surely knew Dr. Dàyóu. The other option was to go to Uncle Sun's house. She could be there in a half hour, hide the truck in the shed, and take time to contact Chase Williams and Black Wasp, organize an extraction, not just flight.

"Uncle, I'm coming home. I will see you very soon."

"Grace—"

She ended the call and pushed the truck ahead and listened for any sounds that were not the throaty diesel engine.

"Who are you?" Yang Dàyóu asked unexpectedly.

"Sir, I am Lieutenant Grace Lee with American special forces."

"Were you sent to abduct me?"

"No, Dr. Dàyóu. I was—watching the base and saw what was about to happen to you."

"You were spying."

"Yes." She had wanted to suggest a better word but there was no point insulting this man's intelligence.

"Were you born here?" the engineer asked.

"My parents were. My Uncle Sun lives in Jinzhou."

"I see. What is your intention?"

"To get to my uncle's home and organize asylum for you in America, if you will have it."

The engineer grew as steely as he could in his state. "I am a loyal son of China. Despite the wrongs visited upon me by General Chang, I will not become a collaborator with your military."

"Who is General Chang?"

The engineer fell silent. Grace realized she should not have pressed; not now.

"Sir, we are here, now, because I saw a man who had been prepared to defend himself with the only tool at hand yet who ultimately chose surrender. Because you are a patriot, because of your family—I don't know. The matter you bring up is beyond my experience and authority. All I can promise you is my full support for any choices you make."

Once again Yang Dàyóu became quietly thoughtful. It was some time before he spoke.

"I am moved by the risks you took."

"Thank you."

"But I am afraid I must ask you to take more or return me to the compound."

"I don't understand."

"I will not leave without my family," Yang informed her.

The extent to which Grace had not thought this out was alarming.

"Where are they?" she asked.

The engineer answered, "My wife, Dongling, and my daughter, Ushi, live on 714 County Road in Wuzhai in a house I saw too infrequently. And my son, Wen, is in Beijing. He was at the University of International Business and Economics. Now he is in Qincheng Prison."

Grace took it all in without being able to process the implications or path forward. This was not a discussion for text; she called Chase Williams.

CHAPTER TWENTY-SEVEN

The Defense Logistics Agency, Fort Belvoir, Virginia
February 18, 10:28 A.M.

"Captain Mann at Naval Support Activity told January Dow that she wouldn't consider coming down here unless she spoke with you first."

There was a trace of satisfaction in Angie Brunner's voice as she relayed the information over the phone; Chase Williams felt a welling of pride when he heard it.

"What did January tell her?" Williams asked.

"She said she was not accustomed to interviewees setting terms, but she would think about it."

"She's not accustomed to people acting with integrity," Williams said. "Be careful. As soon as she has my head, January will be after yours."

The dedicated Black Wasp phone pinged. It was a call from Grace, not a text.

"Angie, Grace is calling—I'll accidentally put you on speaker if you promise not to tell January."

"Not a word," she promised.

This was either urgent news, bad news, or both. Williams punched up the call.

"Are you all right?" Williams asked.

If she answered, "*I'm perfectly fine*," it meant that she was being forced to make the call.

"Admiral, I'm in my uncle's truck, driving back from Taiyuan, about a half hour from Uncle Sun in Jinzhou. Dr. Dàyóu is my passenger—he was trying to escape and had just been captured. I believe he will request asylum if we collect his wife and daughter and his son."

"The women are under house detention in Wuzhai," Williams replied, processing the information. "Where is his son?"

"In Qincheng Prison."

"Of course," Williams said. He would deal with those problems later. "Does your uncle know anything about your activities?"

"None."

"What is the pursuit status?"

"We jammed them up at the main gate but they'll be after us—jeeps, one chopper, a lot of anger."

Williams brought up the regional map on his desktop. "There's a lot of open country to cross to the border. They'd likely have it watched and mined before you can get there."

"I plan to stay with Sun and hope he'll cooperate. If not, I'll detain him."

Williams hesitated. He knew how much Grace's family meant to her. "All right. Are *you* okay?"

"Second-guessing myself, sir. I did some damage getting Dr. Dàyóu out."

Another hesitation. "Casualties?"

"Just a jeep, but there are some broken bones and a non-lethal knife wound."

"They are going to tear the province apart looking for you."

"I know, sir."

"Was your vehicle identified?"

"I don't think so. It will go in a shed."

"All right. Get to Sun's place and stay there. I'll contact the rest of the team and see what we can do about the family members."

"Thank you, sir. Sorry."

"Our business is a fluid one. You were sent to gather intel and exceeded expectations. I'm proud of you."

"Thank you," she said.

He did not tell her about the trafficked women. Breen and Rivette intended to drop them off before reaching their destination. He ended the call and picked up with Angie. "I'm back."

"Christ," was all she said. "Chase, this is not what the president wanted. He asked for surveillance."

"And what he got was the chief engineer of China's hypersonic missile project, defecting."

"At what cost?" Angie demanded.

"So far, none."

"Don't do that. Lieutenant Lee said it herself and you confirmed it. She's trying to outrun PLAA forces for assaulting Chinese soldiers and attacking a missile base."

"She did an amazing bit of soldiering."

"She sounded scared."

"I'd be scared, too," Williams said.

"You're not an American officer attached to our embassy!" Angie yelled. "If she's captured—"

"We are far from that point. Listen, I have to contact Major Breen—"

"Right. Jesus. Who is where?"

"He and Lance Corporal Rivette seized a truck in the Gobi Desert, one loaded with Chinese girls being sex-trafficked. They turned it around and are headed into China."

"Christ," she said again. "This isn't happening."

"That's what the Pakistanis in Abbottabad said when Seal Team Six flew in to neutralize Osama bin Laden. That's how special forces *work*, Angie. I've got to go. Don't do anything. Don't *say* anything. I will work this out."

"Just tell me—is this how you worked with President Midkiff? I watched you extemporize in Philadelphia to follow an evolving situation. But *this*?"

"We nearly blew a few situations all to hell, yeah. But I didn't have to operate sub rosa with that president. He understood the risk-benefit ratio."

"This one won't."

"Grace Lee has kicked a leg out from a major threat against this country. Maybe he'll understand that."

Angie Brunner swore before hanging up. Despite what he had just said, Williams did not blame Wright's chief of staff for her reaction. Williams had defended his people. He always would. But without Major Breen as a stabilizing force, Grace had attacked this mission with an unfailing, laser eye on results . . . not consequences. Williams was worried for her and he was worried about reprisals, both political and military. If the Chinese captured her, a show trial and execution would be swift. Military action against American or allied interests—most likely in South Korea or Japan—would inevitably follow.

Williams needed to get Breen there to arrange a quiet, careful exit. One that might not include the terms Dr. Dàyóu had laid out.

After checking Black Wasp's location on Pit Boss, Williams called the major.

The trip south had been a brisk but relaxing one for Breen and Rivette. Cold air poured around the bedroll in the window; the rush of wind and the hiss of the inadequate heater were almost as loud as the motorcycles had been.

Neither man felt like talking anyway. While looking for the keys to the shackles, Breen had found a map of the landmines. It was old-school, a printout and Rivette was the self-described tour guide.

"Their phones are burners," Rivette had said. "I'm guessing they don't work too reliably out here."

"True, though we'll probably get some good data from them," Breen said.

"Idiots should've put their money into hardware instead of footwear."

They crossed into China without seeing anyone but a man with a pair of oxen at a watering hole.

"I will never take a sink, any sink, for granted," Rivette remarked.

Williams' call was a surprise. The Black Wasps exchanged a look as Breen answered and Rivette muttered two words: "Dammit. Grace?"

"Yes, Chase?"

"I see you just crossed into China. I need you to head directly to Jinzhou, address—33 Tung-wo-lung-shan." He spelled it out so Breen could enter it into the GPS function; the street signs would not be in English. "With luck, Grace will be there with her Uncle Sun and Dr. Yang Dàyóu."

Rivette's mood changed. "Damn, Grace!" he said.

Breen said nothing. He knew that Williams was not done.

"She made some enemies in Taiyuan and they will be out in force. You have to get her and Dr. Dàyóu out, possibly Sun—but there's a complication."

Williams explained Yang's demands and the disposition of the three family members.

"The mother and daughter would be messy but doable, I suppose," Breen said. "But Qincheng Prison?"

"I know," the admiral said. "I don't want you going there. My advice is to get all of you back to Mongolia. I'll see if I can arrange transport out of the country."

"We've got wings," Rivette said.

"For three people," Breen pointed out.

"Right," Rivette said. "The doctor, Sun, and Grace. We'll wait for the second Odval shuttle."

"What if Dàyóu won't go?" Breen asked. "We take him

against his will, he'll complain and rightly so. We're just swapping out one incarceration scenario for another."

"I know that too," the admiral said. "Plus I've got some folks in the White House who are hang-up-the-phone unhappy with how far Black Wasp has taken this. If Grace can get the intel she was sent for and release Dàyóu, we may still accomplish the limited mission we were sent on."

"Or we can finish what the lieutenant has started," Rivette said.

"You are risking more than your lives," Williams warned. "I understand how the president does not want to create an international incident three weeks into his administration."

"Even Genghis Khan Jones knew better," Breen told his companion.

Rivette folded his arms across his chest, stared out the windshield, and shook his head disapprovingly. "Grace got us a big fish. You don't throw that back in the sea."

"You do if you've got a school of great whites rocking your boat," Williams said.

"I've swam with sharks," Rivette said. "And I'm thinking of the young women in the back. What if you do something because it's the right thing to do? You know, freedom. Justice. Major, isn't that what your whole JAG world is about?"

"It is," Breen said, "but those questions were not on Black Wasp's marching orders. Admiral, we have about four hours of driving ahead of us. Let's see where we are when we get to Jinzhou."

"Fair enough," Williams said.

He hung up, restless and unsatisfied. There had not been much else he could have said to Breen. As spelled out in the Memorandum of Understanding, the ranking active-duty officer—Major Breen—was the one who actually commanded military operations. That did not include Williams, which had been the source of whatever real conflict the team had endured.

But this situation was on Williams. Though command belonged to Major Breen, responsibility for the independent backbone and aggressive disposition of Black Wasp came from his style of command. As he considered the paths forward, that approach seemed to be writing a big, messy epitaph to his career.

CHAPTER TWENTY-EIGHT

Jinzhou, Shanxi Province, China
February 18, 11:09 P.M., CST

By the time Grace Lee pulled into Uncle Sun's shed, she was shaking.

She was physically tired; that was a significant part of her reaction. And while they had made good their escape, the distant sound of aircraft and the occasional headlights of vehicles in the rearview mirror had made the trip emotionally tense and exhausting.

That was to be expected. She had felt it all before. Since talking to Williams, doubt had been added to the mix and dragged her down. Williams' reserved, almost—what, disapproving?—tone had brought that on. She had begun the call feeling as if she had overachieved, even for her. She had spearheaded a landing yet his response had not been LSTs and troops but caution. She did not understand how she could have executed her objective so perfectly yet meet with anything less than enthusiastic support . . . and end up questioning it now.

That was new and, detached from anything familiar, it left her unsteady.

Dr. Dàyóu had sat quietly at her side. He had alternately looked out the window and sat back with his eyes shut. She could not begin to contemplate what he had been through these past few days. The only conversation they had was when Grace asked if he had a photo of his son.

"On my phone," he said. "But that . . . all of my photos are gone."

She turned off the lights and cracked the door and looked over at her passenger.

"Dr. Dàyóu, I do not know what will happen when we go inside," she confessed.

"I understand."

"If it becomes necessary, I will take you wherever you wish to go—to your home, if it pleases you."

He nodded in the darkness. Whatever turmoil he felt inside, it did not show.

She wanted to learn from that, from him.

The kitchen light was on and Sun was still awake. Grace ushered her companion in first then shut the door behind her. Her uncle was standing beside the table, in his bathrobe, a cup of tea and his cell phone beside him.

"Uncle Sun, this is the esteemed Dr. Yang Dàyóu of the launch center."

"Welcome," Sun said tentatively. "You are . . . a PLAA private?"

"The uniform is not mine," Yang remarked.

Sun noticed the awkwardly cut cuffs. "I see that now."

Grace walked forward. "Uncle, I am with American special forces. I'm sorry I could not tell you that before. My assignment was to reconnoiter at the base, but I saw an opportunity and liberated this esteemed scientist from captivity."

Sun Fenghe turned to the engineer. "Did you wish to be liberated?"

"I do not want to burden you with my problems, Uncle Sun."

"That choice appears to be no longer mine," he said, with a quick, uncritical look at Grace.

"I was falsely accused of negligence and was facing a lifetime in prison or execution. Your niece risked everything to help me."

That simple statement lifted the terrible weight from Grace's spirit. This time her uncle looked at her with approval.

"The Fenghes are a tigerish clan," Sun said. He regarded Yang. "Forgive me, would you like tea? Something to eat?"

"I would appreciate that very much." Yang smiled, nodding in appreciation as Sun indicated the only other seat at the table.

"You'll also want something less . . . *combative* to wear. Help yourself to whatever is in my closet."

"Thank you," Yang said.

Sun went to the electric teakettle and turned it on. He put biscuits on a plate and brought it to the table.

"Uncle, this is grave business," Grace said. "The military will be seeking us out—"

"I have no love for the authorities, you know that."

"There are also others coming to help us out."

"Americans?"

"Yes."

Sun considered this as he fetched a cup and filled a tea infuser. "What do you need from me?" he asked.

"I don't know. I truly don't."

"What are *your* plans?"

"Dr. Dàyóu has a wife and two children, also in captivity. I have promised to reunite the family."

"Your superiors support this?"

"My superior does. He is taking it up with President Wright's chief of staff."

"The president of America," Sun said appreciatively. "I work at the coal power station in Wuzhai, Dr. Dàyóu. I know from experience that it is useful to have support from the highest levels."

"It is indeed," the engineer said. "If I may, I'd like to accept your offer of a fresh shirt and trousers."

Sun showed him to the bedroom and left him there. When he returned, he walked straight up to Grace.

"You know this, I am sure. The men looking for the doctor are without mercy. If you are found, no one will help you. No one *can* help you. You are safe for the moment because if they knew where you were they would have taken us all by now." Sun cocked his head toward the bedroom. "He knows this too. He is thinking of his family, Grace . . . and so am I. It is unwise to do anything but leave the country as quickly as you can."

Grace looked into those eyes that were so much like those of her mother, compassionate but strong.

"I have trained for this life."

"Maybe you should pause."

"And do what? If I give up here, tell me—what about to-morrow?"

Yang reentered the room. "This is called the inflection point of threat assessment," he said. "Forgive my overhearing, it was not intentional."

"It's all right," Grace said. "I welcome insight."

Yang approached wearing a gray sweat suit. He nodded in thanks to Sun as he approached Grace. "I made compromises in my work that I knew were wrong. It doesn't matter that I was ordered to—I knew better. I did them to protect myself from dismissal. So doing, I caused something much worse." He smiled thinly. "I took the safe path instead of the right path. It was a mistake."

Sun shook his head. "It's easy to tell the difference looking back, Dr. Dàyóu."

"No, Uncle," Grace said. "I know the difference *now*. That's why I asked about tomorrow. I can't *not* try, every day. I can't live being afraid."

Sun sighed. "Your mother was highly competitive too—if not with others then with herself. She had to bicycle farther, grow more lettuce than the year before, her cat had to catch more mice even if she had to help."

Grace smiled. "I didn't know that."

"She had confidence," Sun said, balling his fist and shaking it. "I sought clarity before charging in."

"Your protests against the Greenbelt?"

"What Dr. Dàyóu said. The situation reached an inflection point." Sun sighed again. "These friends—when are they coming?"

"Not for several hours," Grace told him.

Sun turned to the engineer. "You may use the sofa, I'll get a pillow and cover. I suggest we sleep while we can."

"I'll have the tea you graciously prepared, first," the engineer said.

"Of course."

"Uncle?" Grace said. "I don't want you—"

He stopped her with a hand. "Later, when I have clarity. Or, at least, more than I have now."

Sun shuffled off to his bedroom and Grace followed into the cluttered alcove. Yang stopped her with a gentle touch on her arm.

"Thank you. I am sorry for the unrest this is causing."

"Don't be, sir. You and Uncle Sun have shared something I seek above all—wisdom. It's up to me to sort it out."

"Before you put yourself or your comrades in further jeopardy, I must repeat what I said earlier. I will not compound my errors of judgment with treason. If you act, you act for humanitarian reasons only."

The reminder was sobering if not surprising. She said nothing.

Yang patted her arm, went to the small, rickety table, and sat alone to eat his modest snack.

The journey took longer than Hamilton Breen had anticipated. The Gobi assumed its better-known profile as sandy desert, and traction was frequently spotty. For the most part he drove without headlights, except where the ground sloped and was rutted with runoff. Driving by the light of the gibbous moon impeded progress. He was also not as attentive to the terrain as he should have been. His mind was like a corkboard with papers tacked to it and threads running from one option to another, crisscrossing in every variation he could think of.

The situation was a mess without any good options.

The delay did not come from the major being distracted but from Chingmy banging on the back of the cab with one of the discarded manacles. Breen stopped and felt his way along the truck to the back.

Chingmy poked out her head.

"Toilet. Hungry."

"Of course," the major said.

He called to Rivette and the two watched northeast and southwest while the women moved among the dunes. The Altai Mountains loomed in the distance, magnificent and eternal. Breen could not help but think of how many temporal human struggles the peaks had witnessed and wondered what the mute opinions of these stoic judges would have been.

Nothing good, he suspected.

When the women were finished, Rivette gathered the rest of the power bars from the motorcycles and passed them out before they resumed their journey. Coatless, with a heater that struggled, sputtered, and finally died, Rivette curled into an upright ball and tried to picture the sunny beaches of San Pedro.

He managed to sleep, the cold and bumpy ride overwhelmed by his need for rest.

It was just before 4:00 A.M. when, after refueling, the truck rolled through the outskirts of Jinzhou. It was still dark and he pulled up in a dark alley between an old restaurant and a new office tower. Breen gave Chingmy three thousand Chinese yuan, nearly five hundred American dollars.

The women were overwhelmed by his kindness and Chingmy hugged both men in turn. Then, following the direction of one of their number, a Jinzhou native, they set out for the nearest railway station of the Liaozhongnan Metropolitan Region.

"God bless America," was all Rivette could think to say.

Reaching civilization did not quicken the pace significantly. The speed limit was forty km/h on China National Highways—just twenty-five mph—and Breen obeyed every caution graphic they encountered, from turns to construction work.

It was nearly dawn when Breen pulled up to the cottage of Sun Fenghe. The arrival of the truck had wakened Grace and she met them outside. Rivette met her with a crisp salute and a smile that, for a moment, seemed to fix her world.

She, in turn, saluted Breen, who was less salutatory. The lieutenant walked the men to the shed so as not to wake the others. They stepped inside and she shut the unevenly hung door. Orange sun peeked through the slats as they stood in the narrow space between the wall and the truck.

"How are you?" Breen asked.

"All right. I don't think we drilled for this scenario, sir," Grace said apologetically.

"Tactics aren't what concern me right now," Breen told her. "We have no support from anyone beyond the admiral."

"Did we expect that from the new administration?" Grace asked.

"Actually, yes. For a limited action. We are way beyond that now."

"I'm sorry," Grace said.

"You shouldn't be," Rivette said. "You saw your shot, you took it."

Breen was about to say that was not her call, that Black Wasp had grown insubordinate. But from the time Williams had executed Ahmed Salehi on their first mission, that had been their unorthodox, frequently lawless way.

"It was more than just an opportunity," Grace said.

"Explain," Breen said.

"This is my ancestral home. I felt connected from the moment I got here. America is my country but I couldn't just walk away from what was happening to Dr. Dàyóu."

"Like we didn't with those trafficked ladies, and we're not Chinese," Rivette added.

"The women were an unanticipated consequence of our mission," Breen said.

"So was this," Grace said. "I didn't want to walk away but I was prepared to when I didn't know, for sure, who was being held at gunpoint. I remember thinking, 'They wanted intel— here it is, and more.'"

"And you acted," Breen said. "I understand that but where we are now—it's not just about your life or the Dàyóus. We've created an international tinderbox and are deep in the middle of it! Fixing that has to be our top priority."

"Sometimes the best way out of something is not backing up but going through it," Grace said.

Breen shook his head. "We need an exit strategy, not aphorisms."

"I say we finish what we started," Rivette said.

"You didn't hear me," Breen said. "One wrong step and this blows up."

"Then what do you suggest, sir?" Rivette asked. "Should we get back in the truck, turn tail for Mongolia, and fly home? Do we give Dàyóu back?"

"I'm considering that."

"Well then, consider this, sir," Rivette said. "I believe that would be the last thing Black Wasp does, ever, period. Even if the president doesn't shut us down, our spirit will be shot."

Breen suspected that the end of Black Wasp was inevitable and for the members themselves there would likely be court-martials at worst, dishonorable discharges at best.

Still, the words echoed in his mind: *What do you suggest, sir?*

His legal mind strongly advocated rolling back the error as much as possible, pushing forward the success of having stopped the traffickers, and throwing themselves on the mercy of the president. Yet if this *were* the end of Black Wasp, what kind of epitaph did he want to write?

Should it be a legal summation or a moral one?

"I want to go inside and check the Project Blackjack images, see if the computer can pick up a pattern in the pursuit," Breen said. "I also want to see what's happening on his end. Does Uncle Sun have any caffeine in the house?"

"Tea," Grace said.

"I was afraid of that. Okay. Let's revisit this in an hour."

"The door's unlocked," Grace said.

Breen thanked her and went inside, leaving Rivette and Grace in the shed.

The two stood shivering in the cold semidarkness.

"We've got two motorcycles in the back of the truck," Rivette said. "Crossed half the desert on them."

Grace knew from the way he said it: We can outrun the truck. "That would get us to Wuzhai and Beijing," she said. "Then what?"

He laughed. "Are you seriously thinking we'll get out of those places alive?"

The lieutenant smiled. "It's been that kind of a mission, hasn't it?"

"We rode here with stoves. I didn't think it was going to be normal."

"What is 'normal' for Black Wasp?" Grace looked at her teammate. "You lose your coat?"

"Gave it to someone who needed it more."

"You're a good person, Jaz."

"Sometimes yes, sometimes no. At this moment I'm feeling 'no.'"

"Meaning?"

The lance corporal was silent for a moment. "Y'know, I feel like I'm in one of those World War II movies hiding from the Nazis. Except I'm hiding from my own people."

"Meaning?" she pressed.

"I can't do what the major asked. The mission has expanded. Our missions tend to do that, from the time we parachuted into Trinidad looking for a terrorist who we ended up catching in Yemen. If we start picking what is safe, what is not safe, then it's not only Black Wasp that is finished. We are. Walking away is not what we do."

"Following orders?" she asked. "Do we do that?"

"I didn't hear any," the lance corporal answered. "Not yet."

Grace considered the loophole. Then she took in the larger issue. This was not even about self-respect or honor, as Rivette had implied. The question was one she had faced since entering martial arts, one of the few girls in her school and smaller than the shortest boy: *are you good enough?*

Kung fu did not recognize limitations. One of her bibles, *The Nei Gong Zhen Chuan, The Authentic Classic of Internal Practice,* laid out the path to dragonhood and the ability to soar.

Either she believed in the arts, and herself, or she did not. Earlier that evening, she had. Nothing had changed. Major Breen had fretted over them being caught, but what was new in that? It was a risk all special ops took.

"There's something else," Rivette said, his expression pensive.

"What's that?"

He grinned. "The truck heater died and the driver's-side window is busted. Gonna be damn cold."

Grace nodded contemplatively. "Then we better be done before the sun goes down. You have your Blackjack phone?"

"In the cab with my other tools. You?"

She patted her heart.

The lance corporal raised his fist, Grace bumped it, and the two left the shed.

CHAPTER TWENTY-NINE

Jinzhou, Shanxi Province, China
February 19, 4:55 A.M., CST

Hamilton Breen was sitting alone at the kitchen table when he heard the truck growl to life. The fuzziness that had settled upon him after the long, unbroken journey dispelled in an instant.

Sun had made introductions in pantomime, since neither he nor Yang spoke English, and Breen's Chinese was tour-guide rudimentary. Tired and hungry, he accepted the plate of biscuits Sun offered as he sat at the kitchen table to call Williams.

He was still giving his progress report when Sun rushed to the door. He motioned Yang back as he opened it, allowing the dawn to push over the threshold. Their host just stood there, watching and shaking his head.

"They're gone," the major said into the phone. "The rest of Black Wasp just drove away. Goddammit. They couldn't even give me the hour I asked for. A freakin' hour."

"You sound surprised."

"Disappointed."

"Where do you think they'll go?"

"They took the truck Rivette and I seized in the desert. There are two motorcycles in the back."

"Motorized infantry," Williams said.

"Stupid," Breen said, angry after the admiral had said that. Common Article 2 of the Geneva Conventions made a distinction between spying and espionage, and invasion, pertaining to international conflicts. Technically, Black Wasp had just crossed the line.

"Guns?" Williams asked.

"He's got them."

"If you order them back, will they come?"

"I don't believe they will," Breen said. He thought for a moment. "And there's one more thing. If I do order them back, this is on them."

"If not, it's on you," Williams pointed out.

"I'm aware of that."

"All right, we can worry about the legal fallout later. I suggest you find a way to get Yang out of China. We may need a high-value hostage to swap if Black Wasp is taken. Will he go?"

"I don't know and my Mandarin is limited to hello, goodbye, and thank you. I'll figure that out. What about you? You going to tell January about this?"

"Negative," Williams said. "Frankly, I don't trust her not to tell the Chinese there are two rogue agents on the way."

"That's strong."

"Realistic," Williams disagreed. "January's against this,

against us, and she has the Pacific Shield Resolution for cover and precedent. Morality doesn't enter into it."

The admiral was referring to a presidential directive issued the previous year when a live Tomahawk went off course and U.S. Pacific Command let Beijing know.

"Sad times when it's a bigger job protecting them from our people than from the Chinese."

Breen said he would communicate with Yang and Sun and see what could be done. From what Grace had told the admiral, Sun had a truck and—it seemed—the Chinese had not identified it. That was where he would start.

After calling the two men into the kitchen, Breen used maps, gestures, and pointing to try to communicate what he wanted. There was frequent discussion between Yang and Sun and, in a relatively short span of ten minutes, Breen believed he had transmitted his wishes to the two. The major was accustomed to reading expressions in court and depositions; he was relying on that skill now to gauge the men's reactions.

They seemed, in the end, to understand. Then it was Sun's turn to communicate. He seemed to agree that Yang—and he—would be willing to cross the border into Mongolia but, using a palm pressed firmly on the map, they would go no farther until the rest of the Dàyóu family was present. It was not an unreasonable request. Sun also indicated that he would drive and would remain until the matter was settled.

Breen was happy to let Uncle Sun drive. He needed to close his eyes, even if it was in the back of a truck.

Sun made a phone call. From the coughing and moaning, Breen assumed he was calling in sick. Then, resuming his previous vitality, Sun packed the last of the biscuits and nuts he kept for snacks. He also furnished Breen with a winter coat and Yang with a heavy sweater, gloves, and wool cap. When everything was ready, he went outside to get the truck from the shed.

Just as a white car with red lettering on the side pulled up.

It was the Jinzhou police.

There was a surging energy in the cab of the traffickers' truck, the same kind of fire Grace and Rivette had shared charging across Marion Island, South Africa, to free the Point Dunkel bunker from the Chinese.

Rivette wasted no time bringing up a dossier on Qincheng Prison. He described the layout, known locations of the guards, and the fact that there had been no escapes since it opened in 1958.

"Where the Dàyóus are, that's country. It's a little community with—according to this map—a post office and a public toilet. That's it. But the jail is hard-core, Lieutenant. There are five thousand guards."

"I'll think of something. The important thing—and you have to communicate this to Dr. Dàyóu—is that I tried. He has to know that."

"You think that'll make him smack palm to forehead and say, 'Man, I've got to tell the DoD every damn thing I know!' Uh-uh. If his kid doesn't get out, I'm guessing the Dàyóu parents will come back and trade themselves for him. I don't think the president will be real happy with just Wen and Ushi."

"Then I guess I have to get Wen and me out."

Rivette slumped in his seat as he studied the layout. "Penn and Teller couldn't get out of there."

"They aren't Chinese," she said.

The remark had the quality of whistling past a graveyard. Grace was beginning to realize the odds and questioning how much of this was determination and how much was obstinacy. Beyond those driving forces, she had one moving in the opposite direction: a growing sense of foreboding that this might be as reckless as Rivette had said.

Not that it mattered, she told herself. As one of her teachers had said after she had won her first competition, *"Your feet are set on a path they must follow."*

Grace had programmed the GPS for Wuzhai and 714 County Road. The numeric designation was the road, not the home; she did not have a number for the Dàyóu residence but expected there would be official cars parked there. That trip would take only about ninety minutes. Beijing would take nearly four hours more.

They would both go to the Dàyóu home. Together, they would secure the release of the two women, after which Rivette would head for Mongolia. The prison was a different matter. The lance corporal did not speak the language and drawing a gun in a fortress with that many guards would only get him killed. Grace would head to Beijing alone, by motorcycle.

There were two ways she knew she could get in. One was to inform officials that she has information concerning the abduction of Dr. Yang Dàyóu from the Taiyuan launch facility. The fact that she knew about the incident was sure to get her inside. Deep inside.

The other would not likely get her very far into the facility, but it was safer. Dr. Dàyóu had said his son attended the UIBE. He would have had friends, roommates. Perhaps she could persuade one of them to give her something of his to bring to the prison. A book, a sweater. The request would be denied, of course, but that was not the reason for going. The Chinese would be suspicious of any callers and would want to talk to her.

There was time to consider those options. First, they had a date in Wuzhai.

By his crude reckoning, Wen Dàyóu had been a prisoner for a little over two days. It was difficult to tell by the nature of the dull winter light in his cell; it was impossible to tell by the times he had slept. Rest was impossible in Qincheng. If actual noises did not keep a prisoner awake—even simple ones, like the banging of a cell door or the screams of a man who had simply had enough of captivity—then the anticipation of sound had him restless, always anticipating.

And then there were the actual visits.

Wen had been put through two interrogations. But the arrival of the guard in the newly lifted darkness was different from the previous "collections," as he had come to think of them: as in trash pickups, the grabbing of a bundle that was once a man to haul him away. Wen did too much thinking here, talking silently to some faceless enemy; talking quietly to his mother and father, hoping they were well and trying to *think* thoughts into their heads.

I love you. I hope you can be happy. I'm sorry for the cost of my newfound wisdom.

This time the guard entered and, instead of summoning the young man with a sharp word and a push, he grabbed Wen by the arm and yanked him from the cot where he had been watching dust float in the shaft of light overhead.

"I'm coming—" Wen began, stopping as the guard's baton snapped hard against the small of his back. The young man doubled over backwards, his mouth torn wide in a silent scream, the sting having run up his back and robbing him of his voice. The blow was so perfectly placed that Wen's legs did not go out from under him. He was pulled through the door, still bent with his tortured face toward heaven like a fallen angel.

"God help me!" he wheezed, unsure whether the prayer was spoken or merely thought.

As throbbing pain replaced the stinging shock, Wen's legs finally turned to water and he fell forward. Another guard arrived and the young man was dragged by his wrists, facedown, his nose and chin rubbed raw until he managed to turn to his right cheek.

The trip to the interrogation room was mercifully brief. His face burning, his lower back swollen, he was dropped onto a wooden chair. Just that contact with a hard surface caused him to scream out and arch his shoulders over the top of the backrest.

Through watery eyes he saw the smeared features of General Chang looming over him.

"Who are the friends and confederates of your father?" the officer demanded.

"Friends—?"

Chang drew back an arm and slapped the young man hard on his bleeding cheek. Wen shrieked.

"I want names. Now!"

"I . . . don't . . ."

Another slap, another scream, and the question was repeated. Wen was crying, saliva or blood—maybe both—running over his lower lip.

"*You* have friends. The photographer Jiang Yiwu Dan and her husband, Chao Dan. They have cooperated. They will soon go free. You can join them."

"General . . . I swear . . . I have no names to give."

Chang grabbed the boy under the chin, wrapped tight fingers around his throat. "Answer me, boy, or I will have your mother and sister in this seat with questioning far more unpleasant!"

"I swear—" he wheezed.

"*Who* has been at your home? *Who* knew where your father worked? You are his son. You took trips with him!"

The young man gagged and Chang released him.

"Those trips . . . ," Wen gasped. "Not . . . for . . . years . . ."

"When you traveled, what women did he see? What mistress did he have?"

The question was so remarkable that Wen laughed. The laugher helped to cut through his agony.

"My father . . . was loyal . . . ," he said, spitting blood. "He was devoted to . . . China . . . and my mother . . . and to God. In that . . . order."

The general looked down, sneering. "You filth. You lie."

Chang's next blow was more from frustration and rage than to solicit information. The general's fist plowed solidly into Wen's mouth, dislodging teeth and cracking bone and snapping the young man's head back. Chang was talking again but the words were a dreamy, echoing blur. Wen's eyes were open, looking up at the bulb in the overhead light. The yellow-white glow invested him with a calm he had not felt since he was in his bed at the dormitory, reading and contemplating the future and thinking about his day and not his life.

He felt himself being moved and was suddenly reclining and there were fingers in his throat and a raw pain below that.

And then there was darkness.

CHAPTER THIRTY

Jinzhou, Shanxi Province, China
February 19, 5:24 A.M., CST

Sun Fenghe went to the door before the police reached it. He did not open until his two guests had moved quietly but swiftly into the bedroom. They could not be seen from the street; if the officers insisted on entering, these were the last moments of freedom Sun would ever know.

His gut burned. He was glad it had only a few almonds to push back up his throat.

Sun looked out at the road as he waited, saw another official car zip by. Then his eyes returned to the uncommonly grim faces of the two uniformed men who approached. Their shoulder patches said that they were not part of the local People's Armed Police but were Border Defense Corps, based in Jinzhou but provincial. The stars on their uniforms identified them as a first and second lieutenant.

"Good morning, *Wu Jing Zhong Wei*," Sun addressed the senior officer. Then he pleasantly regarded the other. *"Wu Jing Shao Wei."*

The men nodded.

"Mr. Sun Fenghe?" the first lieutenant read from a tablet he carried.

"That is correct. Excuse me, but it's cold. Would you like to come in?"

"This is fine," the man replied. "A truck was spotted in this vicinity at sunrise. It had a pale brown canvas back, the driver's-side window was broken and covered over, and it was seen depositing a group of young women near the train station." The officer looked up. "Did you see such a vehicle?"

"No, sir. I was just getting up then."

"You heard nothing? More recently—within the last thirty minutes—it was seen on this street."

Sun smiled. "So much traffic goes by on its way to the local stands."

"Those carry vegetables and meats. We believe this carried the young women."

Sun found himself asking, "Do you seek the owners or do the owners seek the ladies?"

The officer's expression soured. "Explain yourself, Fenghe."

"I have lived here all my life. In the last few years smugglers of goods and human beings have operated openly between here and the border. Operated in *both* directions. Had I seen such a truck then, on my oath, I would have been the one calling you, not the other way round."

Whether the officer had been exposed as one of those border agents who was complicit in the trade, or whether he was here in support of the law, the man backed down.

"Thank you for your support, citizen Fenghe," he said. "If you see this vehicle, you will report it."

"Of course."

Touching the brim of his cap, the officer turned and the two men got back into their car. Sun watched until they were gone. Then he shivered.

"Sun Fenghe," he said, "next time, you visit your niece in America."

He did not fetch the others until the car had gone away. Then he went to the bedroom where Yang and Major Breen stood stiff and alert like the terra-cotta army of Emperor Qin Shi Huang.

"We are safe," he said to Yang. He looked at the tense American, nodded, smiled, and then motioned to them both. "Let's have some tea until the investigation passes by and then leave this place."

Breen sent a text and then followed the other to the kitchen. Sun had explained as best as possible about the truck. If the American did not quite grasp the entirety of the situation, he would understand why leaving now might seem suspect, as though they were running.

The police visit set them back a quarter hour, and the additional delay of a quick breakfast was fine with Sun. It gave time for more than trucks to begin crowding the roads, providing anonymity and some measure of security.

Grace and Rivette were on the moderately populated China National Highway 108 with mostly trucks and buses around them. Rivette was at the wheel of the truck, guiding it along the spacious, modern roadway. Behind her reduced-glare sunglasses

Grace was drowsing in the passenger's seat. She was sorry she had not been able to bring her military-issue glasses, which also boosted color and contrast, but their distinctive delta wing wraparound might have given her away. She was instantly present and alert when the text notification chimed.

"It's Major Breen," Grace said. "We have to get off the road now. Something about the girls you freed IDing the truck to police."

Rivette maneuvered quickly to try to make an upcoming exit, then saw a sign with a graphic for a low overpass. He swerved back onto the highway, slowing as Grace waved apologies to drivers who had to brake behind them. The next off-ramp was two miles away. Rivette fought the urge to pass his way swiftly around intervening traffic, reminding himself that this was not the 405 and the penalty for speeding would be more severe than losing his license.

"I guess that's on us, the thing with the women," Rivette said.

"Why?"

"Thirteen young ladies looking confused, buying train tickets? Yeah, why would *that* attract attention?"

"What else were you going to do?" Grace asked.

"I don't know," he admitted. "I wonder if the police are after the traffickers or the guys who stole their truck."

Now that they were alerted, Grace watched out for police cars—in case they had to abandon the truck on the highway. She also began to consider the impact giving up the truck would have on the rest of the plan.

"How are we going to get the Dàyóus to safety?" she asked. "We can't very well take whatever car they have. The police will be watching for it."

"Finding transportation has never been a problem for me," he replied.

"Okay, then here's another problem," Grace said. "I've never driven a motorcycle."

Rivette made a face. "You're from New York! I thought you guys did everything."

"I know how to drive—a car. I mostly took Citi Bikes."

"Man, I learned on a stolen CHiPS ride. Next time I hear someone knock street learning, I will tell them your sad story." Rivette considered the problem. "I guess you'll have to wear my backpack and ride caboose with me."

The lance corporal did not like the idea that one bullet could take them both down but decided not to mention it. The discussion ended just as they reached the next exit, roughly twenty miles from their destination. There was no one behind them and Rivette paused at the bottom.

"The Fen River," Grace said, reading the sign at the end and the one below it. "The Waterway Industrial Park is on the other side. Let's go there, leave the truck near some shipping dock."

Rivette turned off the exit ramp and spotted a latticed steel bridge a quarter mile ahead. Crossing, he followed a curving road around to a series of dumpsters in the back.

"What do you think?" he asked.

She looked around. "It'll stand out here. We should park with other trucks."

Rivette drove to a loading area as if he belonged. The nearest platform was about thirty yards away.

"You take the backpack and stay visible out front while I get the bikes down," he said. "I'll feel better if anyone looks over and sees a face that looks like it belongs here."

"That wouldn't be the face of a woman," she pointed out.

"It looks more local than I do," he replied.

While Grace checked her phone for off-highway directions, Rivette pulled up his collar and slid from the cab. He slouched as he made his way to the back of the truck, as much to stay warm as to conceal his features. He flipped over the metal ramp and walked out the bike he had been riding in the Gobi Desert. It still had dried, dead grass stuck to the exhaust and both fenders; that crossing seemed more distant from the present than just a day.

He whistled and Grace strode back. Rivette was already on the motorcycle when she arrived. He held her up a moment to tuck his semiautomatic in his jacket. Slipping the backpack on with the M4 assault carbine inside, Grace held tight to her companion.

"You good?" Rivette asked over his shoulder.

"Good enough," she replied. "Are you going to button up the back of the truck?"

"Why waste the time?" he asked. "Someone calls this in, the police are going to know it's the one they're looking for."

The lance corporal started the engine and headed back toward the bridge. Two minutes later they were following the river on the way to Wuzhai.

CHAPTER THIRTY-ONE

Wuzhai, China
February 19, 7:00 A.M. CST

With his right hand bandaged where it had been kicked—powerfully, concisely, and with fury that still blazed in his memory—Lieutenant Colonel Tang Kun stood with the butt of a Type 77 semiautomatic resting in his badly bruised palm. The weapon was pointed at two women who were seated side by side and holding hands on a sofa before him: Dongling and Ushi Dàyóu.

In his left hand was a walkie-talkie. Like the gun, it was the same one he had been holding in Taiyuan. His arm was stiff at his side, his thumb poised above the TALK button.

The officer had barely moved since arriving nearly an hour before. That was not patience; it was fear of what he would do to the women if he lost control. General Chang had not only vowed to find and personally execute whomever had attacked his base, but he swore he would break Kun if the lone attacker got away with his prisoner, the traitor Yang Dàyóu.

The lieutenant colonel shared the general's outrage, if not his power to inflict retribution. The officer shared the general's belief in this much as well: someone would come for the rest of Dàyóu's family.

Someone will come, Kun kept telling himself, keeping his hate vivid, his purpose true.

There were four PLAA troopers outside the house, patrolling the grounds. Kun had not wanted more than that. Over seventy soldiers from the Taiyuan Satellite Launch Center were seeking the escapees with assistance from local police and aerial support from their helicopter detachments. The enemy would not, could not, move in large numbers. When the one or two radicals or foreign agents or whoever they were came here, Kun wanted to draw them in, make them feel as if there were a chance of freeing the two women.

Someone will come.

Kun hoped it was that woman, the small Asian who had cut through them like they were dumb, helpless things. He would not fall to her a second time.

His grip on the semiautomatic caused Kun's injured hand to ache. It pulsed like a second heart, also cold and resolute.

This time he would kill a Dàyóu without hesitation.

"Stop," Grace said in Rivette's ear.

The lance corporal throttled down as she pointed ahead to a turnoff from the two-lane road they were on. Rivette could not read the sign but he saw the numerals that indicated this was 714 County Road. It was a flat country road with small fields on either side. It curved between low hills ahead. The terrain blocked the view of the small community on the other side.

Rivette pulled onto the road and stopped. He dragged a sleeve hard and slow across his mouth, wiping away grit before he licked his wind-dried lips. "How far to the house?"

Grace was studying her phone. Pit Boss had pinpointed them on the GPS; she switched to the Blackjack view to see the homes in real time. She stopped at the one with four figures and two military vehicles blocking two civilian cars in the driveway.

"It's just under a quarter mile."

She passed the phone to Rivette. "Four-corner deployment," he said. "Plus whoever's inside."

Grace heard a car coming along the main road. "We've got no cover here," she said, getting off the motorcycle. "You should pull it—"

"No, stay," he said. "We need the bike."

"For what? We're not using it to get away."

"No," Rivette agreed. "I'm thinking we use it to get in."

The sputtering approach of the KTM 450 EXC snapped Kun's eyes toward the bay window behind his prisoners. The lieutenant colonel was instantly on high alert.

He raised the radio at his lips. "Hold your positions, protect your perimeter. This could be a distraction. Song, what do you see?"

"Nothing yet, sir."

The road turned past several homes to this one. There were spacious yards and a clear view of whoever was coming. The soldier watched and Kun watched the soldier.

"Does anyone on this road own a motorbike?" Kun asked the women.

The Dàyóu women straightened a little, expectantly. Their captor had obviously not been expecting anyone.

Fearing that silence would provoke the officer, Ushi answered, "The Chunlan boys have a scooter."

"That is not a scooter."

"It could be a delivery," Dongling offered.

Kun had no patience for speculation. "Get up," he told them. "Go to the window with your backs to it."

Still holding hands, the mother and daughter rose and went to the window. Kun stepped behind them. He wanted to have a better view but his uniform made him a first-strike target.

The sound grew louder and the cough of the engine became more pronounced. As the motorcycle finally appeared around the turn in the road, Kun saw a lone passenger struggling with the vehicle. It was a woman.

A woman whose clothes he recognized.

"It's her, the one who took Yang Dàyóu," he said into the radio. "Do *not* allow her near the house. Zhu, come forward a little to the front of the house, give Song cover. Let the woman come as far as the driveway. If she comes farther, terminate her."

The soldier at the eastern side of the house, to Kun's right, took up his position. He shouldered his CS/LR17 SCAR.

The new arrival drove for a few yards more, to within twenty feet of the driveway, before stopping, dismounting, and letting the bike drop in disgust. She raised her arms and walked forward.

"Stop there!" Song shouted.

The woman obeyed. Her eyes moved from the soldier to the women in the window—and the figure using them as shields. She shouted back, "I want to talk to whoever is in charge here!"

Kun said to Dongling, "Break the window."

The woman looked to the sides. There was a ceramic flowerpot on an iron table, the leaves of the braided bamboo bright with sun.

"Now!" Kun yelled. "Or I will push your daughter's head through the panes!"

Dongling reached over, hoisted it in both arms, and heaved it through the glass. The pot crashed on the slate walk outside, shards of falling glass shattering as they fell around it.

"Talk!" Kun shouted back. "Start by telling me where you have Yang Dàyóu!"

"Let the women go and I'll tell you!"

"Tell me or they will die before you do!"

A pistol shot cracked from the west side of the house. Kun turned toward it as, several seconds later, more shots were discharged—rifle fire.

His men.

Enraged, the lieutenant colonel dropped his radio, grabbed Dongling by the hair, and pressed his semiautomatic to the base of her skull.

"Your confederate has failed!" he shouted out the window.

"If there is one more shot, this woman dies! Move one step and *you* die!"

In the ensuing silence, Kun heard moans coming from around the back. He heard the click of a door latch. The lieutenant colonel roughly swung the frightened Dongling around, elbowing Ushi aside when the teenager reached to help her mother. The officer looked into the room.

A man was staring down the iron sight of a CS/LR17 SCAR. It was one of Kun's rifles but it was not one of Kun's men.

The regular troops had reacted as Rivette had expected regular troops would.

The lance corporal had entrusted the motorcycle to the incapable hands of Grace so she could make her uncertain entrance and keep the men distracted. While she did that, Rivette made his way around the backs of the other houses to the Dàyóu residence. The lance corporal neutralized the guard on the west side with a shoulder wound, then ran forward to secure that man's weapon. As Rivette had expected, the soldier stationed out back came around cautiously to investigate. That gave the lance corporal time to go belly-down and drop him with a hip shot from the Chinese weapon.

The familiar sound of the rifle did what it was supposed to do: it made Kun think his team was on top of things, giving Rivette time to enter the house.

Now he was staring into a face of naked hate. Beyond him, Rivette saw Grace and one of the two soldiers who had a rifle trained on her. But his main focus was on the lieutenant colonel.

He was waiting for a tell, a sign that the man was about to fire. Rivette suspected that it would come from the injured hand, the one that would take a little bit of a jump-start to use—

The knuckles moved under the tight bandage.

Rivette made his move.

The lance corporal had drilled for this, repeatedly. Shoot, shoot, move, shoot. Shoot, move, shoot, shoot. Shoot, move, shoot, move, shoot. It was fluid second nature, like Grace with whatever animal form she drew on.

For better or worse, this was what Jaz Rivette trained for, lived for.

Grace had trained with him. Her skills had a range of a few yards. Rivette had a considerably longer reach and she had become adept at watching him, knowing when to move or duck.

Rivette fired a burst at Kun, near enough to his left ear to take most of it off and cause him to jerk in that direction. His pistol moved with him, discharging well to the side of Dongling. When the lieutenant colonel went down, so did Grace, vaulting behind the motorcycle to avoid the twin bursts from the guards. They fired high and it was the only chance they had before Rivette took them both down, in turn, from the near side to the far side.

None of them had been a kill shot.

Rivette kicked the radio a distance from the fallen lieutenant colonel. It would take a while for Kun to reach it and summon help; that was more of a chance than the man had been prepared to give Dongling.

"He'll tell them which car you took," Grace pointed out. "They'll know what to look for."

"I don't do that they bleed to death. Which is it?"

Before Rivette could decide, Dongling went over and drove a heel into the walkie-talkie.

Grace nodded approvingly. "It's that," she said, then looked outside. "Which car are you going to take?"

"The big boy's staff car," Rivette answered. "I do not intend to do the speed limit and I do not want to be stopped. Windows are real dark-tinted; so as long as I don't have to roll them down I'm okay."

Grace went over to Dongling, who stood hugging her daughter. "I'm sorry for all of this."

"Who are you?"

"We are with American special forces. I secured the release of your husband from the launch center. He is with my commander on the way to the Mongolian border. My teammate, Lance Corporal Rivette, will take you to him."

"Our son, Wen—" she began.

"I know. I'm going down there now. I'm going to try my best to get him out."

"I don't know how," the woman said, fighting tears.

Grace smiled encouragingly. "Neither do I. But I've got time to figure that out. The lance corporal is going to take the staff car. May I take yours?"

"Take mine," Ushi said. "It is a Geometry A, very new and quiet. It has GPS and the battery is fully charged."

"Thank you," the lieutenant said. "I accept your offer."

It also occurred to her that if the police were alerted they would be looking for Dongling's vehicle.

"May we collect a few keepsakes?" Dongling asked. "I—I do not think we will be coming back here."

"Of course, but quickly," Grace said. "The neighbors would have heard the shots."

"They are older and hard of hearing," Dongling said, "but we will hurry."

"One thing," Grace added. "If you wouldn't mind—a coat? These clothes have been seen by a number of soldiers."

Dongling nodded graciously and the women hustled off to their respective rooms. Grace went to the front door. She looked out at the fallen soldiers there.

"We should bring those two out back. Even if the neighbors didn't hear, someone may drive by."

"Good point."

They dragged the men to where their companions lay out back.

There was a shoulder injury and a more serious thigh shot that was bleeding heavily. Grace ran to the kitchen and grabbed one of Dongling's aprons. She used it to tie off the man's femoral artery.

"We need help!" implored the first man who had fallen.

Grace looked over. She was alarmed to see that it was the more aggressive of the two men she had met at Ho's Market. It took a moment but he recognized her as well. No words he might have uttered could match the look of confusion and disappointment on his face.

"I'm sorry," Grace said. "There's nothing we can do except leave you out here. The cold will slow the bleeding." She collected the rest of the radios. "All you need to do is get to these and hope that someone is within range. I'll leave them in the kitchen."

The lieutenant did not like how hard she had sounded and the inhumanity of her actions; there was no other word for it. But she and Rivette could not afford to allow these men to sound an alarm.

She turned and went back inside where Dongling and Ushi were waiting with Rivette.

"You sure about what you're doing?" the lance corporal asked his teammate.

"About going to Beijing, yes," she said. "I'm looking at it as a reconnoiter and will make a judgment based on what I find."

"You'll stand down if things get too hot?"

She did not immediately answer.

"Lieutenant?" Rivette asked.

"My fallback position is the embassy," she said. "That's probably where I'll head if I can get to Wen."

Dongling perked when she heard her son's name. Grace smiled at her.

"I've got some reservations, but I always do," Rivette said. "I know you can take care of yourself and won't do anything nuts . . . a second time."

"You mean like trusting you to take out two men who have rifles trained on me?"

"Nah, that was a sure bet."

Grace turned from Rivette to the women. Dongling handed over her long, hooded puffer coat and Ushi gave Grace the keys to her car.

"Thank you for everything you've done," the teenager said.

"It's been an honor to get to know you all," Grace said. "Remember me to your father."

"You will see him later, yes?"

Grace smiled. "I hope so."

Dongling wiped away tears when Grace left. Rivette gave Grace a thumbs-up as she walked out the door. Before following her, he sent a text to Williams:

The women are safe. Grace on way to the prison.

He almost added ". . . I wish she wasn't" but left it at that as he walked the women out to the PLAA staff car. He resisted the urge to text Grace and say, "Let's call it a day." He held back because he knew she would not listen.

With a sense of dread, he watched Ushi's Geometry A disappear around the curve.

CHAPTER THIRTY-TWO

Off The Record Restaurant, Washington, D.C.
February 18, 7:28 P.M.

"It took a drink to get me back to the White House," Matt Berry said. "It's not enough."

He and Chase Williams sat at a small, dark table in the back of the restaurant at 800 16th Street NW. Located off Lafayette Square, the eatery was "in spitting distance to the White House," as Berry often said, "and how many times did we feel like doing just that?" When he had been deputy chief of staff, Berry had come here to eavesdrop to the fullest extent of his hearing. Now, with new staffers from the new administration, and fresh priorities for himself, he did not seem to care.

Williams wished he had that luxury.

It was Berry who had suggested this get-together, knowing that this had been a difficult couple of days for his friend, not just because he had stayed behind on a mission, but he had stayed behind because of January Dow, who still was not satisfied.

"So how're you going to fix this?" Berry asked as he thanked the waiter for his second apricot sour.

"Not with that," Williams nodded toward the drink.

"I never said I was a two-fisted drinker," Berry granted. "To me it's about taste and buzz, not foam and volume."

That last comment was for Williams' second Michelob. The admiral did not drink often, but this was one of those times when he had hit a wall and needed clarity that did not involve thinking.

"You didn't answer the question," Berry pressed.

"It's out of my hands," Williams said. "Objectives were exceeded—dangerously, perhaps, I'll admit—but even Breen can't do much from where he is."

"Do you mean 'dangerously' as to your team or are we talking a potential international incident."

"Both," Williams admitted.

Berry raised his eyebrows and took a sip. He cocked his head in the direction of the White House. "They giving you trouble?"

"Nothing but. And interviewing replacements, I believe."

"You know, I can't say that I feel bad about that. Like I told you three weeks ago, when I was packing up my office, it's good to be out. You should think about that. Consult. You could get a retainer from Trigram, from someone else in a shot."

Williams shook his head. "Like I told you then, I *like* this job. I'm just not sure how this one got so out of hand."

"Don't you?"

"You mean JD?"

"Yeah. Her and the new boss. I'll bet you didn't get the support from them you got from Midkiff."

"That's true. But I've been thinking about the culture I allowed—hell, encouraged in my team. I ran a very loose ship, even when Breen tried to stop me."

"You also got results, Chase. I know. I was there for all of them."

"Thanks."

"I know that 'thanks,' and before you get all sullen and self-reproachful, this job was never going to be like running CENT-COM or even the Op-Center 1.0. You know damn well that the special ops rule book gets rewritten from mission to mission. You know it, even if"—he lowered his voice, looked around—"even if that sanctimonious Pennsylvania Progressive and his self-interested national security advisor don't. I'll add this observation, which I hope you'll take to heart. Stay resolute, my friend. I know you'll back your team to the very end, but more than that you are an heir to, and keeper of, the military's legacy of bold initiatives."

Williams snickered. "No one can dress up a disregard for rules like you, Matt."

"Is that what you think?" Berry's voice got even lower and he leaned over his drink. "You know what my world is about, Chase? Cash for data. In journalism—well, what used to be called journalism—they would've been called confidential sources. Virtually nothing travels through traditional channels. Information that matters comes from payouts."

"It isn't that way in the navy, Matt. Not even among black ops."

"Black ops would have nothing to do if informants didn't tell them where targets were at any given moment."

"Satellite—" Williams began, intending to dispute that point when his phone chimed. He looked at the caller ID and excused himself.

"Wasps or the local rats?" Berry asked.

"Neither," Williams said, rising. "I'll be back."

Grabbing his scarf from the back of the chair, he answered, asked the caller to hold on, then made his way into the cold night. He enjoyed spending time with Matt Berry. He respected every member of Black Wasp. But the time he had spent with the caller, shoulder-to-shoulder with the navy for the first time in years, had been special.

Captain Ann Ellen Mann was a Miami native who, like himself, attended the U.S. Naval Academy. Unlike himself, she made Superintendent's List Honors every semester at Annapolis. She spoke thirteen languages, including Pashto, and had served as an interpreter in Afghanistan. Taking part in a clandestine August 2011 effort to find and destroy the Taliban fighters who shot down a Chinook, the then-lieutenant took a bullet in the hip that put her in the Landstuhl Regional Medical Center in Germany for five months. The Secretary of the Navy Vector 7 Education for Seapower report cited her as being among the top five percentile of "experience-rich" officers. A series of promotions later, she found herself in command of Naval Support Activity in Philadelphia.

And, in a moment of fraternal confidence, she had told Williams that she felt sidelined. A woman, wounded in combat—she felt that she was a poster-person for overcoming adversity.

"*To me,*" she had said, "*I'm a victim of it.*"

The admiral put the phone to his ear as he crossed the street to the park.

"Captain Mann," he said.

"Admiral Williams," she replied.

"How are things at Naval Support Activity Philadelphia?" he asked.

"You know the drill," she said. "Spackle the bullet holes then deal with the real damage. We're working overtime on PTSD."

"How are you handling it?"

"Maybe a little better than most. I hear the echo of the bullets and keep repeating, 'You're not in a foxhole anymore.'"

The internal and external assault on her base left blood and destruction in every corner and—as she said—scars on every sailor stationed there.

"Sounds like you've had your own battles, Chase," she went on.

"It's messy, yeah."

"Ms. January Dow has asked me to take the reins there."

"Only the president has that authority," Williams said.

"I just got off the phone with him. I had told Ms. Dow and his chief of staff I wouldn't consider coming down unless you signed off. The president said he would prefer I do this voluntarily but he was prepared to issue an order."

"As of?"

"Tonight, transfer effective at nine a.m. tomorrow."

"In what capacity? Op-Center cannot have a military director."

"Ms. Brunner indicated that there would be no Op-Center as of tomorrow morning. Just a JSOC team."

"Answerable directly to the president," Williams said. "His own personal commandos."

The captain did not comment. Nor should she. Williams was not military and not privy to the designs of the commander-in-chief.

"Captain, we are in the middle of an operation that exceeded the wishes of President Wright and will not be resolved until the morning."

"His end or yours won't be resolved until morning?"

"The mission. And at this point I don't know what the other side looks like."

That was not entirely true: Williams saw very clearly what Wright intended. Before ordering his beer, Williams had heard from Rivette about the "liberation" of the Dàyóu women and the admiral had texted Angie. She had not responded. The president clearly anticipated heavy blowback from Beijing and did not want a "paper trail." Whether the mission was deemed a success or overreach, Wright had already decided to shut down Op-Center and its unconstrained director as a preemptive political move. Blame for fallout would be back-passed to President Midkiff.

"I understand," the captain said. "Ms. Brunner said there was an active operation and I told her that—well, I guess I was a little simplistic. I said this was not a football game where you changed quarterbacks in the middle. I said there are no time-outs in the field."

"You should have said 'directors' instead of 'quarterbacks.' She used to run a movie studio."

"I know. I checked her bio. My bottom line is this, Admiral. You and your team saved this facility. You had my back when my confidence was shot. I will resign before I undercut the officer, retired, who did that for more than love of country and the call of duty."

Williams had not heard uncynical sincerity like that for far too long.

"Captain—Ann Ellen—I appreciate that more than I can tell you. And I say this with equal sincerity: you are one of the few people I would trust to do the job, whether that means assembling a new team, a larger team, whatever the president has in mind. When he gives the order, know that you will have my full cooperation and support on-the-clock or off."

The woman thanked him and wished him well. When the call ended, Williams knew that the next time he spoke with her it would be at Fort Belvoir sometime between breakfast and lunch.

He stood outside, looking at the lights of the White House, feeling a sense of having been gut-punched by a notion suddenly made flesh: it was over. A cascade of emotions came with that, ranging from pride of accomplishment to disappointment.

Maybe you should tap some of Berry's sources to hit back, he thought. Dig up dirt on January Dow, get into the mud and fight it out.

Williams shook his head. Morality was a funny thing. He had once shot a cornered terrorist out of hand, but he did not want to play dirty politics. Turning, he went back into the restaurant to live vicariously through his enterprising if occasionally amoral friend.

CHAPTER THIRTY-THREE

Serenity.

That was the word and the sentiment that had come over Grace Lee shortly after her departure from Wuzhai. She was feeling proud of what she and Jaz Rivette had done back there; of her actions at the Taiyuan Satellite Launch Center; of every mission she had undertaken with Black Wasp; and of the years of devoted training—*no, obsessive training*, she decided—that had brought her to those landmarks.

As she drove to what she knew would be her greatest challenge she was content with just that fact: that she was heading toward it. The practice of Nei Gong taught that there were only five choices to make at any point in one's life: progress, regress, stand still, anticipate, or fix. She had embraced the strongest combination, moving ahead with the goal of righting a wrong.

And what does the enemy offer? she asked herself. Only two: standing still and anticipating that someone will try to free Wen Dàyóu.

The energetic art also taught—*no,* she corrected herself again, *it warned*—that if one was impulsive, then the body and limbs would be damaged. Rivette had never studied any of the Chinese arts. He had learned that last idea on the streets, as he had rightly boasted. If her efforts were to be successful, she had to embrace that philosophy.

She needed a plan that was unlike her attack on the Taiyuan facility.

Going to the university seemed like the best first move. She would establish a staging area, a reason for going to the prison. Progress, but with steps instead of one leopard-like leap.

Grace reached the University of International Business and Economics during lunchtime. She found a spot on the street to park. She had to assume that one way or another—either by a wounded soldier placing a call or failing to answer a radio check—what had happened in Wuzhai was now known. If the car were identified and watched, she had a better chance of spotting undercover activity in the open than in the on-campus parking garage. If she harbored any doubts she could huddle into her coat and walk right by.

Because it was cold, very few students or faculty were taking advantage of the park-like grounds. She checked a post for directions and made her way to the Information Center, a small white-brick building in the heart of things. She entered a vestibule that opened onto a hallway lined with offices. A young man looked up from his computer and smiled pleasantly.

"Good morning—afternoon," he corrected himself.

"Good afternoon." Grace smiled back, like she had with

the soldiers back at Ho's Market. "I'm hoping you can help me. I'm just in from Jinzhou and was supposed to meet a friend, a student. He isn't here and hasn't answered his phone for several days. I'm concerned something has happened."

"His name?" the man asked.

"Wen Dàyóu," she answered.

Grace felt as though she had stepped up to a bank window and demanded all the teller's money. The man's expression registered distress and remained locked there.

"What is it?" Grace asked.

"He's not here," she was informed.

"I suspected as much. That's why I'm looking for him."

The man's eyes darted past her, as though searching for something. "I don't know where he is. Before you ask, I don't know where his roommate is either."

"His roommate?"

"Kong Yanyong. I had an inquiry from his father, a director of the Beijing Municipal Party Committee. So you see, the information you seek is way above my station. Good afternoon."

The young man went emphatically back to his computer, showing no intention of looking up again until Grace was gone.

She left, the young man's last comment having told her a good deal: the man behind this, General Chang, did not fear reprisals from a ranking official in the civic government of the People's Republic. However, that information did give her an idea about how to approach the prison.

There was a food cart just outside the campus and Grace stopped for buns and coffee. She sat on a bench, watching the street, carefully considering what she was about to do. The presence of Lieutenant Colonel Kun at the Dàyóu home suggested similar precautions would be taken even at heavily guarded Qincheng.

Or would they use him as bait? she wondered.

All this General Chang needed to find the Dàyóu women and the engineer was to catch one of the Black Wasps. Wen was obvious bait.

Going there to ask for Kong Yanyong, claiming to be a friend, might afford her some distance, some cover.

Until they ask for your name and demand identification, she thought. *Then you're dead.*

The only thing to do was to go to the prison. She could wait for Kong, try to talk with him, perhaps find out something about where Wen was being kept. Or she might see something she had not expected, think of something she had not considered, find a new and compelling reason to go in rather than an excuse to stay out.

She walked past the car without stopping, saw no one around that seemed to be watching it, and got behind the wheel. She felt momentum, drive, and inevitability as she pulled from the spot.

Qincheng Prison was not what she had been expecting.

The straight, tree-lined road that led to it was majestic and welcoming. The gate was like the entrance to a shrine. The smooth, gray wall around the compound had a stately quality, emphasizing breadth rather than height—a traditional show of power. The wall was capped with a sloping peak and covered with tiles that resembled dragon scales. There was no evidence of human degradation beyond the magnificent exterior, no hint of broken lives and spirits beneath the low mountains that were visible from the outside.

There was a sentry post beside the massive gate. Video surveillance cameras were mounted on the guardhouse looking into the prison and out.

Grace stopped and pulled over. She did not want to drive within range of the cameras, so she got out and walked toward the sentry post. A very youthful guard stepped out and waved her away.

"You cannot park there!"

"I'm going to move," she said as she approached. "I'm looking for a friend, Kong Yanyong. His father told me he was here, of all places."

"I don't know." He pointed to her right. "Go around to the side. There is a visitors' entrance and a place to park." He pointed ahead. "You cannot park *there*."

"Thank you, I'll move," she assured him.

The road followed the wall for the equivalent of three or four city blocks before turning. The forest continued to line the road all around, just like in Taiyuan; it was utterly Chinese, to create security in a decorative way.

As she drove along the wall she came to the spot the guard had described.

And stopped. There were several cars in the visitors' lot, but two caught her attention. One was a staff car bearing the flag of a PLAA general. The other was an official black sedan with the markings of the Beijing Municipal Party.

The elder Yanyong is here to see about his son, she decided.

Grace pulled into an empty spot and waited for the windowless metal door to open. Here was the unanticipated "something" that happened with most missions. It reinforced the conviction that she was right to "progress" rather than "stand still."

While she waited, Grace pulled up the local bureaucracy to find out what she could about Lu Yanyong. He was the younger brother of Liu Yanyong, the Minister of Civil Affairs—a national figure. That meant, effectively, that Lu Yanyong had the ear of the president of the People's Republic. It was a measure of how desperately Chang wanted the Dàyóu family that he hauled Kong Yanyong in for questioning.

Grace knew that the student would not be there long, and she was right. She had been there just over a half hour when three men emerged from the visitors' center. A middle-aged man in a chauffer's uniform emerged first, his moves efficient and attentive. He held the door for Lu Yanyong, a paunchy, balding man with rounded shoulders. Lu had his arm around the shoulders of his son. Kong Yanyong was a big, powerful man who somehow looked smaller than his father. The student stopped and shielded his eyes from the sun as they emerged; just entering daylight, breathing clean air, caused him to break down.

"It's all right," his father said, urging him forward. The two continued toward the car at a shuffling pace.

Grace opened the door, removed her sunglasses, and approached the three. The chauffeur positioned himself between her and the Yanyongs.

"Pardon me," she said. "I am a friend of Wen Dàyóu. I was told at the university that he is here but the guard—"

"Please do not bother the director," the driver said.

"I don't wish to intrude, sir," she addressed Lu, who was not looking over. "But I can get no information and they will not permit me inside. I only want to know—"

Kong stopped suddenly and turned to Grace.

"I saw Wen inside. They showed him to me."

"Son, come along," Lu urged.

"What do you mean 'showed him' to you?" Grace pressed.

The driver went to stop her with a firm palm on her shoulder; she grabbed his fingers, bent them into a *kote gaeshi* wristlock and put the man's knees on the asphalt.

Grace released the man, stepped around him, and addressed Kong. "I repeat the question, sir."

Kong regarded her, his eyes tearing.

"I saw him in a chair," Kong said. "His face was shattered, his teeth gone. Wen was dead."

CHAPTER THIRTY-FOUR

Tavan Tolgoi Airport, Tsogttsetsii, Ömnögovi,
Mongolia.
February 19, 4:45 P.M. CST

It was the reunion that only one of the four men present believed the Dàyóu family would see: Yang hugging his wife and daughter. It was a spontaneous act by the quiet engineer, who erupted in sobs as they embraced.

Breen and Rivette stood back with Sun Fenghe at his truck, giving the family as much privacy as possible on the darkening tarmac of the freezing airport.

"Nice work," Breen said.

"Thank you, sir."

"Casualties?"

"Five airmen, five bullet wounds. Grace fixed the one who was bleeding heavily."

"You texted the admiral that she was headed to Beijing," Breen said. "Was that your call too?"

"I cautioned the lieutenant about some stuff but wasn't going to stop her, sir. So I guess it was my call. Can I ask, Major, if that would've been your call?"

"Why didn't you ask then?"

"I was afraid you'd order us to stand down," Rivette replied. "Would you have?"

"I don't know, Lance Corporal. I truly do not. Do you think she'll try to make it here?"

"Doubtful. It's a long drive and she's got Ushi Dàyóu's electric car. She talked about going to the embassy."

"Makes sense." He looked out at the three family members still hugging one another by the staff car. "Did the women know where Grace was going and why?"

"I believe she told them, yes sir."

"What about cleanup?"

The major was referring to the materiel and transportation that Rivette had obviously left behind.

"We parked the traffickers' truck in Wuzhai, with one of the bikes inside. The other bike's at the house. Nothing I could've done except burn them, which would've attracted attention faster." Rivette nodded at the stolen military vehicle. "That baby got us through two roadblocks. Folks just cleared a path for the lieutenant colonel."

Breen was impressed with what the two had accomplished and would have preferred if they had stopped there. He could not afford to remain here with the engineer and his family. Not with a porous border and Chinese on the trail of the Dàyóus.

Breen noticed a few members of the airport ground crew eying the military vehicle. Rivette followed his gaze.

"They looking to buy or rat?" Rivette asked.

"Even money," Breen answered. "I'm going to call Odval and see if we can get her cousin Bat Erdene down here with the Piper. If we can't, you'll take the two women back and we'll wait for the second trip."

"I'd rather you—"

"That will be an order," Breen said. "There are at least five soldiers who have seen your face. You'll be safer north."

"Yes, sir," Rivette said.

"Anyway, you have a job to do and it's not going to make you very popular around here."

"Huh?"

Breen pressed the last of his tögrög into Rivette's hand and nodded toward the parking lot. "Go tell Ganzorig Senior and Junior that we won't be returning the motorcycles, as promised."

"But we bought them?"

"Doesn't matter. The Chinese may come. Just give them the money."

While Breen made the call, the lance corporal jogged back to the staff car to get his backpack. He was not going to leave the location unarmed. Yang Dàyóu broke from his family long enough to take Rivette's hand in both of his and shake it warmly. If the engineer was anxious about his son, he did not show it. Dongling had most likely shared the fact that his savior was headed to Beijing, which no doubt gave him hope.

When Rivette was alone on the other side of the staff car, he leaned on the seat and looked down in the dark. He was suddenly overwhelmed by what they had accomplished so far and let his heart fill with pride and hope for his treasured partner.

CHAPTER THIRTY-FIVE

Qincheng Prison, Changping District, Beijing, China
February 19, 5:22 P.M. CST

Grace debated whether to inform Williams now or later about Wen's death. She decided to wait. She wanted to be able to finish the story.

There was, however, no debate about her priority at this moment.

The other cars, only a few in number, had all departed. Whether their business was personal or professional, the cold turned the passengers of the other cars inward. Soon, all that remained was Ushi's electric car and the bold, arrogant contours of the PLAA staff car.

Grace had relocated to a spot just out of the reach of the single light above the door to the visitors' entrance. The early darkness rendered her presence nearly invisible. The passenger's seat was nearest the military vehicle and Grace sat in it still and alert. The driver of the general's staff car had come out once to smoke a cigarette; he stomped his feet to ward off the cold before giving up and going back inside.

Except to take the measure of the man—he did not carry a walkie-talkie but wore a handgun in a holster—the lieutenant never took her eyes from the iron door. It was a way to focus her energies; she needed that. Grace wanted to pull open that metal door and make her way through the prison, destroying the people who sustained it.

They were all guilty of Wen's death. The town around it was guilty. The silent nation was guilty.

China had given the world the profound simplicity of Daoism, the harmony of human and nature exemplified by kung fu and tai chi. It would be well worth the sacrifice of her life to embolden others to stand up against Beijing's monument to domestic terror, this modern Bastille, and encourage a new Chinese revolution.

That would be the true and ultimate test of her skill; it would be the true test of her moral core.

A daughter of the land should *become the mother of a new land,* she thought. She could text Williams to explain that to her parents, to Uncle Sun. They would all understand.

She did not know how much time had passed before the door finally opened. The driver emerged and went directly to the back door of the car. Two men followed him. One was a general. Another wore an olive-green uniform that identified him as a member of the Chinese People's Armed Police Force.

The men were quickly on the other side of the staff car, haloed by the light above. Grace would have to go around or over it.

The lightweight alloy of the Geometry A barely whispered

as she opened the door and stepped into the shadows. She did not remove her knife from its sheath. This had to be done by hand, while she looked in their eyes.

"Captain Laihang, there is no confession so damning as the refusal to confess," the general was saying. "Even the boy's fellow revolutionaries, the photographer and the poet, pointed to his radicalism—"

"General Chang!"

The sharp voice silenced the conspiratorial hush of Chang's voice. As one, the faces of three men snapped to the source of the voice. The driver drew his pistol.

"Get in the car, sir," the adjutant said.

"Before you do," Grace said, emerging from the darkness, "I want you to know that I am the one who went to Taiyuan. I am the one who took Yang Dàyóu from you."

"Don't shoot her," Chang said. "Call security."

Grace walked boldly toward the front of the vehicle, which was just a few feet from the door of the prison. The driver would have to go behind the two men to get to it.

"The inquisitors are afraid," Grace said.

"Who are you?" Chang demanded.

Grace did not answer. Her attention was not even on the man maneuvering behind him. It was on the officer beside Chang. It was not cold that caused him to quiver; Captain Laihang did not have the military constitution of the others.

The PAP officer was about to run for the door or shout for help.

Grace was a few feet from the car when she ran for the hood, placed her right hand flat on it, and landed between the fender and the visitors' door. She put her back against it even as the captain reached for the knob. She pushed his nose across his face, breaking it, with a sweeping ridge hand blow. The man stopped and shuddered and stumbled back against Chang. Startled, the general recovered quickly and threw the man to the side.

Chang and his driver were now side by side, facing her. Falling back on his training, not on the general's orders, the younger man stepped forward to protect the officer. He raised his 77 semiautomatic and was still in the process of aiming when Grace sent man and gun pinwheeling toward Captain Laihang with a roundhouse kick.

Rather than stop and turn back to the solitary figure still standing, Grace continued the arc of the kick. Her back to the general, she put a sharp right elbow in his chest, cracking a rib, and followed immediately with a backfist to the face. She only wanted to stun him. The general staggered back, his gloved hands on his bloody nose and upper lip, as Grace faced the other men. Laihang had stayed down because Laihang was a coward. The driver was attempting to rise. Grace put him down with a high, frontal axe-kick under the chin. His head snapped back audibly; he did not get back up.

She looked down at Laihang, who was considering the pistol a few feet away. A side-kick ended his ambition and sent him skidding into an empty parking spot.

The lieutenant turned back to Chang, who was attempting to call out but only spit blood as he stumbled toward the back of the car.

"You killed a blameless boy and tormented his honorable father," Grace said, stalking after him.

"They were guilty!" he sputtered.

"You have *no* standing to judge innocence or guilt!" she hissed.

"No! Talk to me! I will *explain*—"

Grace wanted him to shut up. She put a foot in his gut. It bent him forward, causing the broken rib to send a sharp pain up his breastbone and into his throat. His knees wobbled a moment before giving out. He was outside the circle of light now but his eyes and blood glistened.

The woman stood over him. She put the bottom of her foot on his face and pushed him onto his back. He went easily. Without losing contact with the man, she had matched his fall and shifted her foot to his chest. She leaned forward slightly, putting pressure on the spot her elbow had struck. Chang wept with the pain.

"You deserve to die," she said. "But more than that, you deserve to live with dishonor."

"S-stop," he implored.

She leaned harder into the broken bone. He squirmed and squealed and Grace knew that someone inside would hear. She removed her foot and crouched beside him. There was just one thing left to do: she reached down and tore away one of the two gold shoulder straps with three stars. Then she clutched it close to his face.

"I will present this to Dr. Dàyóu," she said. "It will not compensate him or his family for what you have stolen. But your lost epaulet, the lost face it represents, will prevent you from ever taking anything from anyone again."

Grace could not tell if the wincing, writhing figure had heard any of that. It did not matter. He was finished.

Leaving the men where they lay, Grace returned to the car and, in near silence, drove from the prison.

"You can't park there, ma'am."

The marine guard at the United States consulate waited for a response from the disheveled woman in the black coat. She looked at him with tired eyes.

"Second time I've heard that today, Mr. Goodman," she said, reading his name tag.

"This will be the third, then. You can't park there."

Grace had driven to the American compound on 55 Anji-alou Road and parked on the street in front, ignoring the sign that said it was for embassy cars only. She walked quickly to the south gate, a barrier of white brick and thick iron. Beyond it was a compound of offices and residences fronted by the L-shaped embassy proper. The building's ivory-colored façade and white poles made it look to Grace like an industrial Olympus, spot-lighted and grand.

To get there, however, Grace had to first pass the gate and the formidable outpost just beyond it. Her experiences with guardhouses on this mission reminded her of the Three Little Pigs: this was impressively the structure made of brick.

"I *am* embassy," Grace said through the bars. "I don't happen to have any ID with me. Call Ambassador Simon. Tell her

that Lieutenant Grace Lee has returned from Jinzhou and requires admission, immediately."

"I will do that at once," the young man said with uncon-
cealed sarcasm.

Eager to transmit the absurd claim of what was surely a
local character, and eager to tell her to go away, the sentry went
back inside the bombproof outpost and explained to his companion about the visitor's claim. The woman at the desk placed
the call.

Less than a minute later Grace was on her way to the main
embassy building with Goodman as an escort. She was shown
to a conference room where the ambassador joined her. Grace
made a point of thanking Goodman before he left.

"You are most welcome," he said, showing deference pro-
portionate to his initial derision.

Ambassador Nell Simon arrived promptly. She shut the
door after instructing a deputy they were not to be disturbed.

"Unless you want food? Drink?" she asked Grace.

"Coffee and any kind of sandwich would be welcome,"
Grace said.

The deputy left and Grace sat and the ambassador took a
chair beside her. "Neither the president nor his national security
assistant kept me apprised of your movements," she said.

"They did not know them," Grace replied. "If I can, I'd
like to communicate with my superior. He can inform them and
they can brief you—I think that's the way it's supposed to go."

"Of course," the ambassador said. "I'm sure it's been quite a
story. I'm pleased that you're all right."

Grace thanked her and sat still and spent until her meal arrived. When the deputy and the ambassador left, the click of the door sounded strangely comforting. She was alone and she did not have to be on high alert. For the first time in days, she could relax.

She took a bite of whatever meatless, five-grain sandwich she had been served and was grateful for it. As she savored the coffee, she took out her phone and composed the messages for both Admiral Williams and Major Breen:

I am at the embassy. Wen is dead. The general
who orchestrated this travesty is alive but
permanently decommissioned. Let me know how
Rivette is?

When that was finished, she thought carefully about the message she would write in Chinese to the Dàyóu family:

My friends: With profound sadness, I must
tell you I was too late to save your son. His roommate
Kong, who was also at the prison, informed me of his
passing. I want you to know that General Chang, the
man who orchestrated this tragedy, will orchestrate
no further indignities on any citizen.

She sent both texts to Major Breen with a photograph of the epaulet attached. He would know what to do with the second.

Aware of the grief she was about to cause, Grace pressed SEND and waited.

Within minutes, she heard directly from Jaz Rivette:

We made it too. Reprimand me if you want but
I can't wait to hug your neck.

CHAPTER THIRTY-SIX

Buyant–Ukhaa International Airport, Ulaanbaatar,
Mongolia
February 19, 9:45 P.M. CST

The Piper Cherokee touched down with a little icy skid, causing Rivette to grab the armrests and Ushi Dàyóu to scream.

"It would suck to crack up now, after all the other stuff," he said.

Breen saw Odval Bayar sitting in her plane, looking at her tablet. She put it down and climbed out as the six-seater taxied toward the hangar.

The major received the text from Lieutenant Lee. He read it quickly and forwarded a copy to Williams; Black Wasp was once more functioning under the normal chain of command. The contents were both disappointing and a relief. There had already been concerns about fallout from the attacks and the resolution of the status of Dr. Dàyóu. He assumed the engineer had come this far to ensure the safety of his family. After that was unknown. The major had no idea how the death of Wen would impact their decision.

Breen would wait until the family could have privacy before showing them Grace's Chinese text. Then they had to talk, unpleasant as that would be.

Breen saw Odval waving at Rivette from the tarmac. They were at a newer, larger airport that somehow made her plane seem ricketier. Williams phoned as they were about to deplane.

"Where are you?" the admiral asked.

"We just landed in Ulaanbaatar."

"Did Uncle Sun come with you?"

"No," Breen said. "I gather from the fist he shook southward that he intended to stay and finish his ongoing battles."

"I'm texting Grace to keep herself available," Williams said. "We're going to need someone who can speak to the family. We've got a potential legal and diplomatic crisis on our hands."

"Yeah. I was just thinking that."

"What are you going to do if the Dàyóus want to go back?"

"What can I do? I'll give them some money to get to the Chinese embassy here. We've no legal right to do anything else."

"Do you think Dàyóu will blame us for Wen?"

"I honestly don't know. I expect he'll talk to Grace. They seem to have gotten close during their escape. How are things over there?"

"Bad. Very. I'll fill you in later. I want to call Angie Brunner and see about getting you home. Let me know about the Dàyóus."

"Will do."

The door was open, the stairs folded out, and Rivette dashed out to give Odval a hug for the way she chased off the

Mongolian column. Breen went back to the three passengers. They were just getting up.

He passed them the phone, indicated the text, then thought of the ridiculousness of him showing the engineer how to make a call off that text—but he did it anyway.

There was a look of uneasiness in Yang Dàyóu's eyes, and the major turned away. Whatever the successes of the operation— and those were clearly undecided—failing to save Wen was what would linger.

Yang Dàyóu read the text before passing the phone to his wife. The engineer's expression had not changed; Ushi, who was sitting behind them, leaned forward so she could read along.

Dongling cried out and her daughter began to sob. Yang took the phone as Ushi threw her arms over the seat to hug her, Dongling grasping at her hands, clutching them tightly. His finger trembled as he touched Grace's name on the screen.

She answered in English, thinking it was Major Breen.

"This is Yang Dàyóu calling," he said, his voice trembling. "I—I have read your text."

"I'm very sorry, Dr. Dàyóu."

"When I learned where he was, I held little hope. I will always cherish the effort you made, the risks you took. And I am grateful that you are well."

Grace choked when she tried to thank him. She took a moment before continuing. "Dr. Dàyóu, do you wish to come home?"

"To what?" Yang replied, his voice choking as he looked at

the pain in the eyes of his wife and daughter. "Our lives there are in ruins."

"Shall I tell Major Breen that you wish to continue with him to America?"

"I believe that would be best. Understand that I will do nothing to cause harm to my homeland. But what they have done to us . . ."

He did not finish. He did not have to.

Grace asked the engineer to return the phone to Breen. Yang went to the door; the major was waiting at the foot of the steps. The engineer passed the phone down.

"Thank you," Yang said in careful English, then rejoined his wife.

"How are you, Lieutenant?" Breen asked.

"Tired. Frustrated. Angry."

"We can debrief back at Belvoir. Did Dr. Dàyóu tell you what they want to do?"

"They'll go back with you, though I would caution anyone who tries to pressure him—don't. He would go back and face whatever waits rather than dishonor himself."

"I don't know that he has to *do* anything, other than not work for the People's Republic."

"Let's hope so," Grace said. "Where's Uncle Sun?"

"He headed back to Jinzhou. I think you inspired him."

"He was always an activist, like his sister. I'm glad he was able to stay clean. What about Rivette?"

"He's flirting with one of our pilots," Breen said. "Doesn't take a whole lot too seriously. Maybe he knows something we don't."

Grace was quiet for a moment. "It's good to have a normal conversation, whatever that means. I told the ambassador I would talk to you about letting her know what to expect—"

"I'll leave that in the admiral's hands. You take it easy now, you earned it."

"Thank you, sir," she said. "But I have to tell you, this is the first time I have looked back on a Black Wasp mission and asked myself a question."

"What question?"

She replied, "Did we solve more problems than we created?"

CHAPTER THIRTY-SEVEN

The Defense Logistics Agency, Fort Belvoir, Virginia
February 19, 10:30 A.M.

No mission was over until everyone who had participated had returned to base. For Chase Williams, the mission would likely end after this phone call.

It was with a sense of vindication that he rang Angie Brunner.

"I will inform the president directly," Williams began, "but I wanted you to know that Grace Lee is safely at the embassy in Beijing and the rest of Black Wasp is out of harm's way."

"Which is where?" she asked. There was no relief in her voice; she was still wound tight. "You said before they were in the Gobi Desert. China or Mongolia?"

"Mongolia," he said. "Right now they are in Ulaanbaatar, at the Buyant-Ukhaa International Airport. They are with Dr. Dàyóu, his wife, and his daughter. All are safe and prepared to come to the United States. Unfortunately, the doctor's son died in Qincheng Prison."

There was a long pause on Angie's end. "Is Dr. Dàyóu pre-pared to request asylum?"

"He doesn't want to go back to China," Williams said. "That's as far as Major Breen and Lieutenant Lee were able to carry the ball."

"Well that's good news," Angie said, her temper cooling. "Do they have transportation home?"

"They do not. I looked at the Ready Air Asset Inventory. We have a C-21A Learjet at Kazakhstan's 610th Air Base that ferries our officers between former Soviet republics. It's just sit-ting there. From Karaganda to Ulaanbaatar is about three hours flying time. We can go from there to Italy or Germany for the trip back."

"All right. I'll call you when transportation has been ar-ranged. And if you don't mind the breach in protocol, I'd like to brief the president about where we are."

"Fine. You can tell him that Breen and Rivette also recov-ered cell phones from the sex traffickers. Should provide a lot of names, locations, methods of abduction and transport."

"I will inform him."

Williams did not know if Angie's intercession was to pro-tect him, to hoard what was generally good news, to freeze Jan-uary Dow out, or all of the above. Whatever the case, Angie clicked off and the admiral texted the plan and timing to Breen. The major said they would stay at the airport rather than go to a hotel. It made good sense. Beijing would have cast a wide surveillance net looking for an older man, his wife, and their

daughter, possibly in the company of Americans; China had
eyes in Mongolia and Breen did not want the Dàyóus to be seen.

Finishing his role in the mission, Williams turned to what
would likely be his last duty as the director of Op-Center: he
started writing his letter of resignation. He had hopes that the
successful resolution of the operation, along with the appointment
of Captain Mann, would enable Black Wasp to continue as is.

Chase Williams had a knack for command but none for
writing, and he struggled between a Nixonian "I resign" and
something with meat on it, an explanation of why Black Wasp
is a valuable asset and that a small mobile unit requires the freedom to adapt to "evolving field requirements" that sidestep the
chain of command.

After a half hour he had written two drafts and discarded
them both. He was about to type out the one-line version when
Angie called back.

"You have your aircraft, which will arrive at three thirty
a.m. CST. It will be flying civilian so military clearance will not
be required. The plane will return to Karaganda to refuel and
then continue to Aviano AFB, Italy."

"Thank you," Williams said.

"I'm not authorized to tell you this but the president was
very happy hearing the news about the phones."

Of course he was, Williams thought. The phones were an
important humanitarian resource but, more than that, the proactive seizure played into Wright's slogan during the campaign:
People Before Politics. The news would resonate with his base and
the adoring press.

"Captain Mann will be arriving in Washington for a four p.m. meeting with the president," Angie went on. "He would like you to be there."

"My calendar is open," Williams said.

"For what it's worth, I've argued on your behalf," Angie went on. "There's always a get-to-know-you period for both parties in a—"

"Angie, this isn't necessary. I'll be there and I'll do whatever I can for Captain Mann. The president could not appoint a better person to command Black Wasp."

This time it was Williams who ended the call. Some of Angie's anger burned in him now. He did not know who first decried the judgment of "those temporary occupants of the Oval Office" but Williams felt that more strongly now than under any administration he had served. The feeling was especially acute when he was surrounded by bureaucrats who were not appointed because of their skill, understanding, experience, and wisdom but because of optics. Who had a specific demographic appeal, even if they were privately inadequate opportunists who put personal advancement above country. During the campaign and now in the West Wing, the government of John Wright was sick with that.

Williams was angry because he still wanted to serve his beloved nation, not the temporal whims of people with tribal agendas.

Maybe Berry was right, he thought. *Do something else before you become embittered.*

"Too late for that," Williams allowed. Besides, he was a fighter. And the president had just invited him into the arena.

He began to type. At three o'clock, *that* was the letter of resignation he would submit.

Odval Bayar had one more cousin. Her name was Naima—short for Naimanzuunnadintsetsegii—and the imposing, gray-haired woman worked at the security check-in point at the airport in Ulaanbaatar. She arranged for Breen and his companions to pass their time comfortably and privately in The Section for Honored Guests. The only window looked out on the tarmac, and it was darkened to protect those honored guests from the daytime sun. Having spent the last of his local currency, Breen "tipped" Naima in American dollars.

"That's probably more money than she earns in a year," Breen said as they were ushered through a locked door with gold lettering and varnish so new it smelled. "I mean legally," the major added.

"God, I'm liking this country," Rivette said. "It's like being home. Things just function better with an underground economy and a handshake."

The JAG officer could not agree; that was the way organized crime operated in America. But he found it difficult to argue with the sentiment.

With Odval's help—and Rivette's charm—the woman had been willing to explain the timing and flight plan to the Dàyóus. Yang accepted the information with a small incline of his forehead. Though he was outwardly neutral, Breen felt sure that the tears of his wife and daughter spoke for him as well.

He would not say it aloud, but their grief helped to conceal their identities. They held one another, faces downturned as they crossed the terminal. Habit caused airport workers and waiting passengers to look away, to avoid intruding.

Odval excused herself after hugging her two new American friends.

"I have to move my plane inside," she said. "Weather is coming."

"Snow?" Breen asked.

The woman nodded. She snapped her fingers. "It comes and goes like this."

Within a half hour a squall blew in. It was brief but it caused the airport to shut down for two hours while the one runway was cleared. Everyone but Breen and Yang slept, and the storm did not delay the arrival of the C-21A. It taxied as close to the terminal as a snowbank permitted. Naima made sure to personally wake and escort the travelers before going off duty.

"That's very kind," Rivette said, yawning as Naima walked them through a side door.

"More than you know," Breen told him. He cocked his head behind them. "A pair of official Chinese cars pulled up on the tarmac about a half hour ago."

"Do you think someone tipped them off?"

Breen shook his head. "They're starting to look under every rock for their chief engineer. I was expecting something like this—"

"Why didn't you say something, sir?"

"I've defended a lot of men and women and I know 'guilty' when I see it. I wanted you to relax."

When the small group reached the door, Rivette saw the vehicles. Beyond them he saw Odval and the Ganzorigs talking to four men in matching black down parkas. The pilot was pointing toward the city, then shrugging, then pointing in another direction.

"Atta girl," Rivette said. "Stall them."

"We better go," Breen said. "You take point. Stay behind the plowed snow. I'll follow with the Dàyóus."

"If they try to stop us?" Rivette asked.

The major replied, "The men are diplomats, not soldiers. Fire at the tarmac if you have to. Getting to that plane is the difference between a clean exit and an international incident."

"Never thought shooting at Chinese could avert a blowup," Rivette said as he used the cover of darkness to slip out his M4 assault carbine and held it concealed along his leg.

The door of the jet was open and the stairway had been rolled over as the Black Wasps and their charges made their way into the frigid night. Whether God or nature was looking out for them, Breen could not say. But as they walked a powerful series of wind gusts lifted particulate ice and swirled it around them, not just concealing them but sweeping toward the terminal where the Chinese were talking to the last of the pilots.

The party reached the jet without incident. The Dàyóus entered first, picking their way up the slightly icy steps as Breen and Rivette waited below. A flight attendant, a young man in civilian clothes, helped them onboard.

"Go, sir," Rivette said.

Breen did not hesitate. If the Chinese came over, Rivette

might be forced to cover their departure. The major entered the hatch and looked back. Rivette looked like he was not just ready for a fight, but eager.

"Lance corporal!" Breen shouted.

"Coming," Rivette answered as he trotted up the stairs. He looked at the major as the door was shut and the jet powered up. "Sorry, sir."

"What was it?"

"They were talking to Odval," he explained. "I wanted to make sure they treated her right."

The passengers sat, the aircraft lurched and rolled toward the runway, and the C-21A was airborne within minutes.

As he texted Williams, Major Hamilton Breen was glad for the connections they had made here and the wrongs they had righted. Even so, he was never so happy to see the lights of a city fall behind him.

CHAPTER THIRTY-EIGHT

The White House, Washington, D.C.
February 19, 4:00 P.M.

Williams felt sad but strangely at peace as he greeted his old friends
Kayser and Miller at the West Wing security checkpoint—most
likely for the last time. His resignation letter folded inside the
pocket of his overcoat, Williams removed the garment and threw
it over his arm rather than hang it in the closet used by visitors.
Squaring his shoulders, he walked through the familiar corridor,
reliving memories and achievements, setbacks and confronta-
tions, none of them regretted. They were the brick and mortar
of wisdom and growth. He had reminded himself to look at this
meeting the same way.

Thomas Deerfoot nodded toward the closed door of the
Oval Office, indicating that Williams should enter. The admiral
stopped.

"I remember when executive secretaries to the president
rose for visitors," he said.

"You may go in," the young man said. He had remained

seated and here was no honorific; the invitation had the quality of a reprimand.

Williams smiled. Privately, he wondered if he should use his retirement to push for the return of the draft. Kids like this could use the discipline and lessons in respect.

The admiral entered and left the door open so Deerfoot would have to get up to close it; it was a small triumph, but one way or another the kid would stand.

Angie Brunner and January Dow were on one of the facing sofas; Captain Ann Ellen Mann was in another. The president was leaning against his desk. They had been here more than a few minutes; Williams saw empty coffee cups and partly eaten pastries on small plates.

Mann smiled broadly, stood, and saluted. She was tall, just under six feet, and solemn-looking. Her dirty blond hair was worn in a donut bun. Her skin was pale, as he remembered, but her hazel eyes had a liveliness that had been lacking in the midst of the fight against the Black Order. Williams heard the door click behind him. He was glad Deerfoot had seen that.

The admiral returned the salute. "It's good to see you, Captain," he said.

"And you, sir."

There was a chair at the near end of the coffee table and the president indicated for Williams to take it.

"Thank you, Mr. President," Williams said.

Mann's feelings were not the only ones open and out there. The other women were equally transparent. Angie was pleased and poised; January was scowling slightly and restless, fidgeting with a napkin.

"Admiral Williams," the president began, "we have just been discussing the future of Op-Center and the transfer of command of Black Wasp from Major Breen to Captain Mann. I am confident that this new structure will serve the best interests of this office *and* the efficient and proper operation of the National Crisis Management Center."

Williams said nothing. He did not disagree with anything the president had said. He was putting reins on Op-Center, which was both his responsibility and prerogative.

"We have also been discussing your role in this new arrangement," Wright went on. His eyes had been moving around the group as he spoke; now they settled on the admiral. "I reject absolutely the way you organized this mission. It was not only unjustified by any interpretation of the NCMC charter, your actions risked undermining our policy toward the People's Republic of China and antagonizing a nation that thrives on overreaction, not just domestically but globally. We still do not know what kind of reprisals there will be as Beijing pieces together what has taken place."

The president allowed that to settle. He clearly was not finished. January's sour expression told Williams that.

"However," Wright went on, "I cannot deny that the mission—to put it bluntly—was a 'win.' From all we're hearing, the Taiyuan facility has not only lost its top officials, the scapegoating of Yang Dàyóu has begun circulating in scientific circles around the world. China is good at spreading online rumors.

They're not so happy to be receiving them, especially when they happen to be true. That is going to force a better balance between the military and science."

"We managed to fix their broken system, Mr. President," January said. "I am not clear on how that helps us."

Williams spoke up before the president answered.

"We demonstrated that we could tear up one of their treasured systems," Williams said. "What can be done once can be done a second time."

"That was *not* your call to make!" January snapped back.

"Ms. Dow, I could not agree more with that sentiment. And the truth is, not only didn't I make the call, I didn't plan it. The situation evolved and, under the direction of Major Breen and myself, we followed opportunities. *That* is what special ops do. That is why Black Wasp was created."

The president raised a hand. "Admiral, Ms. Dow—you make valid points, and you can debate them on your own time." He regarded Williams. "I am not a novice in government. I know how to delegate . . . and to whom. My only requirement is that people follow the policies and standards established by this office. You are a man of exceptional experience and sound, valuable instinct, Admiral. Any president would be foolish to lose you. I would like you to continue as the director of Op-Center, working with Ms. Brunner and Ms. Dow, but with no connection to Black Wasp other than through Captain Mann. Is that acceptable to you?"

Williams was surprised by the offer. He understood that the buffer placed between himself and the field force was a necessary safeguard, not so much tactically but as a concession to

January. Nothing less than his dismissal would have satisfied her. No restrictions would have been too much for her.

More than that, Williams was pleased—not so much for himself but for the president. Wright had displayed an unexpected willingness to learn and adapt. The admiral was inclined to accept the offer. He wanted to continue serving the country, and having Ann Ellen Mann on the team would only sharpen that goal. Still, Williams did not want to accept here and now. He wanted the reality of the new role to settle for a day.

"Mr. President, I'd like until tomorrow to consider your offer," Williams said.

"I understand. But there is something else I hope you'll consider. My offer is more than about righting the course of Op-Center. It is about righting that course in time and in a fashion to deal with new challenges. There is one in particular that we'll talk about if you decide to stay." The president went back behind his desk. "You'll communicate your decision to Ms. Brunner by—let's say nine a.m.?"

Williams rose and grabbed his coat. "Yes, sir."

Captain Mann stood as well. "Mr. President?"

"We're finished here, Captain, yes. Thank you."

"I'll talk to you in the morning, Admiral," Angie said as the two officers made their way from the Oval Office.

Williams looked back at her and smiled. January was still scowling. So was Thomas Deerfoot.

A few hours of live ammo training, belly-crawling through mud, would absolutely cure what ails them, he thought.

"It's good to see you, Admiral, and congratulations on the

mission," Mann said when they were in the corridor walking toward the exit.

"Congratulations to you as well."

"Thank you. I'm looking forward to seeing the team again. I only wish it had been under different circumstances."

"New administration, new rules, old habits, inevitable clash," Williams said. "No regrets."

"If I may ask, sir, what did you do to piss off the national security advisor?"

"You just said it," he informed her. "The mission worked. We didn't start a war with China, the one she predicted."

"Ah. A goaldigger," the captain said.

"*Goal*digger? I haven't heard that one."

"You need to be on social media more."

"Actually, I don't," Williams said. "You have time for a drink?"

"If I can stop by the hotel and get into street clothes, you're on."

The admiral was more than amenable and, walking smartly past security, he threw warm salutes at the two navy guards. He slipped on his overcoat, the resignation still crisp in his pocket. He had not decided for certain to tear it up.

But it was good to have a choice.

CHAPTER THIRTY-NINE

The Trigram Institute, Georgetown
February 19, 6:02 P.M.

If Matt Berry had learned anything during his years in Washington, it was how to stay upbeat under any and all circumstances. The secret, he swore, was not optimism; it was sarcasm. The only way to retain one's sanity and still ride herd on events that shaped the course of human history was to punch sharp, tiny holes in the sheer magnitude of things. Let the air out with funny noises. Very few egos in that history had been large enough to play that straight.

This new matter, however, the one that had just showed up on his screen—this was different. The former deputy chief of staff had fought battles of every stripe during his years with President Midkiff—and for a decade before that bouncing around, collecting names and indebtedness, in various branches of government. He often told Chase Williams, proudly, that he was the very definition of "deep state."

Yet in all that time Berry had never experienced the sense of dread that filled him now.

Berry sat at his desk in his corner office, looking at instant messages reproducing like prompts on a paywall. There had been clusters of them in the last few minutes. They were all from different people who worked in government, finance, the military, and scores of other industries and concerns across the nation. They were all on the Trigram payroll. Over a hundred strong, they furnished Matt Berry with countless options, data streams, and also provided an early-warning system of developing events.

Berry used the data to create algorithms that charted and recognized threats. New or unusual developments in every field were noted and sold to federal and private agencies, especially those with the potential to upset existing geopolitical and socio-economic structures. It was this influx that had noted the spike in imports of new appliances to Mongolia, information Berry had used to help Chase Williams on his latest undertaking. But the imports were only a small part of the picture. Increased spending among Mongolians pointed to the rise in the black market, since the average national wage had failed to keep up with even the normal cost of living. That was directly attributable to illegal siphoning of coal and copper resources, since those commodities contributed twelve percent less this year than last year to the nation's GDP.

The metrics created full and complex pictures of the world, which is why the incoming messages caused Berry deep concern. They were all from contacts in one area of the membership: tech. From component purchases to patent searches, from new hires to criminal break-ins, they pointed to something imminent. Something of which the White House seemed aware, including the "friend" working in the West Wing.

The new messages continued to compound—over thirty of them now, originating in government and business offices. They came from military sources, from energy grids, from communications networks, and now from NASA. Matt Berry did not yet see the big picture. But as the rising or falling numbers massed layer upon layer, one thing became clear: whatever was causing them to reach and then spill past their fail-safe levels, it was not an isolated event. . . .

ABOUT THE AUTHOR

JEFF ROVIN is the author of more than 150 books, fiction and nonfiction, under both his own name and various pseudonyms, or as a ghostwriter, including numerous *New York Times* bestsellers and over a dozen of the original Tom Clancy's Op-Center novels.